WA[RRIOR]S
RETURN

Barry Brierley

By Barry Brierley

BEAR BOOKS
PUBLISHING

Advance Copy Trade Edition 1996

Published by:
Bear Books Publishing
1852 S. Saguaro Circle
Mesa, AZ 85202

Cover art and illustrations by Barry Brierley

This is a work of fiction. Names, characters, places, and incidents are the product of the author's imagination or are used fictitiously.

Manufactured in the United States of America.

ISBN 1-889657-20-4

REVIEWS

"*Wasichu* is a remarkable tour de force, bold in concept and brilliant in theme. An excellent read of what the West has become." ---**Clive Cussler**, Author of *Shock Wave*

"*Barry Brierley is the Tom Clancy of Indian historical adventure. His diligent research shows through on every page. I learned more about the Sioux culture reading these thoroughly entertaining novels than I have in any textbook.*" ---**Marshall Terrill**, Author of Flight of the Hawk: The Aaron Pryor Story

"*Wasichu* is a romping western adventure that vividly captures the Sioux Nation in its glory ... an action packed, authentic tale ..." ---**The Book Reader**

"*Timeless Interlude at Wounded Knee* is one of those wonderful books that is read in one sitting -- not because it has little to say, but because it's said so well that it's hard to put down. The book is so well researched that Brierley's Lakota Sioux leap to life in the reader's eye as they face their darkest hour." ---**The Writer's Showcase**

"*Brierley's writing is so vivid ... his words paint a picture that transports the reader to that time and place. After 20 plus years working with writers developing scripts, I have known few who can translate vision to screen. Brierley is one of those few. I love everything he writes.*" ---**Gay Gilbert**, Casting Director and Film Producer

AUTHOR'S NOTE

I would like to thank all the people who have supported my writing. I may have met you at a book signing, book fair, Western show, or on the street. You may be a friend from my past or present. Thank you for your letters and kind words of encouragement and support.

For all of you who have been asking for this sequel to Wasichu, thank you for your patience. For those who have not read Wasichu, this book can be read and understood without having read Wasichu first.

This book is dedicated to Suella High Elk, whom I have only recently been able to contact since the death of Joe Four Bears. Suella and Joe's friendship were the catalyst that gave me the courage to become a writer.

And, also, for my wife, Barb, whose love and support has been instrumental in my development as a writer.

Contents and Illustrations

GREASY GRASS

PART 1

EXCERPT FROM THE JOURNAL OF CETAN CHIKALA (LITTLE HAWK)

▲▲▲▲▲▲▲▲

I had not yet seen thirteen winters but had been given the honor of keeping watch while my adult companions slept. I do not know why this honor had been given to me. Because of my foolishness, my grandfather was killed by some renegade Crow and Shoshone. I knew that I must be a warrior and face whatever punishment Wakan Tanka (Great Spirit) chose for me.

I glanced toward the bundled forms of my mother, Blue Feather, and my new father, Okute. Beyond them I also saw Wolf's Spirit, wrapped in his blanket. By the moon's pale light, I watched the slow rise and fall of their bodies. Seeing their complete confidence in me made me even more vigilant.

Early that morning Okute, Wolf's Spirit, Ptecila, and a wasichu (white man) named Caleb Starr saved me from certain death. I had been a prisoner of the same renegades who had killed my grandfather; I had been captured while trying to find Okute's horse, The Black. The stallion had been in with a herd of ponies who had been stolen from my people, the Lakota.

Perhaps I should mention that, like Caleb Starr, Okute is a wasichu. Several moons ago, he had arrived among my people as though placed there by the gods. Since that time he proved to be of great value to my people ... a great

3

warrior with humnha (magical fighting skills). Furthermore, he became close friends with Bear's Foot and Wolf's Spirit; both have always been like older brothers to me. The most important news of all was that Okute became my mother's husband. She had been without a husband for two winters since the night my father was killed by a Crow arrow.

After the fight and rescue we watched Caleb Starr's departure and then returned to the killing grounds to look for Ptecila, the Oglala tracker. Okute had said that the plan was if something happened to separate them, Ptecila would meet us in the north. Before moving northward, we first had to be certain that Ptecila was not lying wounded, or dead, nearby.

After a thorough search of the area we did not find the Oglala among the dead. While there, we decided to look for things of use. When they ran away, the renegades were so frightened of Okute's shotgun that many things were left behind. The carrion birds, who had already begun to feed on the dead, did not care what remained, but I did. In the renegades haste to leave, my bow and arrows were among the items they had overlooked.

Before leaving we used the stream to bathe Okute and Wolf's Spirit's wounds and to apply poultices. Soon after we moved north, we met Ptecila, Bear's Foot, and my mother. Bear's Foot was leading a force of Sioux who had been following the renegades' trail to reap vengeance and recapture their stolen pony herd.

When Bear's Foot's raiding party left the big village, my mother rode with them. She claimed that she would not return home until certain of Okute's and my fate.

Later, when the raiding party had met up with Ptecila, Bear had talked him into tracking for them. Ptecila had agreed, but only until the herd was found, then Ptecila would return to us. That is why we were still camped beside the shaking aspen and the talking stream. It is just as well that we waited; my mother had been tending to Okute and Wolf's wounds. The rest gave their wounds a chance to start healing.

Clouds passing in front of the moon reminded me to be alert and brought my thoughts back to the present. My eyes continued to search the darkness for danger. I could hear our ponies tear the grass free as they grazed nearby. I relaxed, knowing that if danger was near they would be the first to know. I watched their dark shapes closely; the horses and the soft babble of the stream were a lasting comfort to me.

Rubbing my sore, chaffed wrists brought back the memory of my pain and humiliation as a captive. The cuts and abrasions caused by the thongs still burned and were a constant reminder of how fortunate I had been. I closed my eyes and was once again thrilled by my memory of Okute as he had appeared at the edge of the vile Indians' camp like a vengeance-seeking wanagi (spirit).

All alone he had sat his horse with Wi, a fiery ball at his back. The renegades had stared as though certain that he was a kanga (demon). When I recalled the big fight, I revelled in my memories of how bravely my friends and Caleb Starr had fought to save me.

Most memorable of all was when Okute turned away from certain safety, and returned to rescue the wounded Wolf's Spirit. I could still hear the thunder of his shotgun and see the ferocity of his war horse, The Black, as he charged into the enemy horses.

My thoughts were abruptly interrupted by the sudden movement of The Black's head as it swung toward me. The *moon was bright so I was able to see the notches in the war horse's ears as they flickered and then steadied. My breath caught in my throat as I realized that whatever it was that he had heard came from behind me.*

After a brief heart-felt moment of watching The Black, the big horse lowered his head and resumed grazing. If he was not upset, then I had no reason to be either.

My earlier thoughts returned. When we crossed a great plain and arrived at the place of rolling hills and trees, we set up camp in a grove of aspen beside the swift moving stream.

While my mother was cleansing Okute and Wolf's Spirit's wounds, I had gone in search of herbs to use for the poultices. I recall the great peace I experienced when I first walked among the pine and aspen. As I approached the stream and felt the nearness of the trees, I had sensed a new closeness with Wakan Tanka. I could feel his holy presence everywhere.

At that moment, sitting alone in the dark, the day's events seemed dream-like and distant. Even the things that had happened late in the day had lost some of their reality, but are important memories that bound Okute, my mother, and me together as a family.

Just before Wi had completed his journey and I had become one with the darkness, I watched Okute and my mother as they worked to repair his 'gun-with-no-barrel'.

It was a shotgun like no other. The most unusual thing about it was that many shots could be fired before having to reload, and in that time and place it was very special. The part that is put to the shoulder had been struck by a bullet during the saving of Wolf's Spirit. Using strips of leather and glue, some of which came from my mother's parfleche bag, they shaped and stretched them as they applied the leather to the splintered wood.

While working on the gun, Okute would occasionally glance toward the sleeping Wolf's Spirit. The lighter color of the poultice was noticeable in the failing light and made the slow rise and fall of his breathing visible. As I watched him, I felt someone's eyes on me. When I looked up, Okute's pale eyes met mine. There was a weariness in their depths I had never seen before. Yet, when he spoke, his words were still full of energy and life.

"You get some sleep, Hawk. We will have a need for your sharp eyes in the morning."

Knowing the sacrifice he was making, I said, "You must sleep, Okute."

From the side of my eye, I saw my mother look up at my words. Okute's gray eyes watched me with a quiet intensity as I spoke again.

"I will keep watch with the same keenness of eye as the hawk for which I am named. I will not fail you, Okute."

I could feel the touch of my mother's eyes as I awaited Okute's response. He smiled and rose to his feet. Even with a bullet wound in his leg, he still could move with the grace of a mountain cat. He gazed down at me for a moment and then jerked his thumb toward Wolf's Spirit as he replied, "It will be as you say. See to it that you have the hearing of his namesake, the wolf, also. "

Okute's tight-lipped smile and his closing of one eye, like hinhan (the owl), made my heart swell with pride. My mother softly touched me as she walked by. I watched as they moved over and spread their blankets near Wolf's Spirit. I was then left alone with the weight of my new task resting heavily on my shoulders.

7

Perhaps it was because death had been so near that morning, but I remember how later, sitting alone in the darkness, I still felt my mother's soft touch. I heard once again, the swish of leather and the tinkle of the hawks' bells sewn onto her dress. The sounds lingered in my ears and thoughts long after the darkness had closed in about me like a blanket.

My random thoughts took flight as quickly as a hummingbird leaves an empty flower. All four horses had their heads up and were staring at a point behind me. I willed myself not to move. My ears strained to listen. Softly, as though it was a part of the wind, a familiar voice came out of the darkness.

"Do not turn around, Little Hawk. It is I, Ptecila."

Before I had a chance to wonder why he was not in the south tracking renegades, he was speaking again.

"Three of the Indians who held you captive are hiding nearby and are watching you at this very moment. Do not look toward me or do anything different."

My heart became like a small animal trapped within the cage of my ribs. While my breath struggled to free itself, I listened to the words of my Oglala friend.

"Take some of your arrows and pretend that you are examining them for flaws. After looking at them, set some beside you in the grass."

I resisted the need to turn my head to look for the enemy. My eyes longed to seek out the shadows, but I forced myself to do exactly what Ptecila told me to do.

"Hawk, in a short time the clouds will again smother the moon's light. Before that happens, you must be near Okute and the others so that you can warn them. When you go, leave the arrows that you have set aside. My quiver is empty."

Wasichu's Return

After a moment, I stood and walked the short distance. My legs felt heavy as though they were wading through water. The stream that only moments before was making happy, comforting sounds had changed. Now, because of my fear, it was a noise that could conceal the sneaking footsteps of an enemy warrior.

The weak light glistened off Okute's open eyes. I rejoiced that he was still awake. In the moonlight, his eyes looked as black as my own.

In a voice as quiet as the whisper of the nighthawk's wing, I said, "Ptecila is here ..."

While I spoke, I pretended to watch the surrounding terrain as I faithfully guarded my camp from enemies.

"...There are enemy warriors nearby."

I heard a sudden intake of air and saw my mother's large eyes peering fearfully at the encroaching shadows.

"How many are there?"

I softly answered Okute and, as he quickly instructed, slowly moved away while my trembling legs managed to carry me near a dead pine tree. Remem-bering Ptecila's words, I removed another arrow from its quiver and pretended to sight along its length as I waited for the total darkness that would come when the clouds passed in front of the moon.

As quickly as water snuffs a campfire the moonlight was gone and the clearing was plunged into darkness. In an instant, I was crouched behind the dead pine with a gooseberry shaft notched snugly against the taut sinew bowstring. Without the pale light I could see nothing but dark shapes.

Once, not long after he had come to us, Okute had come at night to sit with me as I helped to guard our band's pony herd. He taught me how to tell if something is truly moving in the darkness. He said, "If a shadow appears to move, do not look directly at it. Look at something else and watch the shadow from the side of your eye."

Across the stream there was a form that looked darker than others. I used Okute's trick. It was moving!

Slowly I raised my bow. All at once the clouds released the moon's light. The form became a man's shape; he was bent at the waist and carrying what appeared to be a stick. Suddenly, I realized what I was seeing. It was an Indian with a rifle!

At the very instant that I recognized the shape as being one of the enemy, my nose filled with the stench of stale sweat and rancid grease. Before I had a chance to react, my hair was clenched by an iron fist. Tears of pain flooded my eyes as the fist lifted me into the air.

A thought sped through my mind with the swiftness of one of Sky Father's lightning bolts ... I am going to die!

I heard the unexpected hiss of zuzeca (the snake), and a loud choking noise. The fist released me and I dropped to the ground. With a trembling hand; I quickly cleared my eyes of tears and struggled to keep my balance on the rotten pine branches. Through eyes still awash with tears, I saw a large Shoshone swaying behind me. He was clutching at the bloody shaft of an arrow lodged in his throat! His legs buckled and he fell back among the brittle pine boughs. Before his paint-distorted face dropped from sight, the moon was again released and I saw my own markings on the feathered shaft. Ptecila!

A blood chilling scream sent me scrambling for my bow. With his rifle sticking out in front of him like a lance, the Indian by the stream ran toward the blanketed shapes. He was almost to their shadowed forms when suddenly there was a thunderous explosion. Okute's shotgun! The clearing brightened with a flash of orange and yellow light! In the brief second of illumination, I saw several things. The warrior was stopped and flung backwards by the force of the blast. It was so abrupt he looked like a running dog who had come to the end of his tether. His body landed in the stream throwing splashes of pale blue water into the air. In that same instant; I saw my mother crouched behind the sitting Wolf's Spirit who held Okute's shotgun at hip level. Smoke still curled from the gun's short barrel.

My eyes swept the area still lit by the moon. Where was Okute? Where is the third Indian? I could not see a thing. I looked back toward Wolf's Spirit. I felt a chill that wasn't caused by the night air. Both Wolf, and my mother were no longer there!

The quiet that had prevailed since the shotgun blast was broken by the unexpected thunder of pony hooves. Our ponies were running free! They surged across the stream and burst into the open clearing. Directly behind them rode the missing Indian. He began yiping and lashing his pony with his quirt. I loosed an arrow at him but I missed. As I fumbled to notch another, I feared that he was going to get away with our horses!

A lean figure stood up in the tall grass directly in the path of the running horses. It was Okute! I watched The Black and Hawk's Wing swerve to either side of him. Okute had to jump to the side as Wolf's stallion charged by. He crouched and put both arms out straight in front of him. I saw moonlight glint off his pistol's barrel just as a spurt of flame shot from its muzzle. The flat sound of the gunshot echoed across the clearing as the Indian's head snapped back. His arms went slack and his body slipped from the pony's back, disappearing in the grass almost at Okute's feet.

I was surprised to see the horses stop a short distance away. The Black, followed by my pony, had already begun to walk back toward us. Wolf's stallion had stopped and was grazing near the edge of the trees.

On the far side of the clearing, Ptecila stepped into the open just as Wolf's Spirit and my mother appeared soundlessly from the trees on my left. I noticed that Wolf's hand was pressed tight to the poultice on his side, and my mother was carrying Okute's pumpgun.

Just before the clouds again obscured the moon, I saw the white of Okute's smile as he called to Ptecila.

"Washtay, Ptecila! Next time you come to visit, try not to bring such ill-mannered friends."

CHAPTER 1

ᐯᐯᐯᐯᐯ

The rain stopped. The five riders continued to move in a westerly direction. When the sun broke through the towering rampart of fluffy cumulus, Christopher Raven, known to the Lakota as Okute (shooter), removed his blanket-poncho and canvas shelter-half. Twisting in the saddle he looked back at his companions. As usual, he found it difficult to pull his eyes from his Lakota wife, Blue Feather. Her beauty and subtle sexuality totally captivated him. Directly behind her rode Little Hawk, followed by Wolf's Spirit. Ptecila brought up the rear with their short string of captured horses.

Raven noticed that Wolf's Spirit was joking with Little Hawk. That's a good sign, he thought. He was pleased to see that the young warrior's wound was better.

The morning following Ptecila's return they awoke to find Wolf racked with fever. They spent the day tending to his wound and sponging his body with cool water from the creek. The next day his fever broke. When Ptecila brought down a mule deer with one of Little Hawk's arrows, they decided to have a feast. They dined on venison steaks and soup. The soup, Raven mused, was really more like a stew. Blue Feather had put together a delicious concoction adding sage, wild onions, and herbs to the deer meat. They had spent the remainder of the day resting so that Wolf could regain some of his lost strength.

13

A red and purple sunset was the perfect backdrop for Ptecila as he bedazzled them with the story of his escape from the renegade trackers.

After leading Bear's Foot and the other Lakota to within sight of the stolen pony herd, Ptecila had left them and rode north again. It was his bad luck that some of the horse thieves, fleeing the revenge of the Sioux, had stumbled across his tracks. The little Oglala used his vast experience in tracking and was able to temporarily confuse his pursuers; once he had put them on a false trail, and twice he had backtracked and ambushed them as they followed his trail. He was able to kill two of them but was unable to lose the remaining three. Ptecila, his wizened face grimacing with remembered efforts, told them of how he had tried every ruse that he knew to shake them. He smiled as he remarked on the many skills of one of the renegades, a Crow. "This man," he said, "was a great tracker and almost a great horse thief."

Okute grinned at Ptecila, understanding that the last renegade to die by Okute's pistol was the Crow tracker.

Having used all his arrows, Ptecila had told them that his only chance to survive was to find his friends and bring his danger to them.

The sun's warming rays began to raise steam from the flanks of the horses. Raven enjoyed the pungent burnt scent, but it was the heady, sweet aroma of wet sage and the many varieties of prairie grass that made the morning air so fresh and memorable.

Chris' eyes cautiously probed the rolling landscape while his mind flinched at the improbable reality that he was actually in the nineteenth century. He thought of his late friend, Joe Spotted Horse who had been killed in Vietnam and how a promise and a twist of fate had compelled him to perform a ceremony from the top of Bear Butte, a sacred mountain of the Sioux and Cheyenne. A eulogy to his dead comrade, Raven performed this ritual, but made a mistake and awakened the wrath of the Lakota gods. A violent electrical storm ensued that culminated when lightning struck the butte and knocked Raven unconscious. When he regained his senses, things were not as they had been, and he came to realize that he had been transported back one hundred years in time to the year 1876.

While his eyes swept the prairie for danger, Chris' mind continued to drift. The gentle rocking motion of The Black's gait was having a tranquilizing effect. Opening his vest to allow more air inside, he caught a glimpse of the tattoo on his left chest. He stared at the brick-red rendering of the stylized horse carving.

Aside from the fact that the tattoo had probably saved his life, Raven had more valuable memories of the tattoo and horse carving. He closed his eyes letting his thoughts slip back to Vietnam to rare, happy memories.

He and Joe were on R and R in Saigon. They were in civilian clothes, stumbling down a narrow side street; both were drunk but Raven was really wiped out. Joe stopped, grabbing Chris who would have kept moving. He took Raven by the shoulders and turned him so that he was staring at a brightly lit, tiny establishment. In a quiet voice, he said, "Hey Chris, let's become brothers."

Raven, having difficulty getting his eyes to focus on his friend, asked, "You mean you're goin' to have your mother adopt me?" Then laughed hysterically at his own inebriated wit.

Spotted Horse laughed and said, "Heyah! I mean, we'll each get a tattoo."

Chris' expression sobered instantly as he replied, "What a beautiful idea."

Joe grinned and shoved Raven toward the open doorway. He made a grab for Joe and they practically danced into the cluttered tattoo parlor. Joe sat Raven in a chair and stepped back. They both stared at the four walls that were completely covered with tattoo patterns. Raven's mouth dropped open and he muttered, "I feel like I just fell into a comic book."

Joe chuckled, shaking his head. A seedy looking, middle-aged, white man came through a narrow doorway that was covered with long strings of colored beads. A cigarette was dangling from his thin lips. His sallow cheeks were covered with a week's growth of beard. His eyes narrowed when he saw Spotted Horse.

Raven gave the man a sloppy grin and foolishly asked, "Do you give tattoos?"

The tattooist looked with disgust at Raven, then sneered at Joe. "Let me guess, Chief, your friend, Dick Tracy here, must be with Military Intelligence, right?"

Ignoring the man's sarcastic racial slur, Spotted Horse removed an object from a small pouch worn around his neck. It was a small, pipestone, horse carving ... an artifact that had been in his family for generations. He placed the stylized carving on his palm and moved it into the light close to the man's face. The man sneered, pushing his hand away as though it smelled bad. "Git that Injun voodoo shit away from me, Chief!"

Raven's laugh drew the seedy man's attention, then shook his head in mock seriousness and slurred, "I wouldn't get him mad if I were you. You'll be sorry."

The tattooist glanced at Joe and the blood immediately left his face, leaving him as pale as Casper the Ghost. He slowly peeled the cigarette off his lip and dropped it on the floor. It smoldered there, unnoticed.

Spotted Horse's face looked as though it was carved from the same pipestone as the carving in his palm. His other hand was holding a huge, broad-bladed fighting knife. The light from one of the shop's high-intensity lamps glanced off the razor-sharp, ten-inch blade.

Joe glared at the man and softly said, "You talk just to hear your own voice, white man. Tell me the truth. Are you a good artist? Just nod or shake your head."

The very pale tattooist nodded emphatically. Joe nodded also and asked, "Do you think that you can do a tattoo on my brother that will look exactly like this carving?"

Another positive nod brought a brief smile to Joe's face. Raven grinned, looking from the tattooist to Joe and back again. Handing the man the horse carving, Joe said, "Go for it, man. If it's not perfect, I'm going to give you one." Then he smiled again and brandished the big knife before slipping it beneath his shirt.

The man swallowed noisily and stepped over to Raven, who grinned and said, "Told you so."

Chris chuckled as he remembered the incident and rubbed his fingers over the tattoo, as though not wanting to let loose of the memory. He brushed a finger past his eyes and dislodged a drop of moisture that had formed there. It had been quite a while since he had thought of Joe. It still bothered him to think about having lost the first real friend, or brother, he had ever had.

Although it felt like he had been with the Sioux forever, Raven knew that it had only been about three and a half months. Most remarkable was his ability to adapt to this bizarre situation. He had never been happier in his life.

He thought briefly of his friend, Bear's Foot, and grinned. Remembering his wild and unpredictable sense of humor, Raven ruefully shook his head. He could picture Bear hassling everyone; forcing them to hurry so that he could beat Chris to the big village. It would be just like him, he thought, to beat me there just so he could accuse me of trying to miss the big fight with the Bluecoats (U.S.Army). His thoughts suddenly turned serious as he remembered what historical debacle was looming in the near future.

When Chris had left to rescue Little Hawk, he had entrusted Bear's Foot to be Blue Feather's guardian. At the time, he had told his friend of the impending fight with the Bluecoats on the Little Big Horn River. Knowing that he only had a week, Raven didn't know if he would be able to return in time to protect his wife. He felt that he had reason to be concerned. He knew from his past reading that some of the soldiers had made it part way into the village. Knowing that, he didn't want to gamble with his wife's life just because the odds of her surviving were numerically in his favor. What with Blue Feather riding to meet them, his worry was all for nothing.

A surprised pair of mule deer burst out of a small clump of aspen. The Black tossed his head and nickered as the deer bounced over the crown of a small hill. A covey of quail exploded into the air on the opposite side of the hill, causing The Black's ears to flicker even more. The whirring noise of the birds' wings was unnaturally loud in the prairie quiet.

When Raven crested the hill, the deer were nowhere in sight. He pulled The Black to a stop and gaped at the beauty of the land spread out before him. The low hill had given him an unexpected long view. He heard Blue Feather's pony moving in next to The Black, and it pleased him that they would share the moment.

The sweeping vista was a painter's palette of deep and vivid greens with blue and umber adding a pleasing contrast. The distance was swallowed by a massive mountain range that ran north and south as far as the eye could see. Together the plains and mountains presented a canvas of splendor, unequalled to anything Raven had ever seen.

Feeling the warmth of Blue Feather's touch on his arm, Chris turned and was immediately put under the spell of her majestic black eyes, but she broke the magic moment by pointing and exclaiming, "There, Okute! Just below the blue of the mountains lies the great encampment of Sitting Bull."

Blue Feather turned back to Raven before saying, "Our lodge awaits us there beside the river."

Wolf's Spirit and Little Hawk pulled in their ponies beside them.

"*Peji Sla* (Greasy Grass)!"

The excitement in Wolf's Spirit's voice pulled Chris' gaze away from Blue Feather's allure.

Greasy Grass was the Lakota name for the Valley of the Little Big Horn.

With a graceful sweep of his arm, ending with a quick movement that brought his clenched fist to his chest, Wolf's Spirit spoke again.

"Just this side of the mountains is the Greasy Grass. The village and river are at the feet of many warrior bluffs that are standing guard over our people."

Looking beyond the hidden bluffs to the massive mountain range, Raven marvelled how they blanketed the entire horizon. Lowering his gaze he guessed about where the river should be but couldn't begin to guess the distance to the village.

"How many days ride?"

All three turned and looked at Chris with blank expressions. Without thinking he had spoke in English. Feeling foolish, he quickly repeated it in Lakota.

Wolf's Spirit's proud face twisted into what must have been a Lakota expression of perplexity. Speaking in a quiet baritone, he said, "Two suns, maybe one."

Chris looked at Little Hawk. His rising excitement was mirrored in the boy's eyes. A quick glance at Blue Feather's flashing smile and animated gaze confirmed his suspicions. They were as excited as he was!

Raven exclaimed, "*Hopo* (let's go)!"

Grinning wildly, their child-like exuberance spurred them into urging their horses into a headlong gallop down the hill. Wolf's wound forced him to slow up and follow at a more sedate pace.

Ptecila arrived at the hilltop in time to see the pony rumps disappear in a veil of dust over the next rise. His wrinkled, nut-brown face puzzled over his friends' behavior. He stared at the settling dust for a moment. Suddenly his features brightened as though he had discovered the key to a baffling mystery. Nodding his head knowingly, he gave a perfunctory shrug of his narrow shoulders and muttered, "*Wasichus.*"

Feeling that he had solved the enigma of their erratic behavior, Ptecila smiled and led the string of ponies down the slope of the hill.

After their short, exhilarating ride, the four slowed their mounts to a walk. Chris ignored the bite of pain in his leg as he twisted to see how far behind Ptecila had fallen. He looked beyond Wolf, who was readjusting his poultice, to where the Oglala tracker was slowly closing the distance between them.

Feeling the pull of Blue Feather's eyes, Raven turned and allowed himself to be drawn to her gaze. When their eyes met, no words were necessary. The rhythmic stride of her horse's walk created a repetitive sound from the hawks' bells that were sewn onto her dress. To Raven's ear, the distinctive tinkle, united with the memory of his wife's silken voice, flowed through him with the poetic continuity of a Carol King refrain.

A sudden, explosive gunshot cut through Raven's romantic thoughts and brought everyone to a brusque halt. The rifle shot was close and had come from their direct front! When its echo bounced off the nearby hills, it seemed to come from many directions.

Raven's eyes were everywhere at once. His military training had him looking for cover while simultaneously searching for high ground. Not finding a place with both, he quickly directed his comrades to a nearby copse of pine that had a scattering of dead aspen on its northern side. Gesturing Wolf's Spirit to his side, he swiftly told the warrior what he wanted them to do.

With eyes no longer dulled by fever, the fiery Wolf watched Raven's every move and listened carefully to every word. His black eyes snapped and glittered with excitement. When Raven had finished, Wolf's Spirit lifted his left hand to his brow in a Lakota gesture of respect and acceptance. He wheeled his stallion and immediately led the others toward the stand of pine.

Absently stroking the neck of The Black, Chris urged him toward the closest hill. He was certain that the shot had come from the hill's opposite side. Removing the pump shotgun, he dismounted and started up the hill. He had noticed that the small hill was topped with a couple of weathered pine trees. Swiftly, Raven finished his ascent and

21

cautiously slithered up to the base of one of the trees. Its boughs nearly swept the summit's short grass giving him excellent cover. Easing a pale eye around the tree's trunk, Raven felt a jolt of surprise as he absorbed the scene below him.

CHAPTER 2

▲ ▲ ▲ ▲ ▲

Three horseback Indians were visible on the short plain beneath the hill. Two of the three were dismounted, busy tying a deer carcass to the back of a horse. The third was quietly sitting his horse, on a constant lookout for danger signs. He was the one that was getting all of Raven's attention. He knew the man. The last time he had seen him he was leading a pack of hard-riding Sioux, as they swept down on a unit of General George Crook's infantry during the Rosebud fight.

The slight figure quietly sitting his horse was probably the most feared Indian in the northern hemisphere. His name was *Tashunko Witko* (Crazy Horse).

Just in case one of the three believed in shooting first and asking questions later, Chris decided not to show his white face until he was certain that he wouldn't get a bullet hole put in it. Keeping his head down he shouted, *"Hau, kola* (Hello, friend)!"

Peeking through the pine bough he saw that before the second word was out of his mouth, the two by the pack horse had already disappeared into the brush. Crazy Horse hadn't so much as twitched.

In a calm, resonant baritone voice, Crazy Horse asked, *"Nituwe hwo* (Who are you)?"

Leaving his pump behind, Raven stepped into the open and replied, "It is I, Okute! I have some of your friends with me."

23

The Oglala chief gave Chris one of his rare smiles as he said, *"Hohahe* (Welcome)!"

Gesturing the others to join them Raven moved slowly down the hill as the other two warriors showed themselves. When the two stepped into the open and moved closer to their chief, Chris' step faltered as he recognized one of the men.

The man wasn't exactly a friend. His name was Scar, a bodyguard of Sitting Bull. The big Hunkpapa warrior had, mysteriously, taken an instant dislike to Raven.

Continuing to watch him, Chris wondered why he was hunting with Crazy Horse instead of with his chief, Sitting Bull.

Blue Feather was in the lead as the procession came around the hill. Ptecila, as usual, brought up the rear with their string of horses. The instant the foursome saw Crazy Horse, the air was filled with Lakota greetings and respectful utterances of, *"Wichasita* (Chief)!" When he saw Little Hawk, the usually somber chief broke precedence and flashed another rare smile and urged his pony forward to meet him.

The Black, his ears perked forward, stared at Raven as if he hadn't seen him for a while. Chris gave a low whistle. Hearing the soft note, Little Hawk released the stallion's bridle. Slowly, the great horse moved toward him. About halfway he stopped, bobbed his head up and down, and stared at him.

Looking beyond The Black, Raven saw the Oglala war chief embrace Little Hawk and Blue Feather.

He stooped and grabbed a handful of sweet grass. The Black's nostrils flared as he snuffled and stretched his neck toward Chris. While pulling the grass, he had noticed that Scar was walking toward him. Seeing that Little Hawk and the others were still busy talking to Crazy Horse, Raven thought he might as well wait and see what Scar was up to.

The Black and Scar arrived at the same time. Letting the stallion jerk the twist of grass out of his hand, Chris turned and faced the Hunkpapa.

Whenever chance had brought him in contact with the warrior, Chris was shocked all over again by the man's horrible disfigurement; he was covered with horrible scars.

Bear's Foot had told him Scar's story. Raven wasn't certain that he believed it but was still awed by the tale.

'When he was a young man, Scar had been attacked by a grizzly. Armed with only a knife, the youngster had killed the huge bear. Scar's wounds were so terrible, everyone expected him to die. After his recovery, because of his great medicine and courage, Scar rose from obscurity to become one of Sitting Bull's most trusted and revered warriors.'

Scar's hot black eyes stared angrily into Raven's cool gray ones. In a voice made ghastly because of his damaged voice box, Scar snarled, "I see that you have returned, Wasichu." He paused before adding, "Now that the fighting is over."

Raven felt the familiar tingle of his oldest nemesis, anger. Fighting to hold it at bay, he smiled. It wasn't the type of smile that you could hope to build a friendship on. It was more a showing of his teeth ... the very same grimace that you would see on the face of a rabid wolf just before he rips his victim's throat out.

Scar's black eyes with their yellowish whites reminded Chris of an old saying, 'His eyes looked like two piss holes in a snowbank.' The facetious thought turned Raven's wolf smile into a genuine grin.

The smile was still there when he said, "You know that I was at the Rosebud, leaving only because I was needed elsewhere."

Scar continued to glare. Chris dropped the smile and continued, "Your chief, Sitting Bull, must have been needed to help the women take down the lodge poles. I noticed that he wasn't at the Rosebud fight at all."

Scar's jaw clenched, and his knuckles whitened on the haft of his tomahawk. He took a sudden, menacing step towards Raven.

"*Heyah* (No)!"

Crazy Horse's voice cracked like a whip! It stopped Scar about a half-step short of receiving a straight right-hand punch, squarely on his prominent, Lakota nose.

Noticing Scar's immediate reaction to Crazy Horse's shout, there was no doubt in Chris' mind as to who the 'main man' was in their hunting party.

When the Oglala chief stepped up to Scar, his authoritive bearing made his less than average height appear equal to that of the taller Hunkpapa.

Scar stood very still. Slowly he turned, and throwing Raven a final hostile glance, he strode away. Silently they watched Scar's powerful figure until he was no longer within hearing. Crazy Horse turned toward Raven and spat out a rapid mouthful of Lakota. The verbal attack was so sudden that Chris nearly took a step back. The English equivalent would have been, 'What in the hell is going on between you and the Hunkpapas?'

About a month earlier, Raven had an altercation with another Hunkpapa Sioux named Standing Elk. Since that time Bear's Foot had resolved that conflict, but Scar's hostility was ever present.

Having absorbed the young chief's anger, Chris smiled and shrugged. Knowing that most Sioux think that white men are ugly because of their pale skin and hairy bodies, Raven said, "I think Sitting Bull's Hunkpapa are jealous of my white skin and hairy body, so they pick fights with me."

With the twinkle in his eye canceling out his disdainful look, Crazy Horse stepped forward and embraced Raven. Stepping back his warm brown eyes captured Chris with their directness as he spoke, "Perhaps we will speak of this Hunkpapa thing at another time. Right now it is good to see you back safely. That was a very brave thing you did when you rescued Little Hawk. And then my ears heard that you did another when you saved Wolf's Spirit."

Raven's attention was momentarily drawn to the movement of Blue Feather as she and her son dismounted. He turned back to Crazy Horse.

"No, the true bravery was shown by Wolf's Spirit, Ptecila, and the wasichu, Caleb Starr. I had to be there ... he is now my son."

As he was speaking, Crazy Horse turned away facing south. Once again, Raven's eye caught the movement of Blue Feather and Little Hawk walking their horses. She caught him looking and smiled as she waved to him. Chris returned the gesture and let his gaze drift back to the chief.

The war chief of all the Oglala Sioux was still staring southward. A touch of sunlight glanced off a tear that was secreted in one corner of his somber brown eye. Without looking at him, Crazy Horse blinked the moisture away and said, "It saddens me that so many of my brave friends are gone. Okute, if I had a thousand warriors such as you and your three friends, I would be certain to drive the Bluecoats from our land."

He turned and faced him with a melancholy expression in his eyes. When Raven began to tell of Spotted Horse's death, Crazy Horse stopped him. His profound sadness was evident as he proclaimed, "We must be thankful that Wakan Tanka has allowed you and our other friends to survive. We will need you when the Bluecoats return."

Raven's nod of agreement was in step with their walk toward the others. Scar and the other warrior were waiting for some word from their chief as to what was expected of them. Crazy Horse told Raven that he would ride with them toward the big village. Scar and Two Deer, the other hunter, would ride on ahead to look for more game.

Once the group got under way, they slowly moved west. The Oglala chief told Chris that their hunting party was just one of many. Before coming to Greasy Grass, they had reports of a large herd of antelope that was in the area. To date they had been unable to find the sizable herd. Because of the immense size of the village and the thousands of mouths to feed, hunters were constantly foraging.

Raven recalled the thousands of tipis sprawled along the banks of the Rosebud. He remembered his absolute awe when he first saw the vastness of the village. My God, he thought, where has the time gone? It truly feels like it was only yesterday. At the time, he had estimated that there was between six and eight thousand people in the camp. Having since moved to the Little Big Horn, Chris thought it probable that their numbers had increased to even more. Refusing to let himself worry about it, Raven let his thoughts drift to enjoy the wild beauty of the land.

Their file continued to move doggedly westward. All were anxious to resume the normal routine of village life. Soon, Wi finished his journey across the heavens, and it was time for them to stop for the night. In typical Sioux fashion, they made their night camp away from any trees or hills to make it difficult for any enemies to sneak up on them. Tired after their long day on the trail, Raven's group left the hunters at their campfire and turned in early.

Chris' senses were again assailed by the pungent scent of sweet grass and sage, only this time it was much sweeter. His face was buried in the silken tresses of Blue Feather's hair as they lay bundled together in a buffalo robe provided by Crazy Horse. They watched the stars until Chris felt his wife's breathing deepen with sleep as she surrendered to the beckoning night spirits.

With Blue Feather cradled gently in his arms, Raven watched the burly figure of Scar as he moved restlessly around the other campfire. He wondered about the Hunkpapa. Why is he so hostile? Why is he now making such an effort to stay out of my way? It just isn't his style, he thought. He usually does whatever he wants. Could it be, he pondered, that he's here because he wants to switch alliances and take Crazy Horse for his chief?

Among the Sioux tribes, leadership was not hereditary. The people followed whomever they wished. If they tired of one leader they simply chose another.

Raven's thoughts began to drift about like smoke. His sleepy musing turned to food and just before the night spirits caught him, an image flashed through the foggy corridors of his mind ... 'high golden arches against a blue sky, someone handing him a white paper bag and change from a dollar'... it was in his thoughts for mere seconds. His stomach growled. He sighed and surrendered to the pull of needed sleep.

At the other campfire, Two Deer turned the rabbit on its spit before it burned. The delicious smell of cooking meat browning over the open fire dominated the Lakota's thoughts and flooded his senses. Golden arches and paper bags were things that were not of his world and never would be.

CHAPTER 3

▲▲▲▲▲

They had been riding for several hours. The morning sun was no longer pushing their shadows ahead of them; it was content to let their shadows follow along behind.

Blue Feather was riding alongside Raven; the others were strung out single file behind them. Looking back, Chris absently noticed how the varied colors of the horses contrasted the dominant greens and yellows of the rolling grassland. Returning his attention to the upcoming terrain, he let his memory rehash the early morning's conversation with Crazy Horse.

Before leaving the hunters, Raven was determined to find out if the Oglala chief had any idea that there was going to be a big fight with the Bluecoats.

Knowing from first-hand experience how the Lakota believed in the power of visions, Raven told Crazy Horse that he had dreamed that many soldiers had attacked the great village on the Greasy Grass.

Eyes snapping, the war chief had bombarded him with questions such as: 'How many Bluecoats?' 'Where do they attack the village, and when?' These were just some of his rapid-fire questions.

Raven remembered that Custer had followed some deep ravine that led from the top of the bluffs to the river and village below. He was able to add a few other details, but most of the historical details of the fight he couldn't remember. When Raven had finished telling him what he knew, Crazy Horse became very excited. He explained to Chris some of his thoughts.

Before the Rosebud fight, Sitting Bull had a vision of 'many Bluecoats falling into camp upside down with their hats falling off.'After the great victory over Three Stars (General George Crook), most of the chiefs had thought that the prophecy had been fulfilled. Crazy Horse was not one of those chiefs.

Because of Chris' bogus vision, the young Oglala chief believed that an even bigger triumph was forthcoming. He reasoned that with the Bluecoats approaching the village from the bluffs above, it would appear as though they were 'falling into camp.'

Shortly after their morning conversation, Raven and his group had parted company with the hunters and begun the last leg of their journey to the Greasy Grass. As they were leaving, Chris caught a glimpse of Scar glaring at him. It angered him enough so that he could not resist making a childish gesture. Standing in his stirrups and waving, he shouted, "Goodbye, Scar! Say *hau* (hello), to your chief for me!"

Before turning away from the Hunkpapa's hateful stare, Raven saw Crazy Horse behind Scar, shaking his head in consternation and trying to hide his smile.

Raven didn't see his first sign of the village until the mountains dominated the whole horizon. The haze and smoke from hundreds of campfires and the dust from thousands of milling horses rose steadily from a line that stretched several miles across the green landscape. Drawing closer, it became apparent they were approaching the camp from the top of the grassy bluffs that bordered the river and the eastern edge of the encampment. They were on top of the plateau and because of the line of bluffs, the village would remain hidden until they were looking almost directly down on it. Below the bluffs and beyond the river a lush valley sprawled westward. The fertile green grass stretched all the way to the base of the mountains.

We're almost there, he thought. For a split-second he thought he could hear the hum of voices and the laughter of children at play. Knowing that the distance was too great to make it possible, Chris decided that he was hearing one of many sounds created by the shifting winds.

The foursome dipped into a low area then started up the gentle incline that led to the top of the line of bluffs. As they neared the crest, they could hear the strange sound that could only be the vibrant hum of hundreds of voices. The rolling terrain twisted with countless tree-filled gullies and drywashes as they rode upwards.

"IEEOOWAAH!"

The war cry came from behind him! Raven felt the hair on his arms stand on end. He quickly spun The Black. Wolf's big stallion bolted and slammed into The Black and Blue Feather's mount, causing immediate chaos. As they struggled to break clear of each other, Chris strained for a glimpse of the enemy. Little Hawk and Ptecila were spread out far to the rear.

A huge Indian, naked except for a blue cavalry shirt and breech clout, was galloping his pony up and out of a brush-filled gully. Long, unbound hair flowed back from a face covered with vertical white stripes of warpaint. Shoshone! The enemy's identity exploded in Raven's mind. The big Indian screamed his war cry again and quirted his horse straight toward Little Hawk, who appeared frozen in place by shock. The boy had let himself fall behind and was too far away for immediate protection from them, or from Ptecila.

Raven desperately maneuvered The Black, jerking the reins back and forth in an attempt to find a clear lane to ride through. He needed to get closer for the shotgun to be effective. He could see Little Hawk, but his view of the Shoshone was blocked. The boy had stopped his pony and had his bow and arrow in hand. A flicker of sunlight glanced off the arrow as it left Little Hawk's bow. At that very instant, The Black broke into the clear! Raven saw the arrow flash by the Indian's head. His heels pounded The Black's ribs and he rode straight for the enemy Indian. Just as the Indian was drawing within range of the pump, Chris' peripheral vision caught another flash of light as Little Hawk launched another arrow. The big Shoshone threw up his arms and slid from his pony's back. He hit the ground with a loud "thud!" and landed less than thirty feet from Little Hawk. At impact a small cloud of red dust floated up from the body. The boy sat on Hawk's Wing as if he had turned to stone.

Raven's gaze quickly scanned the surrounding slopes for more of the enemy. Finding none he urged The Black forward toward the downed warrior. He could see the feathered shaft of the arrow standing straight up from the Indian's body. It was wiggling. The Shoshone's legs were moving. Chris could hear strange sounds coming from the Indian. He tapped The Black with his heels as he moved closer. Raven jerked back on the reins. He was completely flabbergasted!

Bear's Foot lay flat on his back clutching his stomach with both hands. The white stripes of paint were smeared around his eyes. He appeared to be unhurt, except where Little Hawk's arrow had pierced the flesh of his upper arm.

The sounds coming from him grew louder ... finally, suppressed laughter erupted from the warrior in gargantuan whoops of joy. The smeared, painted area around his eyes was from tears of laughter!

Chris felt his cheeks flush. Anger began to stir deep within his bowels, but even in his fury he had to admire Bear's timing. He had chosen his moment carefully. He waited until Little Hawk had straggled behind. Bear's Foot had then made damn sure he was out of range of the pump before pulling his practical joke.

Behind him, Raven heard a chuckle come from Wolf's Spirit. Then, before he had time to think about it, all three of them were laughing and braying like a trio of jackasses.

Tears had washed away even more of Bear's warpaint, making him appear about as scary as a Barnum and Bailey clown. Paired with the war paint his grin looked ludicrous.

Still holding his stomach from the pain of his held-in laughter, Bear's Foot sat up. He looked up and the smile left his face as suddenly as if a grizzly had slapped it off. A shadow settled over the now worried-looking prankster.

Because of their laughter none had heard Blue Feather's approach. She sat her horse regal as any chief and stared at Bear as if he had just crawled from beneath a very large rock. Bear's Foot wilted before her baleful stare and lowered his eyes. He rose to his knees and when he looked up, Little Hawk was standing in front of him.

Raven could see that his small frame was actually trembling with rage.

"*Heyoka* (clown)! I could have killed you!"

Little Hawk raised his bow overhead, holding it with two hands like a club. Tears pooled in his eyes as, teeth clenched, his whole body shook with the power of his emotions.

Kneeling, Bear's Foot's great size put him near eye level with his young friend. He stared into his eyes and silently waited for Little Hawk's anger to run its course.

The battle raging inside Little Hawk was obvious to Chris. One part of him was furious at being made a fool, while the other trembled with the reality of having come close to killing his good friend.

Staring into Little Hawk's eyes, a somber Bear's Foot spoke with feeling. His voice was as soft as a Chinook breeze as he proclaimed, "*Wonumayin* (a mistake has been made); it was a bad joke my friend."

The bow fell from Little Hawk's trembling fingers as he stepped forward into Bear's waiting arms.

Raven watched as they re-established their bond of friendship and love. He glanced at Blue Feather. She was wearing an expression of disapproval. But as he watched, her face softened and became complacent with understanding. Her gaze shifted and touched Raven. When their eyes met, Blue Feather smiled and looked back at her son and his hulking friend.

Little Hawk stepped out of Bear's embrace and smiled as he brushed away a tear. Seeing the smile encouraged Bear's Foot into making an attempt to bring levity back into the suddenly pensive scenario. The arrow stuck in Bear's arm wobbled and danced as he gave his little friend a brotherly poke on the shoulder. A spark of mischief gleamed in the warrior's eyes as he teased, "It was a bad joke. But it was a good 'bad joke'. . . was it not?"

The sudden sound of hoof-beats captured everyone's attention. Blue Feather had spun her mount around and was galloping away up the incline.

Wasichu's Return

Bear's eyes found Little Hawk's as he prophesied, "I believe I would be a wise man if I were very careful not to let my shadow cross your mother's path for a few suns."

Raven's glance was in time to see his wife arrive at the top of the bluff and then drop out of sight as she rode her pony down into a deep coulee on the other side. He couldn't help wondering if it was the same ravine that Custer would traverse to the village below.

CHAPTER 4

∆∆∆∆∆

From the top of the bluff, Raven looked down on Sitting Bull's great encampment. His head reeled as he gaped at a multicolored sea of tipis and the combined hues of green grass, cottonwood, willow, and plum leaves. The sprawling village was teeming with humanity. Tiny brown and copper figures swarmed amidst the tipis and other shelters that smothered the banks of the twisting Little Big Horn.

Most of the tipis were on the far side of the river, many of the lean-to and brush dwellings were on the near side. A multitude of lodges bordered the looping, serpentine river as far as Chris could see in either direction.

Lifting his gaze Raven looked through the filmy haze of countless campfires. Beyond, far out on the western plain, he could see the billowing dust clouds lifting from the hooves of the vast herd's thousands of horses. To Raven's left was the wide ravine that Blue Feather had ridden down to the village. It started at the very top of the bluff and meandered its way to the valley floor. At the bottom of the coulee the stream-like river widened and whitewater revealed a natural ford. To his right a wider, deeper gully twisted and dipped all the way to the bottom.

Raven's' attention again shifted. The mountains were beckoning. A strange feeling swept over him as he stared westward. He wasn't really sure how it happened, but in his mind's eye, he sensed that he was being transported back to the future. A patina of perspiration glazed his body as his mind rebelled and completely rejected reality. The village below vanished and was replaced with a gathering of grass hootches that evolved into a typical southeastern hamlet. Even the western valley lost its sweep of distance and became a cross-hatch of rice paddies. The far mountains shrunk, moved closer, and became the towering hills of Laos.

At first they appeared to be nothing more than mere random pinpoints of light. With a sudden birth of awareness came an escalating horror. Raven knew that what he was seeing was sunlight reflecting off metal. The cold, wet towel of recognition smacked him squarely in the face. The shock staggered him.

Ten U.S. gunships materialized in the distance like fireflies rising from a swampy pyre. They fanned out into a wide front that was similar to an infantry skirmish line.

Sweat began to slide down his face. He watched helplessly, as the choppers came straight toward him and the defenseless hamlet below. With each heartbeat the gun-ships grew in size until they filled the whole sky.

The entire hamlet was abruptly seized by fingers of terror which created an immediate panic. Chris' ears were assailed by the fearsome screams of women and children. His nostrils became clogged with the stench of their fear. He could taste the bile that rose in their throats as they awaited their horrible fate. He became them. In his mind he crouched against the grass walls of a hootch and awaited the slashing projectiles or agonizing flames of his destiny.

The rhythmic drone of the helicopter rotors increased until the sound covered everything with a blanket of syncopated, totally dominant clamor. In spite of the din, Raven's mind forced him to hear the screams of terror as the villagers awaited the attack of the gunships' rockets. Powerless to stop it, he waited for the explosions to obliterate the guilt induced shrieks of terror resounding inside his skull.

"*Hiyupo* (Come here)!"

Bear's Foot's resonant baritone cut through the mental barrier surrounding Chris' harrowing memories.

With trembling fingers, Raven lifted the reins and turned The Black until he saw his friend sitting his horse at the mouth of the large ravine. With his mind still tingling with the horrors of war, Chris heel-tapped his stallion into a walk. He felt slightly confused and dizzy as he struggled to regain his mental equilibrium. Approaching Bear's Foot, he noticed that Little Hawk and the others had already started their string of horses down into the ravine. When Raven arrived beside him, Bear's Foot's expression lit up with pleasure.

Several changes in Bear's appearance were instantly apparent. Thank God, Chris thought, he's wiped the war paint off his face. The blue cavalry shirt had also been removed, exposing the nasty looking arrow wound. It's probably not as bad as it looks, Raven mused. Bear's Foot, of course, completely ignored it.

"It is good to have you back with us, Okute."

As he spoke the big warrior placed his heavy hand on Raven's shoulder. The two friends quietly sat their horses and grinned, enjoying the moment. Then Bear's Foot unexpectedly dropped his smile and removed his hand.

"Has Blue Feather spoken to you, yet?"

Bear's Foot's query and manner triggered an alarm that buzzed inside the secret place where Chris harbored his anxieties.

"What is wrong?"

His hand snaked out and grasped the warrior's arm.

Throwing his shoulders back and lifting his chin, the Minneconjou looked down at Raven and said, "If she has not told you, then I must. It makes my heart heavy to see my friend so happy to be with his wife again when she does not feel the same."

Finally, Chris saw the tease hidden in his friend's expression. The warrior's eyes snapped with mischief as he continued, "How could she possibly feel the same for you after spending several suns and nights with the greatest warrior and lover in the entire Lakota Nation?"

Keeping a straight face, Raven agreed with him as he replied, "This is true."

As he spoke Raven had pretended to be adjusting his moccasined feet in their stirrups. First he worked on the left one away from Bear. While reaching for the right one, Chris asked, "Is she also aware that you are, without a doubt, the Lakota Nation's poorest horseman?"

Before his last words had left his mouth, Raven had grabbed Bear's Foot's over-sized foot and lifted and heaved with every ounce of strength he possessed. And at the same time he was able to deliver a glancing kick to the belly of Bear's horse. The startled horse lunged forward! Bear's Foot, eyes bulging, appeared to hover for an instant before gravity sent his great bulk crashing to the dusty trail. The loud "thud" followed by an explosive grunt brought a vindictive smile to Raven's face. Grinning from ear to ear he looked down at the 'great warrior' sprawled in the red Montana dust and said, "Because you are my friend, I will be sure to tell Blue Feather how much your riding skills have improved. You have only fallen off your horse twice today."

Raven gave his friend a small salute and moved The Black into the coulee. Bear's Foot's good-natured peel of laughter followed them down the wide trail.

Far below he could see Little Hawk, Ptecila, and Wolf's Spirit approaching the shallow ford of the river. If it wasn't for The Black's muscular back between his legs, Raven could easily have imagined that he was an eagle soaring high over the grassy bluffs.

Instantly, all thoughts of eagles flew from his mind. A lithe figure in a white dress was running between the tipis. When she reached the river she stopped. Blue Feather was coming to meet him. Even with the distance between them, Chris could see that her hair was still wet from bathing and that she had changed into a clean, finer dress. The sight of her, still wet from bathing, made him want her desperately.

During their three days and two nights together on the trail, Raven and Blue Feather had not slept together as husband and wife. They had agreed to wait until they had the privacy of their own lodge before making love.

He felt a tingling, an awareness of the depth of his love for Blue Feather. It coursed through his body like an electric current. The feeling was an unprecedented sensation and the raw power of it frightened him.

As he approached the ford, he watched as she stopped her son and spoke briefly with him. Little Hawk grinned, then turned his pony away and joined Wolf's Spirit and Ptecila as they led their string of horses into the village. Blue Feather's gaze followed her son as he rode off.

Raven coaxed The Black into the icy, swift water of the ford. He let the big horse pick his own way across the rocky bottom. Blue Feather was still facing away from him. The natural beauty of the scene was breathtaking. Backlit by the approaching sunset, her willowy form showed through the finely scraped doeskin, making him ache with desire. Behind her the golden sky created a backdrop of natural radiance. Hundreds of conical tipis were edged with gold in the amber light.

When The Black's hooves inadvertently splashed the water, Blue Feather turned and faced him. Her eyes widened and her full lips parted in surprise.

He felt a tightness well up in his throat as he realized that Blue Feather was play-acting. She was pretending that she was welcoming her husband home from a successful hunt or raid. Her game-playing touched a romantic spot deep inside him.

He felt himself being drawn into the game. Her play-acting was so convincing that he felt compelled to respond. Suddenly, she was running toward him! Her long, unbound hair swirled and danced on her shoulders. The many fringes on her dress leaped and bounced as if struggling to free themselves from their leather bondage. The shallow water splashed away in desperate flight from her flashing legs.

Captivated by the pleasing tinkle of the hawks' bells, that were sewn onto her dress, Chris reached down and swept Blue Feather up into his arms and placed her on the saddle in front of him. She nuzzled against his chest and looked up at him. He could clearly see the mischief in her eyes as she said, "Welcome home, my husband."

Even with the sudden additional weight, The Black's step didn't falter. He continued to cross the ford until all four hoofs were solidly planted on the western bank of the river. He swung his great head around until he could see Blue Feather nestled in Raven's arms. With a roll of his eye and a shake of his black head and mane, The Black expelled air through his flaring nostrils with a quiet whooshing sound.

A familiar scent pulled the fine head around to face the west. Pointed ears stood erect, nostrils quivered. He nickered softly. The Black's questing neigh drifted away in the direction of the distant pony herd.

CHAPTER 5

▲▲▲▲▲

The starlight coming though the lodge's smoke hole touched her unbound hair like moonbeams glancing off a mountain lake. Completely nude, Blue Feather knelt beside their bed of buffalo robes and combed her long black hair. Minute sparks of electricity crackled as she pulled the porcupine quill comb through her ebony tresses.

Reclining on their robes, Raven watched his wife's every move. Feeling his eyes upon her, Blue Feather's gaze captured Chris' as she asked, "Why do you watch me so, my husband?"

Raven shifted so that he was on his side and was completely facing her. The pale light played along the lean muscles of his naked body.

"I watch you because you are beautiful. But I watch you for another reason also."

Taking a deep breath, he quietly continued, "Even if I were able to speak better Lakota, I do not know if I could explain. But I will try."

Chris paused once more and their eyes met. He continued softly by suggesting, "Let me think for a moment, then I will tell you where my thoughts have taken me."

Blue Feather continued to groom her hair; she smiled and shyly looked away as Raven's gaze lovingly explored her nudity.

While his thirsty eyes were refreshed by his wife's beauty, Chris' thoughts reverted to the moments of their

45

earlier lovemaking. They had barely managed to make it inside their tipi before they were tearing at each other's clothing. Raven's excited behavior had been matched by an equally zealous Blue Feather. In their eagerness, neither had managed to get completely undressed. Tangled in each other's clothing, they had tumbled, laughingly, onto their sleeping robes. In a spectacular, frenzy of love and desire, they had joined together. Clutching and grasping, they raced onward through higher and newer levels of sensation. They rode together across bountiful fields of pleasure until, breathlessly, their race toward fulfillment reached a soaring, crescendo of passion. It had left them trembling on the brink of emotional exhaustion.

Reaching with his sun burnished hand, Raven splayed his fingers across Blue Feather's smooth thigh. In the weak light his weathered hand was darker than his wife's skin. He smiled inwardly as he thought of all the world-wide prejudices that were based on the color of a person's skin. His inner grin widened as he recognized the irony that the only people who he had ever loved were of a different race and color.

Feeling his wife's eyes on him, he met her gentle gaze and felt instantly ashamed. Raven had always taken pride in the fact that he was an honest man. At the moment his conscience was bothering him. In his heart, he felt that he must tell his wife about himself. But, how is that possible? He knew instinctively that he couldn't tell her the whole truth, she would think him insane. But Chris felt that he must tell her something ... something close to the truth.

Raven's voice was barely more than a whisper as he said, "Blue Feather, I am a man unaccustomed to making speeches. I have always tried to keep my own council. But now I am not alone and there are some things about myself, and my life, that I feel should be shared with you. You should know that you are the first woman who I have ever loved."

As Chris paused, their gazes intensified. He sensed an alertness in Blue Feather that hadn't been there before. When he continued, there was a new inflection in his voice; a passion that proclaimed a desire to be understood.

"Before I came to the land of the Lakota, I had loved only one other person. That person was a warrior like myself. He was like a brother to me. We did not share the same blood, but we were as close as brothers could be. We lived together and fought side by side. We even watched mutual friends die together. Then the time came when I was forced to watch my 'brother' die."

Raven, before fabricating the remainder of his story, told her what he could of Joe's death and of how he himself had been raised an orphan. Rather than try to explain time-travel, something he didn't understand himself, he told her a tale similar to the one he had told Crazy Horse several months ago. The story went as follows:

After his friend was killed, he had experienced a vision that told him his brother's spirit had come to the land of the Lakota. The vision also told him that his friend's greatest weapon should be brought to him, so that he would be able to protect himself in the spirit world.

At that point in his narrative, Blue Feather interrupted him. Her large, dark eyes appeared larger than normal as she exclaimed, "The many shooter with no barrel!"

Smiling at her description of the snub-nosed shotgun, Raven replied, "Yes."

He felt a small twinge of guilt, but knew that she would not question his story of the vision. Lakota were firm believers in the validity of dreams and he knew his wife was no exception.

"I have told you these things of my life so that you will see how important you are to me. This is why I watch you so often. I am afraid if I look away you will vanish like a *wanagi* (spirit), and I will never see you again."

Blue Feather set aside her comb and took Raven's hand in her small fists, pressing it tightly against her warm body.

Feeling the silky warmth of her belly against his fingertips, Chris felt a stirring sensation as he began to physically respond.

Eyes smoldering, Blue Feather impishly moved his hand and placed it on her breast.

"See, Okute, I am real. I am not of the spirit world."

Maneuvering his hand against her body her lips parted, and her breathing became more rapid.

Raven's thinking process had completely shut down. His mind was drowning in a sea of sensation. Her nipples became erect islands in an ocean of softness.

Blue Feather's head dropped forward. Her hair enveloped her upper body like a cape. Still on her knees, she moved her legs apart and moved Chris' captured hand down along the silken contour of her body.

In a voice, breathless with passion, Blue Feather said, "Come my husband, we will become as one."

Still grasping his hand, she gracefully slipped astride his hips. Raven's hands automatically grabbed the firm flesh of her hips. Blue Feather released his hand and leaned forward, allowing her hair to enclose them in a curtain of black rain.

Her head snapped up, and she gasped, as Raven entered her. Slowly, she leaned forward. Her hands moved up and across the flat planes of his chest until they reached his shoulders. A sudden intake of air hissed past her teeth, as she shifted her hips to keep him captive inside her. Blue Feather's hands left his shoulders, sliding onto the buffalo robe on either side of his head. Neither moved. Her hair again cascaded down and blocked out all light. He could feel the heat of her breath caress his throat. He was trapped in a cocoon of love and sensuality as the sweet grass and sage scent of her made his head spin. She leaned forward. He felt her breasts touch his chest as she breathed words in his ear that captivated his soul. Raven moved his hands behind Blue Feather's shoulders and pulled her to him. She moaned as he rolled over, reversing their positions, and began to move. Her hot breath in his ear spurred him on until he became a hammer to her anvil. Quickly the fuse burned upward, scintillating within the very core of him until it burst in a shower of pulsating sensation as Chris' muffled voice pierced the silence. Blue Feather's back arched and she cried out, her voice echoing Raven's, as spasms of pleasure racked her body.

They nestled in each other's arms and let the cooling night air soothe their damp, heated bodies. Together they listened to the night sounds of the village. They could hear children laughing, voices calling, dogs barking, and horses nickering. The collective sounds were pleasing to their ears, comforting them as they whispered words of love and spoke of forever.

CHAPTER 6

▲▲▲▲▲

When the rising sun peered over the high bluffs on the eastern side of the Little Big Horn River, hundreds of Sioux and Cheyenne were already busy at their morning routines. Not all of the tipis were busy with early morning chores. One Minneconjou lodge occupant in particular had a very disturbing wake up call.

Raven's eyes popped open with the mechanical suddenness of a shutter admitting light into a camera's lens. Dust motes danced within the rays of sunlight that penetrated the tipi's smokehole. Also, because of the porous nature of the tanned-hide walls, a soft, rosy light was filtering into the lodge's interior. Mixed together, the two light sources created a cozy, lustrous atmosphere.

Raven was oblivious to the special coziness of the moment. All his senses were focussed into one unit of concentration. Holding his body taut as a stretched cable, he listened. There! He heard it again! It was the faint, unmistakable sound of a bugle. Custer! In an instant he was on his feet. Chris paused, glanced at the sleeping form of his wife, grabbed his shotgun, and burst through the tipi's doorflap. The direct sunlight stabbed at his eyes. Squinting, he looked to the east, past the tipis and other dwellings, to the towering bluffs. Nothing. He couldn't understand it; everything appeared normal. Children were swimming and playing games, while the women were mending clothes and chattering away with each other. Men were cleaning weapons and gossiping. Just then there was a sharp, off-key blast on a bugle. Raven spun around!

South of him, less than 75 feet away, a Lakota was sitting astride his pony as it walked through the village. He was examining a captured bugle, obviously trying to solve its mysteries. A small group of children were tagging along beside him. Some of them were imploring the warrior to let them handle the horn.

Raven's relief was as immediate as if he had just shed a heavy rucksack. Hearing a suppressed giggle come from behind, he turned around. Blue Feather's mother, White Star, was staring at him with a look of distaste. The two girls beside her looked vaguely familiar. They were having difficulty holding back more giggles with their hands.

Because of the Lakota custom that prohibits a son-in-law and mother-in-law from speaking directly to one another, Chris said nothing. Unfortunately for him, White Star knew how to handle the situation. And she did so with obvious relish.

Still maintaining eye contact with Raven, White Star turned her head toward the pretty girl on her left and said, "There is talk among the people that the wasichu has been sent to us from the gods. If that is so, why would an emissary of such importance wish to flaunt his less than God-like manhood in front of two young women?"

With her last words White Star's eyes dropped. Raven looked down. His mouth fell open with the realization. that he was stark, bare-assed naked! With the shock came an explosion of red-faced embarrassment. His humiliation was so complete that his knees began to quiver. He was certain that at any moment his ears would burst into flames from the intense heat of his blush. Taking a deep breath, Chris stood up straight and fought down the burning desire to cover himself. Trying desperately to ignore the teasing gleam he saw in White Star's eyes, he turned away. With the sound of the girls' giggles resounding in his ears, Raven scuttled quickly to the comforting haven of the dark shadows inside his tipi.

About two-hundred feet from Raven's tipi and across the shallow river was the base of the bluffs. It was there, beside the river, that many of the unmarried warriors had erected their assorted dwellings. Bear's Foot was one of those warriors who had a lean-to close to the water's edge. He was asleep. Sprawled on his back, his snores were as Herculean in volume as the great warrior was in size. Although the open front of his lean-to was just a few feet away from the water, Little Hawk's revenge was only inches away.

It was known far and wide that Bear's Foot feared neither man nor beast. A lesser known fact is that the big warrior was terrified of reptiles ... especially snakes! Too bad for him that Little Hawk was one of the few who knew of it.

With great stealth and the help of two forked sticks, Little Hawk positioned the wriggling snake directly over Bear's Foot's inert form. The harmless bull snake kept squirming and twisting, forcing Little Hawk to give it his complete attention. He concentrated on keeping the snake on his sticks until it was suspended perfectly over Bear's reclining body. Knowing that timing was everything, Little Hawk snatched the sticks away allowing the snake to drop. The very instant that its writhing coils landed on the warrior's chest, the boy's warning cry broke through Bear's Foot's mighty snores.

"*Aa-ah!*"

The big warrior's eyes snapped open! Seeing and feeling the wriggling, brown coils on his broad chest, Bear's Foot let loose a bellow that turned heads a quarter of a mile away.

He catapulted out from beneath his lean-to so quickly that his initial momentum carried him into the shallows of the river, where his moccasined feet desperately battled for purchase on the slippery rocks. Both feet lost their struggle at the same time Bear's Foot's legs went in the air and his breech-clouted buttocks hit the water with a resounding, liquid smack. The ensuing waves of water drenched several waders and swimmers near at hand.

A small boy, who had been thoroughly saturated, took it as a personal affront. He strode purposefully through the thigh deep shallows until he was squarely in front of the sprawled form, Bear's Foot. Bear ignored the boy's approach. His full attention was on the nearby, jubilant Little Hawk.

Suddenly, the little boy scooped a double handful of water and playfully splashed it into the huge warrior's face. Bear's Foot quietly sat and glared at the little boy as streams of river water rolled down his broad face.

Swimmers and spectators of all ages began to taunt Bear with their laughter and shouted insults. The brave, little warrior quickly scampered out of reach.

Several of the men on the shore began to mockingly voice the Lakota courage cry, "*Huhn, huhn.*" Several shouts of, "Brave up, brave up," added insult to injury.

Both the courage and rallying cry sounded ludicrous, mixed in with the teasing and laughter.

Bear's Foot took the time to throw his hecklers a threatening look before returning his glare back to Little Hawk, who was whooping with laughter.

Refusing to avert his eyes from Bear's murderous stare, Little Hawk abruptly stopped laughing and lifted his chin. With haughty disdain, he said, "If you are through playing with my snake, O' mighty warrior, I will now leave with him and leave you to your bath."

Scooping up the harmless serpent, Little Hawk then spun on his heel and began to walk away. He had only taken a couple of steps when all at once he heard a sound unlike anything he had ever heard before. It was a huge splashing sound that blended frighteningly with the bellow of a large, wounded animal.

Without looking back to confirm his worst fears, Little Hawk threw his snake into the air and ran.

Many have said that on that day, 'Little Hawk's fast start was equal to that of The Black.' But then, there were others that have said, 'When someone as large and angry as Bear's Foot is chasing, anyone would be able to show exceptional speed.'

CHAPTER 7

▲▲▲▲▲

Raven was sitting in front of their tipi in the heart of the Minneconjou camp. He had just finished tying the laces that held a leather sheath over the pumpgun's damaged stock. At first, all he could hear was a general murmur of excitement sweeping through the village. It was coming from the south end of the village, near the Hunkpapa and Blackfoot circles. The sound grew nearer and swept into the Minneconjou camp with the speed of a runaway racehorse. He heard the Lakota herald shouting the news, "The chargers are coming! They are coming!"

What in the hell are 'chargers'? The thought had just barely registered when he heard the familiar, crackle and pop, and instantly knew.

"Gunfire!" Raven said aloud, as he stood up. Forgotten remnants of leather fell from his lap.

With the unexpected shooting coming from the south, he then remembered how Reno, with part of the Seventh Cavalry, had attacked the village at the Hunkpapa edge of the village.

His first thought was of Blue Feather. Where is she? His mind did a cartwheel as he struggled for clarity of thought. A flash of memory told him that she was west of the village with several other women, looking for turnips. Relief cleared his mind and he recalled that Little Hawk was also in the west with the pony herd.

55

A tumultuous wave of sound was rolling nearer with every heartbeat. With it came a tide of people of all ages. Raven heard several bullets smack and rattle among the tipis. The sweeping ripple of panic and fear was causing the hairs on his neck to stand on end. Chris' eyes quickly swept to the scattered clouds of dust that were rising in the south. He began to see splashes of blue among the khaki colored dust. Bluecoats! Raven's gaze immed-iately lifted to the northeast and the tall line of grassy bluffs. Seeing the empty skyline came as a surprise. He had half expected to see Cavalry Troopers silhouetted against the blue sky. Where is Custer? His query remained unanswered. Quickly, Raven turned toward the west and began to thread his way through the throngs of people while he checked his pockets and belt, assuring that he had enough ammo for both of his weapons. Everywhere he looked, people were on the move. Warriors were splashing on war paint while hanging on to their wildly excited horses. Women and children were darting here and there, gathering weapons and shields for the men. The crackling gunfire had become a permanent pall of noise over the village; a tirade of staccato sound that was a relentless reminder that death was in the air.

Chris' step faltered and he stopped. A wild-eyed hag came screeching between the tipis. She was waving a pole with a battered human head mounted on it. Its long matted hair proclaimed it to be an Indian head. It was so crushed that it barely retained anything that looked human. The old woman was running up to people and sticking the gory object in their faces. He saw one warrior yell at the woman, push her away, then gestured for her to leave. Raven then saw a fresh blood trail running the length of the pole that had turned the woman's hands a bright red. Her eyes were wild and crazy as she disappeared into the masses.

Fighting down the sour bile that had risen in his throat, Raven once again forced his way through the wild, surging crowd. He heard more bullets slap into the skin walls of tipis. A horse screamed and went down. Old warriors were giving advice to younger fighters that didn't want to take the time to listen, while other older men were helping to round up the young children, who appeared to be everywhere at once.

The shooting became more intensified but the sound fluctuated. The increase in gunfire volume was challenged by the escalation of Sioux and Cheyenne war cries. Dozens of warriors raced by, whipping their ponies in their eagerness to reach the south end of the Hunkpapa camp.

Still moving west, Chris felt he was doing well simply by managing not to be trampled. In the middle of it all, the wild-eyed horses, the dust and shouting, jostling villagers, Raven saw a welcome sight. Sorting his way through the churning mass of humanity and animals was Little Hawk. He was riding his pony, Hawk's Wing, and leading The Black. Having spied Chris, he angled toward him, trying to reach him without trampling anyone.

Raven broke into a run and swiftly moved through and around the milling, panic-induced crowd, until he was at Little Hawk's side. Raven was surprised and pleased by the lack of fear on the boy's face. As he handed Chris the reins, he was vibrating with excitement but appeared unafraid. Taking The Black's reins, Raven reached up and pulled Little Hawk closer so that he would be able to hear him. Raven shouted so that he would be certain to be heard. The noise level was increasing at an amazing rate.

"Listen carefully. We must find your mother as quickly as possible and bring her back here to the village. She is too close to the ponyherd. The Bluecoats will have sent some of their Indians to make a try for the horses."

Swinging up on The Black, Raven looked south. Through the veil of dust he could see that the soldiers' advance had been stopped and that many appeared to be retreating. They look totally unorganized, he thought, as he watched some Bluecoats stopping to fight as others rode for the trees by the river.

Raven hastily turned The Black and wove his way through the lodges toward the rising ground in the west. Little Hawk kept his pony close behind. When they cleared the tipis they urged their mounts into a canter, then a gallop.

The giant ponyherd was situated on top of a flat-topped bench about two miles from them. Somewhere in between would be the turnip hunters. To reach it, Chris and Little Hawk had some obstacles to overcome. Horseback Indians were everywhere. Most of them were moving toward the fighting in the south, but many were still bringing horses into the village.

Raven stared in awe at all the whirling, swirling horses and riders. It's like a busy intersection, he thought, without any stoplights.

All around the valley, clouds of dust were climbing into the air obliterating the clean blue of the sky. Coming from the distant ponyherd, the sound of gunfire could be heard, and then seen, as flashes of color flared within the haze of rising dust.

Crouched over The Black's bobbing neck, Chris urged him to an even greater speed. He felt a growing tightness in his stomach as he realized how close his wife must be to the shooting.

A line of dark, moving dots appeared between Raven and the pastoral western foothills. The images had emerged so quickly and were growing in size so rapidly that it took seconds for Chris to realize exactly what it was that he was seeing. It wasn't until the wraith-like figures appeared to rise directly from the earth's core that he recognized them as being the women turnip hunters. They were running abreast up the slope of a ravine. Because of the distance, the gully wasn't visible and the women looked like dark specters floating up from the ground.

The instant Raven recognized Blue Feather among the running women, the tightness in his stomach eased and he momentarily relaxed. It was immediately apparent that the women had been running hard. Several of the younger ones were helping the older ones, who were struggling to keep up.

With growing horror, Raven watched two riders slowly appear behind the ragged line of running women. Their spector-like appearance caused his stomach to again tie into a knot of anxiety. They were quirting their ponies mercilessly and with each lengthy stride, they gained on the fleeing women.

Because of the flowing long hair and distinctive warpaint, Raven knew that they were the enemy. Then, he noticed that one Indian was even wearing a blue army shirt.

Quickly shouting instructions to Little Hawk, Chris tightened his grip on the pumpgun and dug his heels into The Black's ribs. As he swiftly approached the running women, he shouted a warning, "A-ah!" The shout opened a breach in the line of women. Their frightened faces were a blur as The Black hit the opening in full stride. Wanting to divert their attention from the fleeing women, Raven opened fire with the pump before he was in effective range.

The spray of double-ought buckshot brought the lead rider's pony to a sliding, lurching stop. The injured horse promptly began to buck and spin, completely out of control. The warrior wearing the blue soldier shirt, was having a problem with his rifle and his mount. His pony shied away from coming any closer and kept backing away. The Indian, seeing Raven's hard-riding approach, struggled desperately with his rifle. At a distance of twenty feet, Raven solved the enemy's problems for him. The load of buckshot blew him out from behind his faulty firearm and completely off his balking horse.

Chris turned The Black in time to see the other enemy warrior sail off his bucking horse and land in a sprawling heap on the hard ground. He was on his feet in an instant and immediately began to sprint for the cover of a nearby stand of trees.

Beneath his legs, Raven felt The Black's muscles bunch and stretch as they quickly closed the distance. Hearing their approach, the warrior stopped. His weapons gone, the Indian turned around and stoically waited to die.

By the time he had turned around, Chris was almost on top of him. His pumpgun had already begun its downward arc toward the unprotected head. Within the split-second time frame it would have taken to complete the shotgun's swing, Raven's eyes met those of his adversary. Shock zapped him like a bolt of lightning! He reflexively checked his swing. Unable to stop his stroke, the intended killing blow merely glanced off the Indian's head, stunning him. Stupefied, Chris slowed The Black and walked him back toward the fallen man.

Still shaken, Raven looked beyond the man, who was lying absolutely still, to Little Hawk. He was busy encouraging a faster pace out of the women as they continued their flight to the village. The youngster was also trying to watch for any other impending dangers as he did so.

Stopping beside the downed Indian, Raven looked down on him, noticing that he hadn't moved but his eyes were watching him. The Indian, who looked like a Crow, appeared to be only semi-conscious. Raven's voice was harsh as he barked, "Don't move!"

When he again looked at the paint streaked face, he received another jolt. The man's eyes were as light-colored as his own. Except for the slight Indian features, it was like looking into a mirror. Looking closely, Chris saw that the warrior's eyes were a light blue and that beneath the white paint he wasn't much older than Little Hawk. He remembered how earlier, at the Rosebud, he had been in a similar situation.

Instead of killing a young soldier, he had hesitated and it had nearly cost him his life. He silently vowed to himself that if this light-eyed Crow even looks cross-eyed at him, he'll soon be dead meat. Staring into the youthful eyes, Raven asked, "Do you speak English?"

The disconcerting eyes studied him before he gave a hesitant nod.

Raven's face hardened into taut, rigid planes as he said, "I want you to stay where you are until I'm into the village." He silently stared down at the youth for a moment before continuing. "If I see you again today, I will kill you! Do you understand?"

With his gaze solidly locked onto Raven's face, the young breed slowly nodded.

Raven jerked on The Black's reins. The big horse spun around with ease and they galloped after Little Hawk. As he listened to the decreasing gunfire in the southeast, Chris knew that when he had more time, he would question what it was that had stopped him from killing the youth. He knew it wasn't simply because of the pale blue eyes; it had to be something more.

By the time Raven caught up, the women were already in the village and the sounds of shooting seemed to be farther away. Looking to the south he could still see billowing dust and Lakota and Cheyenne riders disappearing into the tan haze.

A spirited Little Hawk swept by, shouting that he was going for the scalps that Raven had left behind. It took a hard word from Chris to stop him. As Hawk's Wing returned with a dejected Little Hawk, Raven gave him the excuse that they didn't have time.

Suddenly, Blue Feather was at his stirrup. Looking into her shining face, he saw that it was teeming with mixed emotions. He quickly looked around, as riders went whooping by. Things are heating up again, he thought. Animated people and horses were everywhere. He knew something must be done to help the old ones and the young. He noticed that many of them seemed to be instinctively heading toward the river and the shelter of trees.

Bending from the waist, Raven grabbed Blue Feather behind the head. Pulling her close, he kissed her quickly and released her.

"I must go and help with the fighting," he said.

Their eyes met and held. Reluctantly, he turned away from her intending to shout for Little Hawk. When he looked back, the boy was sitting his pony behind him.

Pleased, Chris smiled. With a serious demeanor, he said, "Hawk, you must see that your mother safely reaches the other women and children."

A large group of Sioux and Cheyenne rode by, their war cries and shouts added to the existing din causing Raven to shout to make himself heard.

"Stay with her until I come for you!"

"It will be as you say, Okute!"

Raven was surprised and pleased by Little Hawk's apparent complaisant attitude. He had thought for sure that he would have insisted on fighting with the warriors.

"I am proud of you, Hawk. Be careful!"

He turned away from the fervent intensity of Little Hawk's gaze, only to be met by his wife's beseeching eyes. He smiled and swung away. Pulling The Black's great head around, he touched the black ribs with his heels. He deftly maneuvered the stallion between the lodges and moved north. Lifting his gaze to the top of the bluffs, Raven suddenly pulled The Black to a stop. His breath caught in his throat as he saw the tiny blue-clad figures riding in column along the ridge. He knew, beyond a shadow of a doubt, that he was looking at the doomed command of George Armstrong Custer.

BATTLE

PART 2

EXCERPT FROM THE JOURNAL OF CETAN CHIKALA (LITTLE HAWK)

▲▲▲▲▲▲▲▲

My heart was on the ground. I wanted very much to join Okute in the fight against the Bluecoats. But Okute was right, someone must be there to protect my mother from our enemies. There must also be someone who is willing to stay with those of our people that cannot care for themselves. It was a responsibility that I had to accept.

My mother and I moved closer to the bluffs, gathering as many people as were willing to come with us. In contrast to the children running everywhere, several of the old ones were standing around. It appeared as though they were unsure what they should do, or where they should go to find shelter. They, as well as we, ignored the many empty lodges nearby. We knew from experience, if the Bluecoats made it this far into the village, all the lodges would be burned. We quickly gathered as many people as we could and moved them toward the river.

In no time at all, we were among the trees and beside the shallow, meandering river. As the fighting continued in the south two younger boys and I kept watch. When a sudden burst of gunfire sounded like it was closer to us, I decided to move the group farther north along the base of the bluffs. Some of the women questioned my decision. An old man, who used to be a chief, spoke in my support.

Barry Brierley

"Little Hawk's grandfather was a fine chief of the Minneconjou Sioux. The boy now carries the talisman that had always brought good fortune to their band. It is wakan (holy), surely it has given the boy his grandfather's wisdom. That is all I have to say."

When the old chief ended his short speech, I was certain that I could feel my heart swell with pride. Beneath my deerskin shirt I could feel the weight of the horse carving as it rested against my chest. His words also brought memories of my grandfather, and for a moment, tears stung my eyes. I quickly turned away so they would not be seen and perhaps be mistaken for tears of fear or indecision. After the old one's fine speech it would be unfortunate for the others not to have faith in me because of a few tears. As it turned out, Wakan Tanka was with me, and my leadership was not questioned again.

We moved north as swiftly as our most feeble could walk. The other boys and I kept a constant watch for the enemy. There was still shooting in the south but not as much as before. The activity in the village had lessened, yet there were still Lakota and Cheyenne riders racing here and there.

I jerked Hawk's Wing to a sudden stop. I thought that I had heard the faraway sound of a Bluecoat's bugle. I must have been mistaken, for I did not hear it again. We moved forward again. This time we all listened for any sound that would warn us of impending danger.

We had traveled but a short distance when we came to a sharp bend in the river. Everyone hid in the willows that crowded the west bank while I rode on ahead. I had to make sure that the enemy was not waiting beyond the bend in the river where it turns back on itself like a snake.

Wasichu's Return

Since I was the only one with a horse, it was decided by the others that an Oglala girl named Fawn would come with me. She was known to be a very fast runner. If I ran into trouble, or if I was seen by any Bluecoats, she was supposed to return with the news while I rode away like the ground nesting mother bird who fakes an injury and leads the danger away from the nest.

Shortly after rounding the bend I heard unexpected gunfire. It was coming from the north! The shots were quickly followed by the hated sound of a bugle.

I again jerked my pony to a stop. Fawn quickly slipped into the brush and among some trees. There was more firing followed by war whoops and shouts of, "Brave up! Brave up!"

To my left I could see warriors out by the lodges riding hard toward the new fighting. The shooting in the south still continued but sounded much further away.

Just as I was about to turn Hawk's Wing and return to the others, two Indians burst into view. They came from another twist in the river up ahead and were coming straight toward me. Ree army scouts! They must be running from the new fight, I thought.

The instant they saw me, they yanked hard on their ponies' reins and came to a stop. They stared and began jabbering to each other. I don't think they saw Fawn; she kept out of sight, discreetly peering from behind a tree. Judging from their actions, they looked as though they couldn't believe their good fortune ... a small Lakota boy all by himself, an easy scalp. The biggest Ree was grinning. He was probably thinking of the lies he would tell of his bravery as he displayed my fine scalp. I hoped he was thinking that when my arrow struck his eye and pierced his brain. Startled, the other Ree became enraged. Before his comrade's body had struck the ground, he shouted and whipped his pony into an all out gallop. His rifle came up and with the sound of the explosion, I felt fire kiss my cheek as the bullet buzzed on by. Hawk's Wing had jumped sideways at the sudden noise. I stared in horror as the enemy Ree thundered toward me, his rifle held high like a war club. My shaking hands fumbled for another arrow. In my haste I tipped my quiver, spilling my remaining arrows onto the dirt. Panic gripped me. I could not move!

The charging Ree was grinning like a hungry wolf. Suddenly, there was a sharp pain in my leg. The girl, Fawn, was proffering one of my arrows and staring up at me. Her big-eyed face was alive with excitement. I wanted to shout, why did you not run away to warn the others? But there was not time; the Ree was closing in on me! I felt the pain again. She had jabbed me again with one of my arrows! I snatched it from her hand and was swiftly notching it when I felt Mother Earth begin to shake. The Ree slid his horse to a stop. His eyes were wide with fear as he wheeled his mount in a tight spin and whipped it with his quirt as he tried desperately to ride back the way he had come. It was not until then that I heard the thunderous clamor of many hoofs.

"Hokahey!"

The shouted war cry thrilled me to my very soul. I felt the air tug gently, as my pony shied away from the passage of a hard-charging, spotted stallion. The horse's rider brushed by me so closely that I could smell the fresh blood on his powerful body. I caught a glimpse of a bloody hatchet held high in a massive fist. By the time I got Hawk's Wing back under control, a whole host of Lakota had swept by. My eyes again found the hard-riding leader just in time to see him bury his hatchet in the skull of the fleeing Ree.

Wasichu's Return

The enemy warrior tumbled from his pony as if his bones had suddenly disappeared. The leader quickly pulled his stallion to a halt. As the others galloped by him, he held his pony back as it struggled to join them. He looked hard at me. My heart seemed to stop beating. His fierce face was not unknown to me. It was the famous Hunkpapa war chief, Gall!

Within three heartbeats, my eyes had absorbed every detail of the famous chief. Except for a single, eagle feather, loin cloth and moccasins, his muscular body was naked. His face, right arm, and leg were splashed with blood. A gore encrusted hatchet was his only weapon.

His fierce eyes met mine and he brandished his hatchet overhead as he voiced the Lakota courage cry, "Huhn, huhn!" Spinning his spotted stallion, he dug his heels in and within two jumps had almost caught up with the others. I stared open-mouthed as they disappeared around the bend where the enemy Ree had first appeared.

Later, I was to learn that Gall's wife and two of his children were killed in the initial attack on the Hunkpapa village. It has been said that when Gall heard the terrible news of his family, he vowed that he would kill many Bluecoats and that all would die by the hatchet.

A sudden increase in gunfire reminded me of my responsibilities. All at once, I remembered the girl. Fawn was standing a short distance away. Her hands were behind her back and she was watching me. Her large, soft eyes revealed how she came by her name. I reached out my hand to her and said, "Hopo (let's go)! We must tell the others that we must go back."

She hesitated. I quickly moved Hawk's Wing beside a tall boulder so that the Oglala girl would be able to climb up behind me. As she moved to the boulder I became impatient, forgetting that she was only eleven winters not the thirteen winters that I have lived. Well, almost thirteen.

"Hurry! Why are you so slow? What are you hiding behind your back?"

With my last words her face flushed with anger. She thrust her hand out to me and stepped up on the rock. Then it was my turn to blush. I did so, not out of anger, but from humiliation. In her hand were the arrows that I had dropped because of my fear. The words that accompanied her offering did not soothe my embarrassment.

"Here, great warrior, are the arrows that you so carelessly spilled upon the ground. Did you feel that your medicine was so strong that you did not have need of a weapon against the Ree?"

With those words and a scathing look that made me wish that I were someplace else, she leaped onto Hawk's back and locked her skinny arms around my waist. The instant Hawk's Wing felt her weight, he broke into a gallop and we raced for the southern bend in the river. I liked to think that my pony was hurrying because he also was anxious to rid himself of the insulting Oglala girl.

It was not until we had turned the bend that I realized that I was so upset by the girl's words that I had forgotten to take the weapons and the hair of the two Rees. I was thinking of leaving the girl to carry the news when I heard one of the boys on lookout give the signal that I was a friend. The people immediately began to leave the willows and walk back in the direction from where we had come. It was not necessary for me to tell of the danger ahead. Just the increase in activity, with mounted Indians riding through the village to the north and the sudden roll of gunfire, was enough to send everyone further south.

Wasichu's Return

Fawn slid off my pony's back. She looked up and gave me a bright smile. With a flirtatious manner far beyond her innocent years, Fawn purred, "When you again have a need for an Oglala girl to be a quiver for your arrows, think of me. I will come, Warrior."

Once again my ears were burning with embarrassment. I quickly left Fawn to look for her mother, while I made a hasty withdrawal to find my own.

I found her helping an old one over a windfall that had fallen across the path beside the river. I could see the worry on her face as we heard the rapidly increasing noise of gunfire and war cries. As we steadily moved the people away from the battle, my mother's eyes and mine touched for an instant. I am sure that her thoughts were of Okute, as mine were. I prayed to Wakan Tanka that he remain safe, that his magical fighting skills stay strong, and that he was of a brave heart.

CHAPTER 8

▲▲▲▲▲

Raven felt compelled to continue north, keeping pace with the soldiers on the bluff. Everywhere he looked warriors were either slapping on war paint or racing south toward the popping of the distant gunfire. No one seemed to notice the tiny figures on the bluffs.

Looking back he thought he caught a final glimpse of Little Hawk disappearing into the trees by the river. He was with a large number of women and children, who were trying to encourage the old ones into a faster pace to enable them to get out of sight. Moving north again, Chris saw another large group of people running and hobbling far to the west. He couldn't be certain but he thought that he saw the familiar squat form of Sitting Bull among them. The Hunkpapa medicine man was riding a black horse and waving a rifle overhead as he herded the young and elderly out of harm's way. He disappeared in a cloud of dust as more riders passed between them.

Putting Sitting Bull out of his mind, Raven urged The Black into a gallop. All the lodges nearby were empty. Everyone was either running to the fight or away from it. Superimposed over the faint popping of far away gunfire came the pure notes of a bugle. It drew his gaze back to the grassy ridge of the bluffs and the pale blue of the skyline. The long thin line of blue-clad riders had stopped at the mouth of a coulee. The wide gully moved diagonally down the side of the bluff, ending at the ford of the Little Big

Horn. Spellbound, Chris watched as a troop of cavalry, all mounted on gray horses, started down the ravine. It suddenly dawned on him that it was the same gully that he and his friends had ridden down several days ago.

If Raven hadn't spent most of his adult life in the military, he might not have noticed what he did. It really blew his mind to see that some of the troopers weren't wearing regulation headgear. Their hats were different. Some of the soldiers were actually wearing what appeared to be wide-brimmed straw hats. My god, he thought, they're even white, while regulation is black. While he watched, a couple of troopers were having some difficulty on a steep portion of the coulee. Raven gaped as a couple of their hats fell off and tumbled down the trail ahead of them. "Damn," he muttered, "it's like Sitting Bull's dream, '... Bluecoats falling into camp upside down, with their hats falling off'."

A flicker of movement caught his eye and brought his attention away from the soldiers. Far away, near the bottom of a distant slope that flowed down from one of the more outlying bluffs, several Indians were racing their ponies hard. It looked as though they were making an effort to reach the trees as quickly as possible. Because of the distance, Raven couldn't see who the Indians were, but he was willing to guess that they were returning scouts who had seen the Bluecoats. Maybe, he thought, they're hoping to stop the soldiers from entering their village.

His attention was drawn back to the bluffs. Two more troops, riding matched bays, followed those mounted on gray horses into the descending ravine. The remainder of the cavalrymen stayed up on the ridge and began to follow it north.

Raven pulled The Black to a stop. He was confused and didn't know what to do. His thoughts were bouncing around inside his skull like a rubber ball in a handball court. Where in the hell, he thought, is Crazy Horse? He was certain that he had told him about the soldiers coming down from the bluffs. The steady crackle of gunfire from the south, added to the muffled noises coming from nearby troopers and horses, was disconcerting. He couldn't think! Frustrated and nervous, Chris pushed aside his fears and let his military instincts take over.

He jabbed his heels into The Black's ribs; he squatted and lunged into a gallop. Raven headed directly toward the ford of the river opposite the mouth of the coulee. Off to the west he could still see riders moving south. He was beginning to think he was the only one out of the thousands nearby, who was aware that a column of Bluecoats was but minutes away from riding into their village.

Breaking clear of the tipis he was just in time to see the first of the soldiers approach the ford. They stopped. It was so unexpected, Raven was flabbergasted. To his disbelieving eyes, it looked as though a few of the officers were in a heated discussion. Near the guidon and standard bearer, one officer stood out from the others. It was mainly his mode of dress that set him apart. He was dressed in buckskins, wearing a white hat and a red scarf around his neck. Chris watched as he pointed and gestured toward the village. He couldn't understand why they had stopped.

The buckskin-clad officer stood in his stirrups and waved his arm. The soldiers spurred their mounts and surged toward the shallow river. The village waited a mere two hundred feet away.

While closing in on the crossing, Raven saw four horseback Indians abruptly appear from behind the empty lodges. All at once, they used their quirts, and their ponies charged into the shallows toward the oncoming Bluecoats.

All four warriors began firing their weapons the instant their horses' hoofs hit the water.

The cavalry stopped their advance! Raven couldn't believe it. They stopped because of an attack by four warriors. Unbelievable! All Chris could figure was that the soldiers were awed by such a display of raw courage. Had the troopers continued their forward progress they would easily have ridden right over the Indians and been in the village.

The troopers, trying to control their milling horses, began to return the warriors' fire. The four Indians quickly made for cover on the village side of the river. Finding protection behind a sandbar that was near the far shore, they returned gunfire on the soldiers.

Raven was incredulous. What were they waiting for? Even as he speculated, the mass of blue-clad soldiers was growing at an alarming rate. He was close enough then to see that the mouth of the ravine was becoming bottled up. Several saddles had already been emptied, but still they hesitated.

Suddenly, he began to draw fire. Ignoring the snap and hum of the bullets, Raven maneuvered The Black toward the four warriors, firing from behind the narrow sandbar.

Why haven't the Bluecoats acted? His silent question went unanswered. They're but a heartbeat away, he mused, from having the advantage of being inside the village.

Hooves driving hard into the water The Black splashed in behind the natural fort. Oblivious to the rattle and buzz of bullets slicing through the brush and trees, Chris leaped from the saddle. He slid into a space beside one of the warriors and was greeted by a grinning, red and black striped face that must have been created in hell. From the middle of the demonic war paint came a voice that Raven knew as well as his own.

Barry Brierley

"What took you so long, Okute?"

Bear's Foot's facetious question left Chris speechless, as usual.

CHAPTER 9

▲▲▲▲▲

A sudden acceleration in the hum and smack of deflecting bullets were like punctuations to his friend's ribbing words. Raven marveled at how Bear's Foot always seemed to be the most content when his life was in danger. He shook his head in awe of him. Chris interrupted his musing long enough to fire two thunderous blasts of buckshot toward the milling cavalry mounts. Glancing at the other three occupants of the make-shift fort, Raven noticed that they were Cheyenne. He only recognized one of them ... a fierce, reckless fighter named Bobtail Horse.

Being unable to resist the opportunity to tease, Bear's Foot raised his voice above the steadily increasing noise level and asked, "Where have you been hiding, Okute? Or were you simply resting, as you did at the Rosebud?"

Bear grinned, then levered another round into his Spencer, firing over the slab of driftwood that they were crouched behind.

Ignoring his friend's needling, Chris added the pump's throaty roar to the sharper reports of the assorted rifles and pistols. With a wry smile he remembered the last time Bear had accused him of shirking.

He had become separated from the main fighting during the Battle of the Rosebud. His horse had been shot, pinning his leg when he fell, and Raven had been trapped for hours. Later, he had been stalked by two Crow warriors. After resolving that problem, Chris had finally managed to dig himself free just before Bear's arrival. Bear's Foot had greeted him with a smirk and the caustic query, "How long have you been hiding here?"

Raven chuckled over the remembered tease. He jacked another shell into the pump's chamber. In spite of the clamor of gunfire, a sudden rhythmic splashing announced the arrival of the hard-riding scouts who Chris had seen racing down the slopes. There were five of them, all Sioux, and they joined them behind the narrow sandbar.

A bugle sounded and the troopers closest to the river quickly deployed into line. Indecipherable shouts were heard as the Bluecoats shouted commands. The bugler sounded 'charge,' and a solid wedge of dusty blue uniforms on wild-eyed horses stampeded into the shallow waters of the Little Big Horn River.

Firing as they came, the soldiers appeared determined to push on into the village. Vastly outnumbered, the ten defenders increased their rate of fire as much as possible. Just when it appeared certain that they were going to be overrun, a buckskin-clad figure riding in the very front of the charging mass was shot. When he slid off his roan mount, it was as though the riders had hit a solid wall. The charge came to a sudden, unexpected halt, right in midstream. Troopers flanking the wounded man jumped off their horses to help him. Totally ignoring the hiss of arrows and the deadly howl of bullets, the troopers carefully lifted the man back onto his saddle. The big roan held fast as the man grasped his reins and slumped over his saddle's fork.

The men behind the sandbar continued their relentless onslaught of arrows and bullets. In between random shots at the milling troopers, Raven saw a flash of red cloth at the buckskin-clad man's throat as he slumped and his men straightened him in his saddle. Suddenly, Chris realized that the wounded man was the officer he'd seen urging the others on toward the village. Out of the blue, the thought struck him like a thunderbolt. Could the wounded man be Custer?

His theory was interrupted by a swarm of buzzing, snapping lead, as the soldiers laid down a solid wall of covering fire while holding their ground in midstream. More saddles emptied as dozens of Sioux and Cheyenne began to arrive. Not being able to withstand the increased firepower of the new arrivals, the cavalrymen fought their way out of the river and back into the crowded mouth of the ravine. Some of the officers were attempting to organize a withdrawal to the north, across the slopes. It appeared hopeless. Everywhere that Raven looked he saw new Indians arriving. And when they arrived, they came at full speed, not wanting to be left out of the coups or any other part of the slaughter. All were motivated by one common goal; kill the hated Bluecoats.

The sudden blare of a bugle drew Raven's gaze back to the coulee. A good half of the troops that had filed down the long, shallow ravine spurred their big cavalry mounts into action and rode up into an adjoining gully. The ravine was deeper than the other and took a much more direct route up to the top of the bluffs.

Chris watched for a moment as the powerful horses labored up the steep incline. Dun colored clouds of dust, blending with the acrid, gray gunsmoke, momentarily blocked his view of the hard-riding cavalry unit. When he saw them again, all riding bay mounts, the troopers became a living portrait of animated blue and brown on a tan and green landscape.

The dust was rising from everywhere: the ravines, the bluffs, slopes, and even the village. Over the escalating din of battle came a blood-curdling scream followed by a jubilant, *"Hokahey!"*

The war cry was followed by the shrill of eagle-bone war whistles. Their piercing sound was like a nail driven into Chris' skull. Eyes burning from dust and smoke, Raven rubbed them vigorously and threw his gaze in the direction of the war cries and whistles. As he cleared his vision of grit, he saw a stocky, powerful warrior on a black and white pony leading a swarm of Sioux. They splashed across the shallows as though they weren't even there and smashed into the wedge of withdrawing soldiers with a wild fury that was frightening to behold. The stocky leader fought like a man possessed. His war hatchet rose and fell with such abandon it appeared to be alive, as did his long, fur-wrapped braids which leaped and writhed like a pair of snakes across his broad back.

Suddenly, Chris became aware that he was staring at the great Hunkpapa War Chief, Gall. He had just met him the day before and had been impressed by the man's quiet strength. The war chief was anything but quiet now; he was a shrieking demon, a whirlwind of death ... a killing machine. When first seen, Raven thought the man had splashed red war paint all over his body. A shudder followed his awareness that the paint was really blood. Gall's right side, arm, face, and leg were heavily splattered with the fresh or drying blood of his victims.

The troopers still in the bottleneck gave ground, backing away from the madman with the bloody hatchet and his equally fierce companions. A warrior on a big black stallion unexpectedly broke through the wall of soldiers and was instantly surrounded by animated blue figures. Striking left and right with his heavy bow, he drove a wedge into the very heart of the Bluecoats, as his comrades savagely attacked the perimeter.

Raven could feel his heart race. Even with the distance separating them, he could see the light-colored poultice tied to the warrior's side. Wolf's Spirit! He held his breath, as he watched his young friend fight like a crazy man. Attacked from all sides Wolf's Spirit swung his horn bow two-handed, using it like a broad-sword. A trooper slipped from his saddle with blood pouring from a glancing blow to the head; another clasped his face and slid forward over his horse's neck. A panicked guidon bearer was facetiously trying to keep the young Minneconjou at bay by pointing his empty revolver at him and continuously pulling the trigger. Chris would later swear that he saw the white flash of Wolf's Spirit's smile as he knocked the man senseless and ripped the guidon from his weakened grip. Leaving the trooper reeling in his saddle, Wolf's Spirit brandished the Company E guidon overhead and spun his horse as he fought and turned, left and right, trying to get into the clear. Unable to maneuver, he used his horse's great size and strength to batter his way through the maze of combatants.

Raven's gaze was ripped away from Wolf's Spirit by the violent intrusion of an overly zealous army scout. A large, bearded man in buckskins acted like he was going to single-handedly ride over the defenders of the sandbar. He rode low, keeping his head down, and was firing a pistol from each hand. He had almost made it to the barricade when Bear's Foot apparently figured he had come far enough. The big warrior dropped his rifle and, with war club in hand, leaped over a pile of driftwood, landing in the knee deep water squarely in front of the scout's charging horse. In one motion, Bear's Foot skipped aside, avoided the slashing hoofs, and swung his four-foot club. The club's leather-wrapped stone caught the scout flush alongside of the head. His skull split open like a dropped melon. The revolvers fell from lifeless fingers as he slid off his galloping mount like a stringless puppet. He hit the water right next to Bear's Foot who didn't waste a glance on him.

Several of the Bluecoats couldn't resist the large target Bear presented, and the air around him immediately began to fill with the hum and howl of hot lead. Balancing his war club in one hand, Bear's Foot turned his back on the soldiers and slowly followed in the wake of the scout's horse as it lunged and splashed through the water. Bullets buzzed by like angry hornets, but the big warrior would not be hurried. Raven saw a bullet spout in the water between his legs; another clipped about three inches off one of his eagle feathers. Bear ignored it all, refusing to be intimidated or rushed.

By the time Bear's Foot had comfortably resettled next to Chris, the fight at the ford was all but over. Most of the troopers had fought their way clear and were racing for the slopes. An orderly retreat was almost impossible because of the persistence and accuracy of the Indian marksmen. Arrows began falling like hail among the dismounted Bluecoats.

When cavalry are dismounted every fourth man is a designated horse holder, leaving the other three men free to concentrate on fighting. In the past it had been an effective procedure, but as the troopers fought their way up the grassy slopes, the Indian snipers focussed on killing or wounding the horse holders.

As soon as a 'holder' went down, warriors would dart in on their quick ponies and wave blankets and scream, frightening the cavalry horses into running away, and the soldiers were either too busy or too tired to try and stop the horses.

Raven couldn't understand why Custer's troops were so exhausted. Earlier he had noticed that some of the Bluecoats had stumbled and staggered when dismounting. Even as he watched, others were tripping and falling. Some didn't even try to rise; they fought from where they lay. Yet everywhere he looked troopers were fighting for their lives and trying to gain some high ground.

Piercing through the steady hammer of gunfire was the shriek of the eagle-bone war whistles. Sometimes they were used for signaling and other times as good luck charms. It had to be demoralizing to the soldiers, Chris thought, not knowing why the whistles were being blown. He could almost see their confidence dwindling as the shrill sound of whistles pierced the many other noises. The soldier's morale and hope seemed to be shrinking as rapidly as the Sioux and Cheyenne numbers were growing.

Raven and Bear's Foot left the protection of the sandbar and quickly mounted their horses. The atmosphere nearby banged and crackled, with the constant noise of gunfire, near and far, and the steady hiss and hum of arrows. War cries, shouts, and screams added to the endless clamor.

On the opposite bank Gall led his howling, hard-riding Sioux away from the fighting on the slope. Suddenly quiet, the wild horsemen rode up the same gully that the soldiers mounted on the bays had taken earlier. Raven watched for Wolf's Spirit but had either missed him, or he wasn't with them anymore. While he watched Gall's force relentlessly quirt their ponies up the ravine, Chris silently thanked God that he wasn't wearing blue and with the unit at the top of the hill.

A sudden increase in firing drew Raven and Bear's attention back to the slope. Most of the troopers who had ridden down the coulee were now fighting desperately to form together and reach higher ground. Chris noted again how tired the soldiers appeared. Yet, everywhere he looked, the troopers were stubbornly battling on against overwhelming odds. The sound of distant gunfire captured his attention.

Looking to the bluffs Chris saw the minute figures of men and horses running to and fro. From that distance it looked like some kind of game, but with the smoke and dust encompassing the ridge he knew better. He knew the fight up there had to be just as bad, if not worse. Interspersed with the immediate clamor of battle, Raven again heard the definitive crackle and pop drift down from the grassy heights.

Several dozen Sioux and Cheyenne splashed across the busy ford and raced toward the fighting on the grassy hillside. Bear's Foot turned to Raven. His grin was infectious as he said, "Come with me, Okute. I wish to visit some friends up on the bluff."

Seeing the devilment in his friend's eyes, Chris again lifted his gaze to the top of the bluffs. Gunsmoke and dust hovered above the line of the ridge. The steady popping of gunfire was an affirmation of the heavy, hand-to-hand fighting that was going on up there. Then he looked at Bear's Foot and replied, "Will you be sure to introduce me to your friends?"

Bear threw his head back and laughed wholeheartedly.

"Yes, I will do that for you ... white man."

CHAPTER 10

▲▲▲▲▲

Raven involuntarily ducked as a couple of wayward bullets whistled by. The Black high-stepped across the few remaining feet of the Little Big Horn River and followed Bear's Foot's long-legged sorrel up into the deep ravine. It was the same coulee that Gall had used moments earlier.

Although deep within the gully, they still could not escape the clamor of the battle. It was everywhere. It had become as much a part of the day as the ever present dust and smoke. The noise and gritty smog hovered over the bluffs and grassy scarp like an impending storm.

About halfway up the gully they twisted hard to the right. The Black and Bear's red horse eagerly lunged upward toward the smoky ridgeline. Near the top, as the pitch of the trail sharply increased, they began lunging and thrusting in shorter, more powerful strides. Raven noted that the din of battle was becoming more disconcerting with every climbing step.

With a startling spray of sand and gravel preceding them, two riders came sailing over the northern lip of the gully. Their wild, unbound hair identified them as enemy scouts. Their dark faces expressed total surprise as they fought to control their terrified ponies; they were on a collision course with Raven and were unable to stop.

Grabbing a fistful of mane, Chris slammed his heels into The Black's ribs! The stallion squatted and swiftly lunged forward. With powerful thrusts of his long legs he carried them clear of the Indians' angle of descent. Raven heard a shout and the clatter of the ponies' hoofs striving for footing directly behind him. Twisting in the saddle he swung his Winchester pump around with one hand.

In the split second it took for the shotgun to swing into line several things happened all at the same time. The Indian closest to Chris made a fatal mistake; he turned his pony uphill toward Raven. There was no mistaking the murderous gleam in his eye or the deliberate quirting of his pony to enable him to close with Raven and Bear's Foot. Down trail from him, the other scout had turned the other way in an attempt to get away.

As the stubby barrel of the pump came into line with the menacing face, Chris pulled the trigger. The blast of buckshot removed the sneer and the whole right side of the scout's face. Through the resulting red mist Raven saw the dying scout's partner, struck in the back of the head and neck, slide from his pony's back like a sack of grain.

When Raven shot the first scout the outer edge of his shot pattern had missed, but by chance had struck and killed the second scout. He got both of the enemy with one shot.

What happened was an example of why a shotgun will make even the deadliest of gunmen hesitate when confronted by an enemy armed with one. You can miss badly and still hit something.

Bear's Foot had stopped his sorrel short of the top and was staring down at Raven. There was a stern expression on his broad, painted face. He shook his war club at Chris in mock anger as he raised his voice above the din of the nearby fighting.

"If you wish to become a true Lakota, you must learn to share your enemies!"

The glint in the man's eye belied the seriousness of his tone. With a fierce scowl he turned away and kicked his mount into lunging up the few remaining feet. Bear's Foot roared, "*Hokahey!*" and disappeared from view as he went over the top. The Black hop-jumped the remaining yards. Raven's head hadn't come level with the top and all ready he was hearing bullets buzzing by like supersonic bees. With pump in hand he urged The Black up over the verge.

Frantic, desperate hand-to-hand fighting was raging along the grass-covered ridge. At first glance it appeared to be utter chaos but with a second look, Chris was able to spy a couple of organized pockets of resistance.

Dust and gunsmoke had instantly coated the insides of Raven's nose and mouth. He spat and coughed. Everywhere he looked he saw someone dying. He felt a wave of fear pass over him and then it was gone as he concentrated on evaluating the fight.

To Raven's right, a group of Bluecoats were being smothered by a host of blood-crazed Sioux and Cheyenne. Leading them was the imposing figure of the hatchet-wielding Gall. Nearly all the warriors were fighting on foot. Bear's Foot and Gall were the only exceptions, yet with all the smoke and dust Raven couldn't be sure. He saw Bear abruptly spin his sorrel and charge into a crowd of brawling Bluecoats, who were momentarily holding their own against the swarm of Indians. Bear's formidable war club was sweeping to the left and right with deadly accuracy. Nobody was safe within its deadly, wide arc.

Over on his left, Raven saw that the soldiers were putting up a savage, if hopeless, defense. An officer mounted on a big claybank was single-handedly holding two platoons of soldiers together. He kept riding back and forth, exhorting his men to keep firing and to stay low behind cover. The troopers had apparently shot their own horses and were using them as barricades.

The Black unexpectedly reared! He screamed with rage and pain. A bullet had put a new notch in one of his ears. Another projectile creased a bloody groove across the arch of his neck, splattering Raven's hand and wrist with blood. The very instant the stallion's hoofs dropped to the turf, he bolted!

It took all of Raven's strength and coordination to stay on him. By the time he had regained his balance, The Black was in full gallop. He was heading straight toward the two platoons of troopers. Too late to stop him, Chris crouched over the sleek neck and let him run. And run he did! Bullets were snapping and humming all around them. Indians and soldiers alike were scrambling out of the way of The Black's driving hoofs. Between the flying black tresses of the mane, Raven caught several glimpses of startled, angry, even frightened faces. The big Appaloosa catapulted through them like a runaway locomotive.

Up ahead, the officer on horseback was alternately cajoling and haranguing his men to continue to fire rapidly. Their numbers had already diminished in the short time Raven had been on the ridge. Hatless, wearing a torn and bloodstained leather shirt, the officer continued to move his staunch buckskin back and forth, trying desperately to rally his troops.

Suddenly, directly in front of The Black, a trooper deliberately left the cover of his dead horse and stood up so that he could get a clear shot at Raven. The Black bared his teeth, stretched his neck forward, and screamed! The trooper's mouth fell open, his aim faltered as he hesitated. It was all the time Chris needed. He had been carrying the pump in his right hand; all he had to do was drop the muzzle and squeeze. The recoil nearly tore the gun from his grip as he saw the trooper grab his hip and spin to the ground.

What happened next occurred so swiftly that it wasn't until much later that Raven would remember the details. The Black leaped! They soared over the wounded trooper and his dead horse. Then the hatless officer slid into view as he pulled his buckskin to a grinding halt, blocking their way.

Judging by the epaulets sewn onto the shoulders of his fringed leather shirt the officer was a captain. In Raven's eyes, from his fierce demeanor to his sweeping mustache and bristling beard, the man was every inch a professional soldier.

Fully expecting the big, black Appaloosa to swerve aside to avoid a collision, the captain held his ground. He was in the act of bringing his revolver into position for a snap shot when the stallion laid his ears back, bared his yellow teeth, and attacked. The Black lunged forward, his shoulder drove into the buckskin with great force. The black-maned, yellow horse staggered but didn't go down. It was then that Chris saw the many wounds on the buckskin's neck and body. He was amazed by the horse's courage and endurance.

The brave captain was frantically trying to stay in his saddle as The Black screamed again and slashed with his teeth at the yellow horse's neck. Face flushed with anger and exertion, the captain swiftly brought his pistol up and aimed at Raven's head.

Raven instinctively jerked on the reins and swung his body to the left just as the pistol went off, belching smoke and fire into his face. The hot blast of the muzzle blast seared his cheek and singed his eyebrows. Before the soldier could fire again, Raven sawed hard on the reins and swiveled The Black's spotted rump, slamming it into the buckskin's shoulder. This time the cavalry horse went to his knees, then bravely staggered to his feet as his owner swore and tried to stay in the saddle.

The Black pivoted and broke clear. Over the constant clamor of battle, Raven clearly heard a thick Irish voice shout, "Come on back here and fight, you black-hearted, heathen bastard!"

He let The Black run. Still wild he immediately jumped into a gallop. He swerved to the left and before Chris could stop him, The Black charged through a group of newly arrived, mounted Sioux. One warrior took a futile swipe at Raven with his wicked-looking war club, as he flew by. Behind him, Chris heard a loud, "*Heyah!*"

Thank God, someone recognized him, he thought. The Black swerved again, running diagonally down onto the grassy slope of the hillside.

Raven wrestled with the reins until he regained control and then slowed him to a trot. The Black was gasping, heaving for air, and slowed to a walk. The atmosphere on the hillside was also thick with dust and smoke, but the air wasn't nearly so busy with humming arrows and flying lead. There were even gaps where there was no fighting, so that Raven could take a deep breath without having to worry about catching something sharp or penetrating, that might be hazardous to his health.

As soon as The Black settled down and got his wind back, Chris didn't stay out of the fire zone for long. He had begun to think about Blue Feather and Little Hawk, thoughts that just led to useless worry.

In spite of the constant sound of firearms, Raven distinctly heard a ragged volley come from the far right. In the northeast, just below the bluff's highest point, he saw a large body of men in faded, dusty blue. They were enshrouded by a hovering cloud of dust and smoke and circling horsemen, but they were still fighting and holding their enemy at bay.

Raven stared. He became mesmerized by the distant fight. A wayward bullet snapped and hummed by his ear. A riderless cavalry mount breezed by, headed for the river down below. His focus remained on the distant confrontation. In a voice so quiet that only The Black could hear, he said, "Custer."

CHAPTER 11

▲▲▲▲▲

Without thinking about it, Raven pointed The Black north and easily moved him into a canter. Above him, to his right front, hundreds of Indians were fanned out on three sides of the beleaguered soldiers. Although quite a distance away he could see what they were doing.

Many of the Sioux and Cheyenne would stay hidden in the long grass and sage, waiting for the right moment to pop up and shoot their arrows or rifles. After doing so, the warriors would then disappear back into the grass and sage and reload. There were some who would remain hidden and launch their arrows high into the air and let gravity deliver the feathered shafts to the Bluecoats like a lethal, pointed rain.

When Raven first saw the tactic used he was amazed. He knew he was looking at one of the forerunners of modern warfare, used by a nomadic people who had not yet discovered the wheel.

Farther down the slope he saw what looked like another deep ravine. Curious, Raven decide to check it out before swinging up to the fight on the hill. As he rode he kept a sharp watch, he didn't need any surprises. It was bad enough that every few minutes an errant bullet came buzzing by from God knew where. Up the hill his attention was drawn to a frenzied knot of thirty or forty horsemen who seemed to come out of nowhere and were fighting their way through a throng of garishly painted Sioux. The troopers looked like they were heading for the same ravine that Chris was going to investigate. Riding hard they broke into the clear. Just before they vanished into the gully he saw several of the troopers carrying canteens. It's a water run, he thought; they're haulin' ass for the river!

The loud gunfire that suddenly came from the ravine caused Raven's hands to tighten on the reins and brought The Black to an unexpected halt. All at once, a whole host of Sioux and Cheyenne came surging out of the ravine like a flushed covey of quail. Once they cleared the lip of the gully, the Indians spun their ponies and returned to the edge. As a group they peered down at the Bluecoats, boxed in the ravine like a flock of vultures.

Not liking the idea of showing his pale face around a pack of agitated Indians, Chris began to edge The Black away from the gully. He stopped. Directly in front of him, looking down into the ravine, was the Cheyenne subchief, Deer Catcher, who had fought at his side during the Rosebud Battle. He was wearing the same buffalo-horn headdress he was wearing when Raven had last seen him.

A startling fusillade of shots erupted from the gully! The Black leaped sideways like a cat! The other Indian ponies were just as surprised. Several continued to act up as the firing intensified. The warriors were all staring into the gully with expressions of disbelief and disgust. Sporadically the shooting continued.

Not being able to control his curiosity, Raven reined The Black in next to Deer Catcher who didn't even look up. Chris looked into the ravine and felt a chill move up his spine. It took him a moment to accept what he was seeing as reality. The soldiers were shooting each other! He couldn't believe it. As far as he could tell, not one shot had been aimed at the hovering Indians. When the shooting stopped, four troopers were left unscathed out of the approximate two score that had ridden into the gully.

Four faces, white as snow, looked up at the surrounding hostile expressions and uniformly whipped their mounts into motion. At the gallop, they attempted to break through the ring of Sioux and Cheyenne. Only one trooper succeeded to make it out of the ravine. Raven, still shaken by what he had witnessed, watched as the soldier raced for the river with three Lakota hot on his tail. He didn't get very far before the Sioux pulled him down like a pack of wolves would a deer.

The Indians suddenly began to disperse. A few stayed behind to collect some scalps and other booty while the others rode north to join in the fight on the hill. Raven again wondered, where is Crazy Horse?

His eyes were again drawn to the ravine where several bareback riders were rounding up the terrified cavalry mounts. When Chris looked up, a painted Indian was sitting his pony on the other side of the gully and was staring at him. He felt his stomach twist and churn. It was Scar. The two men locked eyes.

The Hunkpapa was a fearsome sight. He had painted a red mask over his eyes and then had smeared vermilion onto the many bear claw scars that covered his body. He had applied the paint so that the old scars appeared to be fresh, bleeding wounds. The effect was mind boggling.

Deer Catcher turned his pony, breaking the spell-binding staredown. When the Cheyenne saw Raven, he stopped his horse and smiled. He greeted Raven in his bad Lakota, shook his head, and looked back into the ravine. Chris returned his greeting and turned to look at Scar. But he was gone! Maybe I just imagined him, he thought.

Face grim, the Cheyenne raised his gaze, caught Chris' eye, and again looked at the twisted, blue-clad bodies. Raven watched as a few of the horses trotted around the bottom dragging the bodies of their owners. Somehow, in spite of the military tapaderos, their feet had become caught in the stirrups.

Deer Catcher again faced Raven. There was a sadness in his dark visage that was only partially hidden in his black eyes. In Lakota he said, "*Witko* (crazy)! Perhaps the Everlasting Spirit was angry with these wasichus for all the bad things they had done to us in the past. Maybe he turned their hate and forced them to use it on each other."

Still numb from what he witnessed, Chris nodded and reined The Black around so that he wouldn't have to look anymore. He stopped, his reflexes having jerked the reins. A young Cheyenne woman was sitting on a pony staring at him. Her black eyes burned with hatred.

Raven returned her stare; he did so with awe. This is no ordinary Cheyenne woman, he thought.

She was wearing a man's fully beaded war shirt and leggings. There was a horn bow and a lynx fur quiver of arrows slung across her slender back. In her right hand she was carrying a long, feathered lance; on her other arm was a shield decorated with feathers, paint, and red trade cloth.

What caught Raven's attention was the point of the lance. It was pointed straight at his belly, and the first three feet of it was covered with dried blood.

Keeping his eyes locked with the woman's, Raven heard Deer Catcher say something to her in Cheyenne. Whatever he said she ignored it. She paid as much notice to his words as she did to the occasional bullet that careened by.

With a tap of her finely moccasined heels, she moved her pony closer. The lance point was now so close that Chris involuntarily tightened his stomach muscles.

Her glaring, black eyes were emphasized by horizontal bars of red and black paint that had been slashed across her high cheekbones. She was beautiful., Raven thought ... and like most beautiful animals very deadly.

While continuing to pierce him with her blazing eyes, she spat out a mouthful of rapid-fire Cheyenne. As she was speaking, several more bullets buzzed by. Chris was willing to bet that she didn't even drop a vowel. Nor did her gaze waver in the slightest. Not daring to so much as twitch, Raven thought, what a woman.

Deer Catcher intervened with several forceful words of Cheyenne that finally got her attention. Her eyes snapped and glittered with rage as she slowly lowered her lance.

Damn, Chris thought, this is one very tough chick.

She tore her gaze away from Raven and jerked her pony. Spinning him in a tight circle, she sped away at a dust raising gallop. She raced by several horseback Sioux who called out to her. She ignored them and rode off toward the distant fight.

Raven felt strange. He was both relieved and saddened to see the woman warrior ride away. She was so extraordinary that he knew he would never meet anyone of her type again. She adds credibility, he mused, to the legends of ancient cities protected by armies of Amazons.

Chris flinched as another bullet hummed by, reminding him that he had to stay alert. He noticed that there were times when he would unconsciously block out the battle noise and ignore the violent activity around him. If he didn't stop such foolishness he was going to wind up dead.

Deer Catcher's voice gave him a slight jolt, causing him to keep his eyes busy as his Cheyenne friend spoke.

"She is Buffalo Robe Woman. Her brother was killed fighting Three Stars down on the Rosebud. Since there is no longer a male of fighting age in her family, she has taken up his weapons and is fighting to avenge him."

He paused for a moment and joined Raven as he scanned the nearby area for danger. From the corner of his eye, Chris saw the horned headdress turn toward him as Deer Catcher said, "She is a ..."

There was a loud noise, like smacking a pumpkin with a stick. Suddenly, Raven couldn't see! Something hot and wet had struck him in the face. Letting the pump dangle by its sling, Chris pawed frantically at his burning eyes until he could see. His vision cleared in time to see Deer Catcher, the upper half of his face a bloody cavity, topple from his pony. The Black shied away from the fresh blood smell. Furious, Raven jerked the hammer back on the shotgun and sawed on The Black's reins as he looked for someone to shoot. He wrestled The Black into a circle as he searched for a target, anything or anyone to squelch his helpless rage. Nausea set in and as he fought hard to keep from vomiting the distraction over shadowed his fury. He rubbed his eyes, which burned from splattered blood and dust and smoke.

Another bullet buzzed by! Raven twisted and turned, looking everywhere for a sniper. Finding none, he had to assume that the bullets were just wild strays. He slumped in the saddle, completely drained by his shifting emotions. He cleaned his face with his bandana and glanced down at his friend's body. Shaking his head in sorrow Chris retied the stained cloth on his head. While adjusting the knot over his right ear, he looked up toward the fight near the top of the bluff. They were still fighting but the gunfire was more sporadic than earlier. Raven squinted his sore eyes and tried to see better through the haze of dust and smoke. He stared for a moment, then slapped The Black on the neck as he said, "Well boy, I think we'd better ride on up there. Maybe we can help end this nightmare."

His thoughts switched to Bear's Foot on the ridge and of Wolf's Spirit. Are they still alive? Where are Blue Feather and Little Hawk? In his heart Raven knew that his wife and son were safe. He knew this with the same inexplicable certainty that he knew he was being lured into joining Custer's final fight just as a moth is drawn to a flame.

CHAPTER 12

⋀ ⋀ ⋀ ⋀ ⋀

Riding up toward the big fight near the top of the bluff, Raven looked back. The fighting down by the river looked like it was over. Many Indians, mainly women and children were moving across the base of the bluffs on foot. Probably looking for loot, he thought, or scalps.

The noise level increased dramatically as he drew closer to the fight. He let his gaze travel along the ridge to where the Irish captain was fighting. There was still some activity up there, he noticed, but nothing compared to the madhouse it was earlier. For the umpteenth time Raven wondered, where is Crazy Horse? As though in answer to his query a bloodcurdling scream shattered a brief lull in the shooting. The scream, which was really a signal, was so loud that it was certain to have chilled many souls. Raven's attention swung to the extreme north as two columns of Lakota poured across the grass and sage covered hillside. They wheeled to Chris' left and attacked the defender's front and right flank simultaneously.

Under his breath, Raven muttered, "Crazy Horse."

War cries, shrieking eagle bone whistles, and the hammer of thousands of hoofs nearly drowned out the escalating, gunfire of countless rifles and pistols.

Close now he could see better through the haze. Because of the thickening atmosphere the stars and stripes banner had become a faded replica of the colorful standard.

It was spiked into the ground at an angle and the Seventh Cavalry's red and blue guidon hung listlessly at its side.

Crowded around the banners, Raven could see several crouched figures in dusty blue and gold. They were firing over the backs of their comrades, who were also firing and using the bodies of dead horses as protection against the hundreds of bullets and arrows.

Refusing to think of what he could be letting himself in for, Raven dug his heels into The Black's ribs as hard as he could. The big stallion's response slammed his buttocks hard against the saddle's cantle as he broke into an immediate gallop.

Closing in, the tumultuous sounds of battle took on the aspect of a giant wave. It pushed and bullied until it rolled over and dominated the entire battlefield with a relentless deluge of noise.

Near the perimeter Chris stopped The Black and made a hurried assessment of the fighting. In spite of the clamor and veil of clinging smoke and ever present dust, he was able to see and understand what was happening. From a soldier's point of view it appeared that the Indians' whole attack was a concentration of a frontal and right flank, mounted assault. In reality the Indians were using the mounted attacks as diversions while the most effective fighting was being done on foot.

While the wild riding warriors were the ones that held the Bluecoat's attention, their Sioux and Cheyenne brothers were running through the grass and sage and attacking on foot. This subtle tactic was steadily and surely whittling away at the enemies' dwindling numbers. Using whatever cover they could find, they would get in close and keep a steady flow of bullets or arrows pouring into the soldiers. Others would lurk in among the downed horses and clumps of sagebrush and wait for the right opportunity. When the time came they would attack with the ferocity and determination of a grizzly bear.

Just as Raven was about to join the action, the Sioux changed their tactics. Large groups of Indians began rushing up to the outer perimeters, launching their arrows, firing their rifles, and then whirling away to make room for the next group.

The sudden snap and hum of bullets by his ears reminded Chris that he was a stationary target. His heels raked The Black's ribs. With a quick burst of speed the stallion carried Raven into the very heart of the fight. In that close, the sound became a monster. It lived; it breathed fire and smoke. Roaring and screaming it attacked and violated all his senses with a symphony of noise. He half expected his ears to bleed from the constant onslaught.

Raven was finally close enough to see the troopers as individuals. One of the dusty figures standing beside the Seventh's banner was a reddish-blond, hatless officer in buckskins. There was a red bandana around his neck. Chris saw that his left hand was clasped against a bloody hole on the same side. He was calmly aiming and shooting a large revolver with his right hand. Even with the billowing smoke and dusty haze, Raven knew. It had to be Custer. There was no mistaking the high forehead, bushy mustache and fierce demeanor. A handful of swirling, centaur-like horsemen erupted from a huge plume of dust, blocking his view. The sudden air-stirring activity brought with it the stench of sun-heated dead horses, torn entrails, blood, and smoke. All thoughts of Custer were driven from his mind as the wild bunch crowded in close: shooting, screaming, taunting the soldiers. Just staying alive was taking his full concentration. Faded blue and paint-streaked brown was everywhere!

Horses screamed, warriors whooped, troopers shouted, arrows hummed, and guns banged incessantly.

Raven was trying to ride into the clear when a horse swung his rump around and bumped into the healing wound in Chris' leg. He gasped, grabbing his leg. Excruciating pain momentarily dominated his senses.

From the corner of his eye, he caught a glimpse of a paint-daubed face just before a glancing blow from a war club detonated painful fireworks in his skull. The resulting starbursts and imploding pain left him reeling in the saddle. He was forced to drop the pumpgun and grab The Black's mane just to stay in the saddle. Fighting to regain his senses Raven shook his head. Pain throbbed and pounded to get free as though trapped within the bony walls of his head. His black bandana slipped unnoticed down among the stomping hoofs and churning dust. Chris' eyes regained their focus in time to see the same paint-daubed face glaring at him. The Sioux, who apparently thought Raven was the enemy, had swung his pony around and was moving in for the kill. He gave a high pitched screech as his pony lunged forward and closed with The Black. The Lakota's club was held high for a brutal, finishing stroke.

Mustering every ounce of strength he had left, Chris put his weight into his right stirrup. His focus was centered on his fists full of mane and his injured left leg. With blurring speed, Raven's left leg cleared the saddle's cantle and moved into what was surely the first and only time Karate's 'Spinning Back Kick' was ever attempted from the back of a horse.

His left foot smashed into the Indian's upper chest! The blow took him off his pony as suddenly and quickly as a low hanging oak branch. Upon impact a stab of agony lanced through Raven's injured calf. The pain was so intense and disconcerting that he lost his grip on The Black's mane. As he fell toward the hoof-trampled turf, his moccasined right foot caught in the stirrup's tapadero. His foot was trapped just long enough so that his body twisted and he took the full impact of his fall on his back and shoulders.

The air left his lungs with a sudden, forceful whoosh! He felt paralyzed. He couldn't breath! Dust and grit were pouring into his gaping mouth. Horses and fierce riders loomed overhead while menacing hoofs slashed and stomped all around him. At last he was able to suck in some air. Raven choked. A spasm of retching wracked his body with pain. Still not thinking clearly he knew instinctively that if he didn't get up he was going to die. With a mighty effort, Chris stumbled to his feet. A spinning Indian pony brushed against him, knocking him to his hands and knees. A horse's hoof struck his bad leg. He fell flat again clutching his leg and gasping for air.

The noise and dust intensified. Raven knew that if he didn't do something, he would suffocate or be trampled to death. In his weakened state he felt a sudden helplessness in the forest of thrusting, stomping legs. The lung-searing smoke and dust was strangling him. Fighting off his fears Chris clawed his way upright. Swirling horses and riders were all around him. The din of their gunfire and savage screams assailed his ears relentlessly. He staggered, seeking his lost balance, as his eyes swept the dirt and grass for his dropped shotgun. A sweeping stroke from a Cheyenne coup stick knocked him to the ground. He lay there stunned ... his mind spinning with visions of feathered,whirling dervishes and broken blue-clad toy soldiers.

CHAPTER 13

▲▲▲▲▲

Along with his burning eyes, the choking from cloying dust, and the constant hammer of loud, excessive noise, Raven experienced another sensation. He felt hands under his armpits. They lifted and pulled, then they were dragging him. He could hear heavy breathing and all the other little gasps and grunts of exertion. With a concentrated effort, Chris was able to open one eye. The other one didn't appear to be functioning. He saw that the threatening hoofs were receding, and he silently rejoiced that he could breath again. He shut his eye and gulped in the life-giving air. Incapable of rational thought he surrendered to the constant pull and tug and allowed himself to be transported into a false state of euphoria. He still heard the howl and hum of bullets and arrows: the shouts, war cries, and gunfire. But for the moment, those life and death sounds had become incidental to him. Raven sucked in the air. He tasted it like a drunk relishing his first drink after a long dry spell. He rested, savoring the indolence, the freedom of responsibility.

Chris' contentment was short-lived. He opened his one eye that was intact and his normal powers of reason began the slow climb back to reality. Still woozy, he felt powerless to move. The hands had left him with his back propped against something solid, so he was able to see what was happening around him. Raven's return to full awareness was coming back, but he was still confused. The Sioux were no longer close at hand. He could see them through veils of dust. Some looked as though they were pointing their weapons at him and shooting. In a move that was unexpected, they began to back away.

Suddenly exasperated by his handicap, Chris pawed at his sightless eye. He rejoiced to discover that dried blood had sealed his eyelid shut. Clearing the blood away he was elated to discover that the eye's sight was still intact. When the Sioux began to renew their attack, Raven wanted to shout at them, 'Can you not see that I am Okute of the Minneconjou?' Instead, it was at that moment that reality jumped up and smacked him between the eyes. The truth of his predicament pierced his shell of complacency with a frightening clarity.

Voices began to encroach upon his newly found awareness. The hodge-podge of voices mixed with the battle clamor sounded strange yet familiar. With growing horror he began to understand the words that were being shouted.

"Look out, Sam!" "Eat that, ya red-skinned sonuvabitch!" "Help me!" "Here they come again, Gen'ral!"

The English rang in Raven's ears like a death toll, confirming his worst fears. All at once, the 'hands' were back! They slid underneath his arms and hooked up onto his shoulders and began to drag him backwards up the slope. A breathless voice near his ear said, "Hang on, fella, I'm gonna move ya up with the rest of us."

Shock had made Chris powerless to act. He was completely at a loss as to what he should do. While the hands labored and backed him up the incline, Raven's indecisiveness left him in limbo. He watched the men in gray shirts and blue blouses, as they ferociously fought for their lives. Absently, Chris came to realize that if he survives, he will be the only white man able to bear witness to their courage. Befuddled by all the twists and turns his mind was taking, he watched in a daze as the troopers bravely inched their way up the incline, firing their weapons every step of the way.

Raven's rescuer gasped with fatigue as he dragged him over a dead trooper. Chris felt the pressure leave his armpits as the man stopped. His raspy breathing sawed at Raven's nerves as he tried to formulate what to do. What can I do? Chris' silent query was tearing himself apart. The man saved my life, he thought. Do I thank him and then shoot him, so that I can make my escape? Deep inside, Raven knew that he would do whatever it took to escape. He did wonder how he would be able to live with himself afterwards.

An acceleration of the battle's deadly gunfire was the perfect background for what Raven had to do; his hand shook as he covertly snaked it out from underneath his vest. His fingers closed tightly over the worn ivory grips as he eared back the hammer. Twisting his body, Chris looked over his shoulder and the first person he saw was Custer. He was standing exactly as he had been before, calmly firing a pistol. Kneeling beside him a wounded trooper was supporting their guidon with one hand and firing a big revolver with the other.

Movement lifted Raven's gaze. Beyond Custer, at the top of the hogback, the summit suddenly bristled with horseback Indians. The Sioux kept coming until they rimmed the whole ridge in a breathtaking display of color and force.

A momentary hush settled over the hilltop. Even the gunfire dwindled away into a pregnant lull.

The men in blue were unaware of the new turn of events until a loud, frightened voice fractured the uneasy moment.

"Oh, my God! Say goodbye, boys. We're dead men!"

Heads turned, bodies twisted. A collective groan rose from the bloody, tattered remnants of the Seventh Cavalry.

Feeling compelled to see the face of his rescuer, Raven twisted and looked at the harried face of a middle-aged trooper. The man was staring uphill, horrified. Raven noticed the dark patches on his faded blouse where chevrons had been. Oblivious of Chris' scrutiny, a low moan came from the man's blistered lips as he studied what was waiting for them on the ridge.

At the very front of the mass of Indians, a warrior quietly sat his white and tan pinto. His long hair was worn loose and adorned with a red-tailed hawk headdress. Naked except for loin cloth and moccasins, his body was painted with pale yellow dots, called 'hail spots' by the Lakota. They were supposed to protect him. Down one side of his face a lightning bolt, painted in blue, slashed from temple to chin.

"Crazy Horse!" The name had leaped from Raven's lips involuntarily. The soldier who had saved his life flinched, and slowly turned to look at Raven. His eyes, wide with fear, quickly absorbed the quillwork on his moccasins and vest. His gaze lifted and met Raven's pale eyes.

At that precise moment, staring into the man's terror-filled eyes, Chris realized that he must have uttered Crazy Horse's name in Lakota. He saw the blood leave the man's face as truth pervaded his brain with a slice of perception.

A solitary shot rang out! As though on cue, the hovering mass of Sioux and Cheyenne swept down off the hill. A ragged fusillade of gunfire and arrows preceded them, spanning the slope with a deadly shower of death-dealing missiles. Raven rose to his knees. The harried trooper, his face begrimed and sweaty, grabbed him by the arm. He shouted over the escalating gunfire, "Who are ...?"

An arrow struck Chris' revolver and glanced off it. Twelve inches of the gooseberry shaft passed through the trooper's throat! His eyes bulged and his mouth gaped! He was still staring with disbelief into Raven's eyes when he hemorrhaged, choked, fell onto his side, and died.

The soldier was still gripping his arm with fingers of steel. Oblivious to the turmoil raging all around him, Chris gently removed the trooper's fingers.

Raven was so traumatized by what had happened he was unaware of what was going on around him. While Crazy Horse attacked from above, the Cheyenne chief, Two Moons, struck from below. The noise, dust, and smoke intensified. Chris stared into the trooper's dead eyes. His own eyes burned; dust had lined his nostrils and throat. He continued to stare, totally immobilized.

"Okute!"

His shouted name penetrated the shell he'd withdrawn into and raised his bloodied head. The pale eyes, once again, became agile and alert. Indians and troopers were fighting hand-to-hand everywhere.

Warriors hacked and flailed with tomahawks and war clubs, while the soldier's fought back using rifles and pistols as clubs. Others battled on with their bare fists or whatever weapon they could pick up.

"Okute!"

The familiar voice pulled Raven's attention toward the center of the fiercest fighting. With his great size and mounted on his rangy sorrel, Bear's Foot towered over the other combatants. His red horse powered his way toward Chris. Every step of the way the warrior's war club reaped a bloody harvest with each scythe-like swing.

Raven stumbled to his feet and began to hobble toward Bear's Foot. With each step pain knifed through his injured leg. Invisible wasps zoomed by his head as firearms were discharged all around him. While he moved Chris desperately knuckled the smoke from his tearing eyes. Chaos was everywhere!

Through the churning dust he saw a figure rise up alongside Bear's Foot's horse. Completely unaware of the danger, Bear's attention was centered on the other side of his pony. Because of his burning eyes Raven didn't know that the figure was a soldier until he saw a flash of red stripes on a blue sleeve. By then the trooper had stepped in close and swung a cocked revolver up to Bear's head.

Thinking fast, Chris shouted, "Sarge, look out! Duck!"

Raven's intuitive yell, delivered with such convincing urgency, caused the soldier to duck and spin around.

Before the sergeant's eyes found him, Raven fired. The pistol leaped in his hand and the heavy .44 caliber slug struck the soldier squarely in the chest. Even with the thick, swirling dust the surprise was clearly evident on the trooper's face as he staggered backward and crumpled to the ground.

With Bear's Foot's close encounter with death, Chris' fighting rage suddenly asserted itself. The white-hot anger cut away the residue of his guilt with the precision of a surgeon's scalpel.

His revolver was still bucking and smoking when Raven felt an unexpected blow followed by an abrupt tightening and pressure between his shoulder blades. His elkskin vest pinched underneath his arms as he felt himself snatched into the air! Bear's Foot's massive arm unbelievably lifted and swung Chris around behind him. Raven barely managed to hook a leg over the sorrel's broad back before Bear released him. The big, red horse squatted from the additional weight and surged forward.

With one hand firmly clutching Bear's Foot's silver-studded belt and the other busy thumbing shots at dusty blue phantoms, Raven added his own yells to the din of the battle. Augmenting Raven's deadly pistol and the whistling horror of Bear's war club were the slashing hoofs of the sorrel. Within seconds they fought their way clear of the hand-to-hand fighting and broke into the open.

CHAPTER 14

▲▲▲▲▲

Wolf's Spirit's face was a welcome sight when Bear's Foot reined in beside him, on the fringe of the fighting. Another pleasant sight was the presence of The Black, nervously dancing alongside Wolf's stallion.

Raven eased his pain-wracked body off the sorrel's back and gave Bear's Foot a playful slap on the leg, thanking him for his timely rescue.

The warrior looked down on Raven, who was already busy reloading his revolver. A smile lit up his dark, fiercely painted face as he proclaimed, "Do not thank me, Okute. As anyone can plainly see, we were whelped by the same mother."

As Bear's Foot rode back into the fray, his whoop of laughter was clearly heard over the steady uproar of battle.

Raven shook his head and grinned. Taking The Black's reins from Wolf's Spirit, he saw that most of the warriors were now circling and firing into the dwindling number of exhausted, desperate soldiers. Chris swung up onto The Black and grimaced from his accumulated aches and pains. The week old wound in his leg began to throb with a vengeance. He flinched as a pair of bullets buzzed and hummed overhead. Raven thanked the young warrior and said, with a grin, "We must be close to the hive; the wasps seem angry."

Wolf looked baffled. Another wild bullet buzzed by. The Minneconjou's face lit up as he answered Chris' grin

113

and replied, "Yes, Okute. They are very angry! I am going now. I will find their hive and taste their honey."

Lashing his quirt across the stallion's rump, he left at a gallop and headed straight for the heart of the fight.

Raven watched the warrior disappear into the smoke and dust. Staring at the hundreds of circling Indians, he was perplexed. He felt that the Sioux and Cheyenne were now playing with the survivors; like a cat tormenting a mouse. Let's get it over with, he thought, I'm sick of all the killing.

Suddenly concerned for his reckless, young friend, Raven shelved his objections. He tightened his grasp on his sliding loyalties and urged The Black into a gallop, riding directly for the spot he had last seen Wolf's Spirit. Within seconds of joining the hard-riding bunch, Chris heard the penetrating shriek of an eagle-bone whistle, and then he heard it again. The circle of riders immediately broke; they turned their ponies in toward the center and charged the remaining defenders. In an instant they were in among them. Most were trying to kill or maim while some struck with coup sticks or their bare hands in attempts to gain honor and recognition.

Near the edge of the fiercest fighting, Raven spied the buckskin-wrapped stock of his Winchester pump. The shotgun was lying across the chest of a dead Cheyenne. The slide was pulled back exposing the empty chamber. The Indian had apparently been trying to discover how to make it shoot again when he'd been killed.

Ignoring the snap and whistle of flying lead, but keeping a wary eye on nearby combatants, Chris quickly slid to the ground and recovered his gun. While examining the action parts of the pump, the steady hammer of gunshots and screams tore at his nerves.

114

Wasichu's Return

He blew into the pump's chamber and knew there was an obstruction of some kind in the barrel. He grabbed a nearby arrow, broke the metal point off, and was using it as a ramrod to clear the pump's barrel when suddenly he stopped. He knew that he was being stared at; he could feel the man's eyes.

Amidst the swirling action, a soldier in a red shirt was standing still, watching him. Frantically, he tried to free a jammed cartridge from the chamber of his Springfield rifle. Frustrated, he threw the gun aside. Eyes riveted on Chris, he groped for his holstered pistol.

Seeing that he wasn't going to clear the pump's barrel in time, Raven dropped it and dove to the side just as the trooper aimed and fired. A white-hot kiss caressed his ribs! His pistol had already cleared his vest before he hit the ground. Ignoring his burning side, Raven's Colt was out and just coming into line when Red Shirt fired his second shot. The heavy bullet plowed into the dead body Chris was lying behind. For the second time that day blood and gore splashed onto his face. Fighting down his revulsion Raven steadied his aim and shot the man dead center. The heart shot killed him instantly.

Raven cleaned his face with a handful of grass and struggled to his feet. His calf screamed in protest as he gimped over to the discarded pump. His side burned as he cleared the barrel. He threw the arrow down and began to punch shells into the magazine. As he worked, Chris' eyes were everywhere. He didn't want a repeat performance of the last act.

Everywhere he looked the fighting was now point-blank, tooth and nail. The crunch of war clubs and tomahawks were now heard over the diminishing slam-bang of fire arms.

115

Raven sneaked a quick look at the bloody furrow along his ribcage and decided it wasn't anything to worry about. He pressed his elbow against it to staunch the light bleeding. A shadow crossed his face. Startled, he looked up to find a wild-eyed Wolf's Spirit standing before him. He was smeared with blood and paint. His poultice had torn loose and the wound in his side had reopened. The only weapon he carried was a slender wooden coup stick.

Before Raven was able to say anything, Wolf shook the stick in his face. A white grin flashed across his dark face as he voiced the Lakota war cry. He had to shout to be heard over the constant uproar.

"*Hokahey*! Come, Okute! It is a good day to die!"

Wolf's Spirit turned and passed through a gauzy veil of smoke-filled dust and disappeared before Raven was able to stop him.

Chris grabbed a trooper's crumpled hat and hobbled over to The Black, who was nervously skittering from side to side. After Raven did some spirited yelling, he waved the hat in his face and he finally got the message. As he cantered away the stallion snorted and shook his head in protest of being mistreated.

Chris felt a bullet whip by his face causing him to inadvertently duck. After making sure it wasn't an aimed shot his gaze again found The Black trotting clear of the fight. Hopefully, he thought, he'll get far enough away so he won't be shot by accident.

Ignoring his sore leg Raven quickly followed in Wolf's footsteps and moved rapidly into the thick of the smoke and dust. A gun went off next to him, causing him to spin away and grimace from the sudden pain in his leg. His ears rang and his eyes burned as he squinted and tried to see through the filmy atmosphere. It was becoming difficult to tell friend from foe. Straight ahead of him, he saw two men locked together, belly to belly, eye to eye. They were grasping each other's wrists with silent determination.

For the moment everything ceased to exist for Raven, except for the two men in front of him. His whole being was focussed on their violent struggle for dominance and survival. He stood motionless, as if his feet had been nailed to the ground.

He whispered softly, "Sweet Jesus."

Custer and Wolf's Spirit were both bleeding from bullet wounds in their sides. Custer had a pistol in his left hand but the young Minneconjou was holding onto both of his wrists. Wolf suddenly let go of the one wrist and used both hands to grasp the gun hand. Slowly but surely the younger and stronger Lakota was turning Custer's revolver inward. Beneath the sunburn, the fierce-eyed Custer was turning pale. Desperately he began to punch Wolf's Spirit in the face with his free hand. Blood poured from Wolf's nose as he relentlessly forced Custer's gun hand toward the pale, freckled face. Custer quit punching and tried to pull the young Lakota's hands off his own. He couldn't do it! Custer's strength had diminished rapidly. Suddenly, his power was depleted and Wolf's Spirit was able to turn the revolver.

Upon seeing Wolf's finger extend over Custer's trigger finger, Raven impulsively stepped forward.

Custer turned his head toward the movement. Wolf wrenched hard on the gun hand and pulled the trigger.

The bullet smashed through the left temple and lodged in George Armstrong Custer's brain!

Twisting the pistol free from Custer's lifeless fingers, Wolf's Spirit watched the body crumple to the ground. The

Lakota's braids swirled out away from his body as he swung around in a circle, arms uplifted in triumph.

Beyond the flying braids, Raven caught a glimpse of a bearded, angry face that suddenly appeared through a plume of dust and came swiftly up behind Wolf's Spirit. Before he was able to shout a warning a bright red flower exploded from the center of Wolf's chest. His jubilant expression instantly turned to surprise as his body was propelled forward by the impact of the heavy bullet.

Chris stared down at his young friend's convulsing body with dismay and shock. Another explosion sent one more bullet ploughing into Wolf's Spirit's midsection.

The man behind the gun, an officer, stepped forward and stood over the dead warrior's body. He looked up and saw a white man pointing a gun at him. He looked closer. From a face smeared with dirt and blood, a pair of pale eyes burned with such a consummate fury, the officer knew that he was a dead man.

Nine double-ought buckshot struck Wolf's killer high in the chest! He was a big man, but the concentrated, powerful blast of the twelve gauge blew him off his feet. He was dead before his blue-clad body hit the trampled grass.

A stillness settled over the battlefield. Coincidentally, Raven's shotgun blast apparently ended the gunfire on the hillside. The metallic clatter of the slide-action sounded unnaturally loud, as Chris pumped another shell into the chamber. Sick at heart he looked all around to be sure no other enemy was near. He gripped the pump tightly, almost wishing he had another enemy available on whom he could vent his anger.

Raven's grief for the young Minneconjou felt like it went bone deep; yet he was able to stare down at Wolf's Spirit's killer without hate. The man was just doing a soldier's job. Judging from his shoulder insignias, the man was a lieutenant. He leaned closer. What had looked like a beard turned out to be long, luxurious sideburns. His chin was clean-shaven.

"*Aaiiee!*"

Startled, Raven looked up and saw Bear's Foot slide from his horse's back.; grief-stricken eyes fastened onto Wolf's sprawling form , he moved quickly to his side.

Not wanting to see the sorrow on his friend's face, Chris turned away and studied the aftermath of the Sioux and Cheyenne victory. Except for Reno, who was four miles away, Custer's command was no more. As Raven absently watched some of the looters putting on the soldier's clothing, he sadly realized that the only men in blue still alive were Indians.

He glanced back in time to see Bear's Foot rise from his young friend's side. Unforeseen, the grief swiftly fled from Bear's eyes and was replaced by the ominous glitter of a murderous rage. Light filtering through the settling clouds of dust and gunsmoke glanced off the blue steel of his big knife. Bear's Foot, knife in hand, knelt beside the dead officer.

Seeing what his friend was about to do Raven stepped forward, saying, "*Heyah!*"

Bear's Foot ignored him. Raven grabbed his shoulder to pull him away. He couldn't budge him! It's like trying to move a mountain, he thought. Chris made another grab at his arm, but the big warrior shook his hand off as if he were nothing but a pesty fly. Apparently finished with the grisly job, there was a wet sucking noise as Bear's Foot stood up and faced Raven. There was a ferocious gleam in the Minneconjou's eye.

Raven glanced at the dripping object dangling from his friend's hand. He let his gaze slide down to the dead Bluecoat. One side of his face was a bloody maw. Bear had taken one of the beard-like sideburns as a scalp!

In Vietnam, Chris had seen countless mutilations committed by both sides, but his friend's creative disfigurement of the cavalry officer bothered him more than others he had seen.

Staring hard into Bear's Foot's hate-filled eyes, Raven said, "Do not do this thing, kola. He was just a warrior avenging his chief."

After trying unsuccessfully to stare down Chris' intimidating gaze, Bear's Foot's hot black eyes slowly cooled. He looked down at the crumpled form of his friend and looked again at Raven. Unformed tears were in his eyes as he murmured, "You are right, Okute. He was just an enemy warrior."

The bizarre scalp slipped from Bear's fingers as he stooped and gathered his young friend into his arms. Carrying Wolf's Spirit's body as though it were a sleeping child, the big warrior collected his horse's rein and walked away.

As Bear's Foot slowly moved up the hill Raven noticed that he carefully stepped over and around the many bodies, both red and white, that were sprawled in his path.

CHAPTER 15
▲▲▲▲▲

The quiet after the battle was like the comforting return of a good friend. An occasional gunshot or warwhoop would bounce across the battlefield, but in retrospect the hush was resounding.

Raven stared at the pale, freckled face. Reaching down he closed the light blue eyes. Carefully he untied the scarlet bandana and pulled it free from Custer's neck.

Chris stood up and looked south. Once again he was able to hear the weak, sporadic popping of gunfire coming from Reno and his besieged troopers. As he listened he absentmindedly tied Custer's red, silk scarf around his own neck. Reno's still hanging in there, he mused. An errant gust of wind whipped the bandana up against Chris' face. The faint scent of sweat and cologne that still clung to the scarf saddened him. He looked down at the 'Boy General, Darling of the Potomac' and felt the sorrow leave so quickly that he wasn't sure that it had ever been there. Anger was in his voice as he said, "The way I see it, General, your epitaph should read, 'The Man Who Would Be King.' And if there's room they should add, 'A man who didn't give a damn how many graves he filled to attain that goal'."

Stepping over the dead troopers Raven gingerly walked the short distance to the top of the bluff. His leg was still bothering him, but it was getting better. Another gust of air cooled his sweaty face and lifted some of the hovering smoke. The breeze also raised several oblong pieces of colored paper. He noticed that wherever dead troopers were, there seemed to be an abundance of the same paper. Another puff of wind swept the slope and the paper refuse rose in the air like confetti. Chris snatched one that was blowing by. His mouth fell open when he realized that he was looking at some kind of paper money. Probably, he thought, some type of military script. I'll bet when the warriors were looting the bodies they just threw it away, not having any use for it.

His attention was drawn by movement down near the river. A number of women and children were making their way up the long, grassy slope. Raven turned away. He knew what was coming. Further down the hill, near the ford of the river, he saw the sun reflect off a few busy knives. The mutilations had already begun. One thing for sure, he thought, the Cheyenne women will be the most savage. They will be remembering what had happened down in Colorado, at Sand Creek, twelve years ago.

Raven remembered the article as though he had read it yesterday. He had been a kid living in a foster home in Wyoming when he had first read the story. At the time it had made such an impression on him, he had read it twice.

In November of 1864, a village of peaceful Cheyenne and Arapahoe was attacked by a force of seven hundred Colorado Volunteers. When the soldiers attacked, most of the adult males were away on a hunting trip hoping to bring back game for the winter. Black Kettle, chief of the village, had an American flag flying in front of his tipi. He wasn't spared and neither were one hundred women and children, nor the remaining twenty-eight men in the village.

The one thing that really stuck in Chris' mind was the statement made by the civilian commander of the Colorado militia, Colonel J.M.Chivington. When asked what should be done about the women and children, he had replied, "Kill them all. Nits become lice!"

Because of the terrible atrocities committed by the Volunteers several chiefs from other tribes, who had always smoked the peacepipe with the whites, began to fear extermination. They collectively turned to their war chiefs and declared an all out war on the white man.

In an attempt to get his mind off what he knew was going to happen, Raven looked south along the broad ridgeline and saw The Black. He was a couple of hundred yards away, standing beside another horse. They were the only riderless horses in sight and were standing in the middle of a host of dead bodies dressed in dusty blue and gold.

With pumpgun in hand Chris limped his way along the grassy crest. He approached another group of scattered dead. The air was suddenly thick with flies. He hadn't noticed the flies over by Custer's group. Must be more wind over there, he thought. He shrugged the thought away and let his gaze drift on ahead and kept moving. Raven made it a point not to look at the faces of the dead. A long time ago he decided that he had enough nightmare memories from Vietnam to last for three lifetimes.

Chris' thoughts began to turn toward Wolf as he tried stubbornly to push them away. Now is not the time for grief, he thought. It is the time to help your people in any way that you can. And, he mused, if I remember my history right, it's also time to gather up the loved ones and look for a place to hide because the entire U. S. Army will be out to avenge Custer.

Movement caught his eye. The Black had apparently caught his scent and was coming to meet him. He slowly walked toward him, and it appeared that he was avoiding stepping on any of the dead. That's strange, he thought. He remembered how Bear's Foot had done the same thing. The Black stopped and waited for Raven to come the rest of the way. He tossed his head at Chris' approach and nipped at his fingers as he stroked the velvet muzzle. As Raven gathered the reins and was about to step into the stirrup, he stopped. Someone had tied up The Black's tail, Lakota style, with an eagle feather thrust through the knot. Bear's Foot, he thought. Sure as hell, he reasoned, Bear was worried that some Indian would see the McClellan saddle and think he was a dead Bluecoat's horse.

Leaving the tail as it was, Raven winced as he swung his leg over the cantle. Moving The Black over by his four-legged friend, he saw that the horse was in a pretty bad way. A buckskin gelding, all bloody and shot full of holes, was standing squarely in the middle of a cluster of blue-clad bodies; the buckskin's saddle had twisted so that it was hanging beneath his belly. The chin strap on the bridle had been cut and the bit was swinging free, outside his mouth. Raven shook his head when he saw the extent of the horse's wounds. The buckskin's head drooped so low it almost touched the ground.

Chris stared hard at the wounded horse. Why does this horse look so familiar? His wondering allowed his gaze to follow the reins down into the trampled, bloody grass where the leather ribbons were still clutched in the fist of the horse's dead master.

Recognition brought with it a sudden twinge of remorse. It was the black-bearded captain who had fought so bravely. Raven stared at the sunburned Irishman with compassion and regret. Remembering how the captain had screamed, 'Come back and fight ya heathen bastard!' brought a smile to Chris' lips. Taking note of the bloody hole in the captain's chest and the leg twisted at such an unnatural angle, Raven thought, *if his wounds weren't so obvious I'd swear he was just asleep.* Still reflecting, he muttered, "It's too bad, you and I would have enjoyed having a few beers together."

A strange sound whipped Raven's attention over to his right. An Indian was busy stripping the blouse off a cavalryman. Raven relaxed; he knew the Indian. He was a Hunkpapa Sioux named Little Soldier, a warrior who was known as small in size but with a very big heart ... the later meaning very brave. Chris became aware that there were others up on the ridge collecting weapons, clothing, etc. *Thank God,* he thought, *they haven't done any mutilating yet.*

Little Soldier walked up to him and grinned. *"Hau,* Okute."

Chris tried not to let his disgust show when he saw that the Lakota brought the bloody blouse with him. *I guess I've just seen and smelled too much blood today,* he thought. Gesturing toward the dead captain, Chris asked, "Were you here when the Bluecoat died, Little Soldier?"

The Hunkpapa's smile got even larger as he replied, *"Han* (yes). This warrior was the bravest of them all."

Raven gestured again, only this time at the buckskin. "Why have you not taken his brave horse?"

Little Soldier's smile disappeared so quickly, Raven half wondered if it had ever been there. The warrior glanced nervously at the captain and said, "Spirits."

"What?" Raven asked.

"Spirits, Okute. The horse is commanded by a spirit. All of this man's warriors killed their horses and fought from behind their bodies. But not this warrior. At the end he crouched between his spirit horse's legs, holding the bridle and firing his pistol until he was killed."

Curious, Chris asked, "Why has not another warrior, who does not know of the spirits, take the horse?"

The brave shook his head, saying, "No Indian would take a horse that is still being held by a dead man, Okute."

Raven glanced at the reins still clutched in the captain's fist and understood. The Hunkpapa grinned again and stepped closer to The Black. He held the blouse up, stuck his finger through the bloody hole and said, "I think ..."

With an abrupt sidestep, The Black shied away from Little Soldier. Looking to see what had spooked his horse, Raven saw a sight that was destined to stay with him forever.

The Irish captain, a gaping hole in his chest, was sitting up and looking around! He had a dazed look in his eyes; a revolver was clutched in his right hand.

Chris' peripheral vision caught Little Soldier's sudden side-step away from the horror. The warrior's eyes were big and his mouth was sagging open. Then, before Raven was able to react, the little Hunkpapa's mouth clamped shut and he rushed forward. His sudden movement caused The Black to do a nervous dance step, as Little Soldier threw the bunched up blouse into the captain's bewildered face and twisted the pistol out of his hand.

It all happened so quickly; all Raven could do was watch as Little Soldier reversed the revolver and shot the captain in the head. A peculiar calmness overcame the officer's countenance as he stiffened and fell back onto the grass, dead.

Calming The Black, Chris felt a knot of regret forming in his chest. He saw the buckskin staring at his captain. A shudder racked the brave horse's body as he jerked his head up. Because of the reins still wrapped around his hand, the head-jerk dragged the captain's body closer to the gelding.

Because of the Lakota belief, Little Soldier kept one eye on the 'spirit' horse and the other on the captain as he edged in close to the dead man. He pointed at the captain's chest and looked at Raven.

"Okute, look."

Moving The Black in closer, Chris saw a large, shiny medallion peeking out from beneath the captain's fringed, leather shirt.

As soon as he saw Raven look, the warrior stepped away from the body, keeping one eye on the buckskin.

"Strong medicine, Okute. He had a great fighting spirit. It is only fitting that he is the last to die."

Numbed by the bizarre chain of events, Chris nodded in agreement and pointed The Black south. While waving a goodbye to Little Soldier, he noticed that many more looters had arrived, and he could see others in places more distant. Anxious to get away from the battlefield, the distant crackle of Reno's gunfire beckoned to him. He moved The Black into an easy canter.

As he rode, Raven's thoughts remained focussed. It's strange, he thought, how I can't seem to shake loose from thinking of the Irishman and his horse. When comprehension came, it was so unexpected that Chris jerked The Black to a halt and looked back. Far away, along the twisted plateau, he saw the buckskin. He still hadn't moved. He felt lightheaded as he thought, the buckskin gelding and the Irish captain. Aloud, he said, "It must be him."

He continued to stare. He absently sawed on the reins as The Black tried to leave. A shiver shimmied up his spine as he quietly spoke his thoughts out loud.

"I can still remember how it read, 'Comanche, a buckskin cavalry mount, was the sole survivor of the battle. He was owned by the fiery Captain Miles Keogh, former Soldier of Fortune, who was one of the fallen in the infamous battle'."

Eager to go, Raven allowed The Black to move into a lope toward the distant, sporadic gunfire. As he rode, he facetiously thought, it's only a few miles away in distance but one hundred years in time.

TRACKS

PART 3

EXCERPT FROM THE JOURNAL OF CETAN CHIKALA (LITTLE HAWK)

▲▲▲▲▲▲▲▲

Riding Hawk's Wing around the battlefield was frightening. Everywhere my eyes gazed I saw the startling white of the stripped bodies of the wasichus. It also bothered me to see the hatred of the women as they viciously mutilated the bodies. My fears smothered the joy I should have felt over our glorious victory. I was worried that the Bluecoats would be so angry over our triumph that they would be relentless in their pursuit of revenge. But, of more immediate importance was my concern for Okute. Why have I not found him? Is he wounded, bleeding to death in some hidden bushes? I would not allow myself to think that he was killed.

It was not until my pony carried me south along the top of the bluffs that I began to have hope. A Hunkpapa named Little Soldier had seen him a short time ago. He was last seen riding The Black south, toward where the Bluecoats were still fighting on the hill.

I continued on toward the south and the far away gunfire. Suddenly, I pulled Hawk's Wing to a stop.

"Hey, hey!"

A Lakota was calling for help! Disappointment filled my soul as I saw the warrior, Kill's Twice. He was grinning and gesturing for me to come over. I had thought the shout had come from Okute.

131

Since the man was from my band of Minneconjou, I took the time to see what help was needed. My pony gave a nicker greeting as I walked him up next to Kill's Twice's mount. Flies, disturbed by my arrival, swarmed into the air like bees chased from their hive. The handful of dead Bluecoats scattered at the warrior's feet, like life-size dolls, explained the new rifle and bullet mold in his hand.

Kill's Twice explained that he had called me over to help him with his looting and scalping. He even offered to share the scalps. When I told him of my mission and asked if he had seen Okute since the fighting had ended, the grin left his face and he looked down at the sprawling dead at his moccasined feet.

I held my breath as my gaze swept the dead. When I saw that all were Bluecoats, except for one Ree scout, my relief was instant. My respite was short-lived.

Kill's Twice lifted his eyes. They met mine as he said, "I have not seen Okute. But I have seen Bear's Foot over there."

He pointed east, away from the bluffs. "He was leading a black horse with one of our fallen draped over the saddle. Because of the distance I could not see who had been killed."

My heart plummeted to the ground and turned to stone. Somehow, I managed to thank him and leave. I had to fight off the desire to gash my arms and wail like a grieving woman. My head spun with fear and anxiety. I was afraid to find out if it was Okute, yet I knew that I must.

Hawk's Wing eagerly responded to my urgings and we moved swiftly toward the east, along the gradual diminishing slope. I was certain that I would find Bear's Foot among a place with trees selecting a burial place to prepare the dead for his journey. We had travelled only a short distance when the land changed. The rolling hillocks, with their deep gullies, became larger hills with toppings of juniper and pine.

Rounding one of the large hills I suddenly yanked my pony to a stop. Less than an arrow's flight away was my friend, Bear's Foot. He was part way up the side of a smaller hill that adjoined the one I had just come around. He had climbed one of two small trees that were supporting a crudely fashioned burial platform and was placing the dead warrior's weapons beside him. I did not know whether to laugh or cry. The horse standing quietly beneath his master's platform was not The Black; it was Wolf's Spirit's black stallion. I felt joy that it was not my new father, Okute, who had left us, yet my heart bled tears for my friend, Wolf's Spirit.

Bear's Foot stepped down from the tree and moved away from the platform. He stopped when he saw me. The smile that was usually there to greet me was missing. I saw a great sadness. A deep sorrow that lurked behind his eyes and spread across the broad features of his face.

As was customary, Bear raised his left arm in greeting. We Lakota use the left arm because it is closest to the heart and has not been used to kill. It will also convince the person we are greeting of our sincerity.

I was returning the gesture when I heard, "Karaack!" The loud rifle shot startled me.

Bear's Foot's hands plucked at his chest and he stumbled backwards and fell onto the buffalo grass.

Stunned, not really sure what had happened, I dug my heels into Hawk's Wing's ribs and we leaped forward with the quickness of a mountain cat. Movement pulled my eyes to the larger hill on my left. A puff of gunsmoke was still drifting upwards. Below it was the Hunkpapa, Scar. He was *struggling with a Bluecoat's rifle. It looked like he was having trouble making it work again. It wasn't until that very moment, when I saw Scar try to make the rifle work, that reality hit me and I realized that Bear's Foot had been shot ... by one of our own people!*

I leaped from my pony's back and glanced back at Scar. My look was in time to see him throw the rifle aside in disgust. I ran to my friend's side. Seeing the blood that had spilled from his upper body, I stopped before I reached him. My heart soared when I saw the slight rise and fall of his chest. He was alive! I stopped myself from moving any closer. I thought of Scar. Slowly I turned. The Hunkpapa Sioux had already mounted his pony. Unless I did something to stop him, I knew that Scar was going to ride down and make sure that Bear's Foot was dead. My head spun with indecision. What could I do?

"Murderer! You have killed my friend!"

Scar, who had already started his pony downhill, stopped. He stared at me. I could see the scar beside his mouth curl as though alive. He sneered and hefted the war hatchet clutched in his hand. I was terrified! What if Scar came to be certain Bear's Foot was dead. How would I stop such a formidable warrior? I was shaking so badly that I was certain that Scar would notice and would understand what I was trying to do. The Hunkpapa continued to stare. I prayed that Wakan Tanka would keep Bear's Foot from moving. If he were to move in the slightest, I knew in my heart that both he and I would die.

For the first time I noticed the red paint that was applied so that it appeared to ooze from Scar's old wounds like blood. When the warrior spoke, a spirit fist grabbed my throat and squeezed. His damaged voice added fuel to the fire of my fear.

Wasichu's Return

"Tell your wasichu that I have avenged my friend's murder."

His words were spoken while still wearing the sneer. I knew that the 'friend' he spoke of was a warrior named Standing Elk who had been killed in a fair fight.

With all my heart I wished that I had my full growth so that I could remove his sneering smile with my two-blade knife. Knowing that I stood no chance against him, I waited. I prayed that he would leave, and would do so quickly, so that I could find help for my friend.

His eyes glittered like zuzeka's (snake) as he said, "If the wasichu has a heart, tell him I will watch for him in the north."

My heart began to beat strongly as he turned his pony to leave. Then he stopped and I felt that my heart had also stopped. I feared that he had changed his mind and was going to make certain that Bear was dead. My heart began beating again as Scar merely faced me once more and shouted, "Leave, now! Go find your pet wasichu. I go to the north to scout for my chief. Tell him I will be waiting."

On trembling legs I walked to my pony. Mounting him, I rode away toward the bluffs. I had longed to look closer at Bear's Foot to see if he was still breathing but had not dared. I used my quirt on Hawk's Wing and he burst into a gallop. I looked back. Relief washed over me like a splash of cool water. Scar was leaving! I used the quirt again. Having rarely felt my whip, Hawk's Wing responded to its bite with a burst of speed. Frantically, I watched for someone to help.

There! I spied Kill's Twice still searching for loot among the dead Bluecoats. An old one had joined him in his quest. Their heads turned at my shout. Pulling my pony to a sliding stop, I recognized the grandfather. It was One

Horn! I was overjoyed with my good fortune. The old one has been long known for his clever use of herbs and poultices.

I quickly told them of Bear's Foot and where to find him. They assured me that they would hurry to his side and tend to his wound. One Horn asked me questions about Bear's wound that I could not answer. I begged that he forgive my rudeness and turned my pony away. I must find Okute!

The urgent thought was still bouncing in my head as I dug my heels into my pony's flanks. Riding away, I heard One Horn already imploring Kill's Twice to keep watch for certain herbs as they moved in the direction toward where Bear's Foot lay wounded.

We swiftly drew closer to the distant gunfire. I knew in my heart that if Okute was not lying dead or wounded somewhere, he would be where there was still fighting.

I let Wakan Tanka guide my pony's hoofs along the narrow, twisting trail. The wind and dust were in my eyes, making it difficult for me to see beyond the brightness of my tears.

CHAPTER 16

ΛΛΛΛΛ

The hovering clouds of smoke and dust had dispersed revealing a sky of startling blue. Christopher Raven was totally unaware of the change in the atmosphere.

His heels relentlessly pounded The Black's ribs. He thought of Bear's Foot lying on some remote hillside bleeding to death as his murderer, Scar, rode away to the north.

Following Little Hawk's directions, Raven swerved The Black toward the east. He could still hear the faint pop of firearms coming from the south. He rode wildly through a sprawl of dead soldiers that looked like a warehouse of broken mannequins. Their stripped and mutilated bodies were a stark white and reddish pink against the green grass and the gray of the sage. He rode hard, anxious to leave the stench and horror of the ridge behind him and to find his friend. The Black sensed his urgency and increased his stride. In no time at all he was in among the pine-scented hills. Coming around one of the larger hummocks, Raven abruptly pulled the stallion to a haunch-sliding stop.

Filled with mounting apprehension Chris walked his mount toward a small group of Lakota gathered on the side of a smaller adjoining hill. During his approach his pale gaze absorbed every sobering detail of the tiny assemblage. What truly frightened Raven was how reminiscent the small group was of a wake.

137

While his throat constricted with dread, Chris moved closer. An old Lakota was kneeling beside the sprawled form of Bear's Foot. Raven's apprehension diminished somewhat when he saw that the old one was staying busy trying to fan flies away from Bear's face and wound. Relieved, Chris acknowledged that he must be alive.

As The Black slowly approached, he saw that the big warrior's head and shoulders were in the shade cast by the burial platform. Even after death, he mused, Wolf's Spirit was looking after his friend.

Standing silently nearby were three men. Raven was surprised to see that one of them was Crazy Horse. Somehow, he reasoned, the young chief had heard of the shooting and had come to help, or as a show of respect for his friend. Beside him stood a tall Sioux with a strong chin and slanted eyes. Chris recognized him immediately ... He Dog, Crazy Horse's closest friend and faithful lieutenant. Standing apart from the other two was the blade-thin warrior, Kills Twice, who was staring somberly at the fallen giant.

Quickly stepping down from the saddle, Raven exchanged nods with Crazy Horse and the others and moved swiftly to Bear's side. His breath caught in his throat when he saw all the blood. At first he couldn't tell if he was breathing. Feeling at the base of the neck, Raven's breath left his lungs with an audible hiss. There it is! Thank God, he thought.

Noting that the wound was high on the chest, he prayed that the bullet had missed the lung. He quickly checked for blood on the lips. Finding none, he checked the pulse again. It was a very rapid pulse! Frantically, he thought. Suddenly, he exclaimed aloud, "He's in shock!"

Jumping to his feet Chris rushed over to The Black and grabbed his blanket poncho from behind the cantle. In spite of the afternoon's heat, he spread the blanket over his friend's body. Carefully, he looked beneath the poultice the old one had prepared and was relieved to see that the bleeding had stopped. He took the time to grin and nod at the old Indian. It was probably his herbs, he thought, that had stopped the bleeding. Looking again, Raven was thankful that Bear wasn't wearing a shirt. I'd probably be trying to hopelessly pick leather from the wound right now, he mused.

Gesturing to the others, they came to his side and together they were able to move Bear's Foot to the base of the incline. Raven explained that Bear must remain warm and kept flat on his back. He also explained that his head should be positioned lower than the rest of his body. They stared at him like he was *witke* (crazy) but agreed to abide by his wishes.

"Son of a Bitch!" He brought his hands to his face in a gesture of frustration as he swore.

The Lakota stared at him, then at each other. Raven shook his head in embarrassment at having spoken English. Not taking the time to explain, Chris bent over Bear's Foot's great bulk and gently rolled him onto his side. As he did so, he chastised himself for having forgotten to look for an exit wound. He prayed that the bullet had enough velocity to go all the way through.

"Shit!" He swore, vehemently.

He cringed when he saw there was no exit wound. Lowering Bear's Foot back onto his back, Chris clenched his trembling hands and felt overwhelmed by helplessness. Raven knew that he didn't have the skills to go in after the bullet. He couldn't remember ever feeling so helpless. His mind raced. What can I do, he thought. He knew that if the bullet stayed in him, the wound would turn septic and his friend would die.

Not having been a medical specialist in Special Forces, all he could do was think hard to remember what he had learned about treating wounds in combat.

Deep in thought Raven was unaware of Crazy Horse's presence until he felt his hand on his arm. The Oglala war chief stared with his solemn, brown eyes at Bear's Foot's unconscious form. He squeezed Chris' arm as he proclaimed, "He will live, Okute. He is a great warrior, and we will need him when the Bluecoats come again"

Raven nodded, knowing full well that the chief's optimism was probably wasted breath. "Tell me my chief, does anyone know from where the shot was fired?"

Crazy Horse's strange hawk eyes studied Chris with quiet intensity. He probably thinks that's a dumb question, Raven thought, and he's probably right.

The young chief suddenly stood up and pointed toward the large hill on their left. He said, "Kills Twice and He Dog found Lakota tracks and a Bluecoat rifle up there. The rifle had a bullet jammed in its chamber."

Staring up at the nearby hill, Raven felt a subtle stirring of excitement. When searching Bear's back for an exit wound, he had seen something low on the back that he had assumed was a bruise.

Trying to hold down a rising surge of hope, Chris rolled Bear onto his side once more. There! Midway down his back and just to the right of his spine, there was a purplish lump. He pushed on it. An involuntary gasp erupted from the unconscious warrior. Raven looked closer. The discolored protuberance, about the size of a thumbnail, obviously didn't belong there. His optimism rejoiced while his pessimism whispered negative suggestions.

Chris looked again at the top of the adjoining hill, thinking, by God, it fits. It must be the bullet! He was elated! Had the bullet struck any lower on his chest, he would be looking at a 'sucking' chest wound. That, he thought, would have been it. Bear would have been a goner. He couldn't believe his luck. The bullet was just sitting there under the skin like a boil waiting to be lanced.

Raven quickly showed the bullet to the others and explained what he was going to do. Sensing Chris' newfound confidence evoked a desire to participate and help save Bear's Foot's life. Kills Twice got busy building a fire, while He Dog went to the horses to fetch some water. As the others went about doing his bidding, Raven delved underneath Bear's inert form and came up with his friend's huge knife.

The drywash separating the two hills was mostly grass and gravel but here and there were patches of sandy soil. Grabbing the water skin that He Dog provided Raven hurried to a nearby sandy area. He longed for the medical supplies that had been available to him in Vietnam. At the moment, he thought, a bar of soap would do wonders for stabilizing his confidence.

The old one watched Raven's every move as he began to prepare what was needed. Wetting his hands, he scrubbed them briskly in the wet, abrasive sand. He did the same with the large knife. Returning to the group he began to heat the twelve-inch blade in He Dog's fire. While waiting for the steel to heat, he thought back to the day when he had given the Randall fighting knife to Bear's Foot in an attempt to buy his friendship. The offering of the knife had been the beginning of a friendship that had grown in a few short months to the status of kinship. Smiling, Chris recalled Bear's remark during the battle, '... as anyone can plainly see we were both whelped by the same mother.'

Turning the blade in the fire, Raven threw a glance toward the mouth of the wash. Blue Feather and Little Hawk should be here soon with the travois, he thought.

Stepping over to Bear's Foot, Chris stopped and stared. The old one was preparing a new poultice to apply to the new wound that would result from removing the bullet.

"Jesus H. Christ," Raven muttered. The old one was chewing the herbs to create a malleable pulp to apply to the wound. Why am I even bothering to wash anything, he silently grumbled.

With a huge sigh of resignation Raven knelt beside his friend. Crazy Horse was there to help him roll Bear's Foot onto his stomach. Before starting, he had the chief pour more water over his hands and knife. If only, he wished, we had the time and sanitary facilities to at least boil the water.

At Raven's urging, Crazy Horse also poured water over the discolored lump on Bear's back. Sunlight flashed off the broad blade as Chris moved in close for the incision. The razor sharp knife bit deeply into the warrior's flesh. Bear's Foot jerked and a loud grunt exploded from his throat, startling everyone. The incision gaped open. Blood welled and coursed down his back. Much of the blood followed the deep indentation caused by the protruding muscles that bordered the spine.

Raven could see it! More water briefly washed away the bright blood and exposed the purple-black bullet. The bullet was lodged in the muscle just under the skin's surface.

Not hesitating at all, Raven plunged the point of the knife in against one side of the lead projectile. Hands grabbed Bear's Foot's arms and legs as he unknowingly jerked and twisted away from the pain. Chris quickly thrust the point behind the bullet and levered upwards! A low, pitiful moan came from the unconscious warrior as the dark lead slug surfaced. It tumbled out of the bloody hole and left a red, tacky trail as it traversed Bear's coppery skin. Exclamations of surprise and relief came from all.

The extraction also pulled an exclamation of surprise from the old medicine man. He followed it quickly with an abbreviated Lakota courage growl eerie enough to make the hair on Raven's arms stand up.

Picking up the misshapen bullet, Chris moved out of the way so that the old one could clean up and apply his poultice. Respite, coupled with the congratulations of his Lakota brothers, left him tired but happy. Wiping the perspiration from his brow he watched to see if the old man did what Raven had asked.

Some subtle sound caused Chris to look around. There, he heard it again. A soft nicker came from the southern end of the wash. The noise compelled five heads to turn toward the sound and nervous hands to reach for weapons.

Little Hawk and Blue Feather appeared at the end of the wash. Blue Feather's pony was pulling a travois.

Leaving Bear's Foot in the old man's hands, Raven walked to meet them. As he drew near, the apprehension on Little Hawk's face was too much to bear. Chris called to him, "*Washtay!* *Wakan Tanka* has smiled on us. He will live!"

A dazzling grin spread across Little Hawk's face. Blue Feather smiled, also. Their smiles were so infectious, everyone was smiling. Even the old medicine man, who didn't look like he had a single tooth left in his head, was grinning.

Adding to Raven's happiness was the sight of his wife. He hadn't seen her since the start of the battle, so her presence was even more pleasurable than usual.

Walking beside them as they continued on toward the small group of Lakota, Chris let his weathered hand rest on Blue Feather's leg.

To outward appearances the contact was used as a point of balance for Raven as he walked beside a moving horse. The truth was that Raven couldn't be near his wife for more than a passing moment without touching her in some affectionate manner.

Their eyes met. Raven asked, "You are well?"

Blue Feather grinned. "I am well, my husband."

He looked away for a second. When he found her gaze again, he spoke softly. "I must leave you again."

A cloud of concern passed over her face as her smile faded away, leaving behind only the sorrowful black pools of her eyes.

Gently, he let his determination show as he quietly said, "I must find Scar and kill him. Bear's Foot must be avenged as soon as possible. If I do not end this now, he will try again. Do you understand?"

Blue Feather stopped her pony. They both watched as Little Hawk waved and rode ahead, joining the others. Still seated on her pony, Blue Feather looked down on Raven. "You must be very careful, Okute. There is more to this than you know."

She paused for a moment and watched the men greet her son. Turning back to Chris, she said, "Ever since my husband was killed two winters ago, this man Scar has wanted me. Whenever the bands would join together to hunt the buffalo, or to dance, this Hunkpapa would always be nearby. Sometimes he would try to court me. When I would refuse to notice him, he would stop. But always he would be watching me. I could not even bathe without him skulking in the bushes like a coyote."

Chris was totally surprised by her words. It certainly explained the scarred man's hatred for him.

Blue Feather paused. Raven saw an intensity in her manner that he had never seen before.

"Hear me, my husband. This man did not want revenge for Standing Elk. He is looking for an excuse, and the opportunity, to kill you. Perhaps he thinks that after you are gone, he will be able to have me."

In contrast to the flush of anger that already heated his cheeks, Raven felt a sudden chill move up his spine. This explains everything, he thought. The son-of-a-bitch knows how close Bear and I have become. Scar knew this would trigger an angry, vengeful reaction from me. One thing he doesn't know, he raged, is that he is already a dead man. You're dead meat, Scar ... you just haven't laid down yet.

Seeing the concern in Blue Feather's eyes, Chris grinned as he said, "Do not worry. I am not some toothless old bear for Scar to wrestle with. I will be back, but he won't be. This I promise you."

Blue Feather's searching gaze saw the resolution in the pale eyes and the tenacious set of his jaw. She also recognized the solid confidence hidden within his relaxed stance and small smile. Suddenly, the worry on her face vanished and a dazzling white smile emerged.

"I hear you, Okute. I believe what you say is true. Little Hawk and I will be waiting for your return."

CHAPTER 17

▲▲▲▲▲

Raven and Ptecila left the great encampment and rode north. Behind them they left thousands of jubilant Sioux and Cheyenne. It was late afternoon and color was just beginning to show west of the mountains. Had they waited until morning they wouldn't have lost much time, but Chris didn't want to be a part of the victory celebration.

A lot of good men died today because of one man's driving ambition, he thought, and I'm not going to be a part of the festivities that celebrate their deaths.

Another reason he decided to leave right away was because some of the tribes were already moving south and he didn't need to get caught up in the resulting hassle. For the moment, he needed all of his focus to be on the dangerous task ahead of him.

He turned in the saddle and looked back. The stripped bodies were clearly visible, appearing as tiny white dots scattered along the rolling sweep of the green hillside. He noticed the number of carrion eaters circling above the grassy bluffs was increasing with every passing moment. Raven pulled his eyes away from the disheartening sight.

He watched as Ptecila, eyes fixed on the turf, swiftly rode his small pony back and forth over a patch of rocky ground. In an unexpected move the tracker rode his mount away from the stony terrain and cantered north. As usual, his eyes stayed riveted to the ground. He rode on for a short distance and stopped. Throwing a glance at Raven, he waved his arm, relaxed, and then waited. He turned at Chris' approach and nodded a greeting as though they had been apart for awhile.

Raven had to chuckle to himself as he, once again, saw the circle of ochre painted around the tracker's right eye. Earlier, when he had asked him about it, Ptecila had said, 'It will help me to see the difficult sign and to tell the truths from the lies in Scar's tracks.'

Ptecila snapped Raven out of his musing by suddenly pointing to the northwest and exclaiming, "Okute, they are riding for that mountain, the one that looks like a sleeping mountain cat."

Chris looked but couldn't tell which one he meant. Perplexed, he asked, "How do you know this?"

Ptecila smiled as he replied, "Because we Lakota use landmarks when we travel. This mountain will be their first if they continue to travel north."

Raven glanced sharply at him as he asked, "That is the second time you have said 'they,' Why is that?"

The smile left the Oglala's wizened face as he said, "Because, Okute, Scar has taken two Hunkpapa warriors with him."

Raven felt a sinking feeling in the pit of his stomach. He looked toward the distant mountain and thought, that's just fuckin' great. Turning to Ptecila, he said, "I thought he would be alone, my friend. I cannot ask you to track for me, now. There is too much danger. You could be killed."

Ptecila put his small brown hand on Raven's arm as he softly said, "*Wahi* (I am coming), Bear's Foot is a friend of mine, also. We will not speak of this again."

He studied the older man's wrinkled face for a moment before replying, "*Waste* (Good). I would not find them without you, *kola* (friend). They would find me."

Ptecila grinned. "These are truthful words you speak. I will teach you how to track. We will find them together."

They started out in a lope with Ptecila's small pony leading The Black. True to his word their tracks were moving in a straight line toward the distant mountain. By nightfall they were at the base of the mountain range still moving north. Shortly thereafter they came to a grove of aspen and set up camp. To be on the safe side they didn't build a fire, just gulped some greasy pemmican. After wrapping themselves in their blankets they took turns staying awake. When it became his turn, Raven managed to stay awake by watching the starlit sky and thinking of Blue Feather and Little Hawk.

By the time the morning sun was filtering through the aspen they were already on the move. They breakfasted on jerky and drank from a mountain stream. The water was so cold it made Chris' teeth ache. In no time at all their mounts had left the trees and carried them into the warmth of the sun. The mountains loomed above them as they cantered their horses through the grass covered foothills. Rather than risk an easy ambush, the trackers traversed the drywashes and ravines. Had they taken the easier route over the hills, they would have presented an inviting target every time they crested a hillock.

By afternoon they were approaching the monolithic landmark and were well into the timbered hills surrounding it. They were now far enough from the big village so that wild game had become more abundant. From a high point they saw, far to the east, a herd of antelope grazing on the valley grassland. But it was the woodlands that offered the most plentiful wildlife. Deer, grouse, quail, and rabbit were everywhere.

The increase in altitude created a special freshness in the air. The sharp scent of pine and cedar dominated the woodland aromas. After the dust and smoke of battle, Raven was invigorated by it all. Even The Black was more lively with the atmospheric change. He noticed that the fiery spark that had disappeared in the aftermath of the battle was back in his eye once more. Sometimes Chris would see him testing the air. The Black's whole appearance was reminiscent of a wild mustang on the lookout for danger.

When they were so close to the landmark that its presence dominated their view, Ptecila stopped and looked up. His gaze wasn't fixed on the mountain but on the blue sky to their right front. Following the tracker's line of sight, Raven saw a hawk, or eagle, circling high above.

"What is it, Ptecila?"

Pointing at the circling bird, he asked, "See the eagle, Okute? He was coming in a straight line from the mountains. When he reached the plains, beneath him, he began to circle."

Ptecila continued to watch the gliding speck, soaring majestically. He quietly said, "Soon, he will go back to the west."

Raven watched the eagle utilize the thermals. Just as he began to have his doubts the great bird stopped circling and flew back toward the mountains. Chris stared in wonder. At the very moment he was about to ask Ptecila how he knew, the Oglala tracker explained. "The eagle is telling us that 'man' is below him. He only acts in that specific manner when he sees man."

Impressed, Raven teased, as he asked, "It is unfortunate that he cannot tell us who it is that he sees." He smiled at Ptecila, letting him know that his remark was a joke.

149

Ignoring the smile Ptecila nodded and looked about until he spied a tall, rocky outcrop. He heel-tapped his pony over to it, stepped from his mount's back onto the rock and began to climb. Near the top there was a flat ledge. The Oglala bellied onto it, cupped his hands around his eyes, and studied the terrain far ahead and below them.

Raven chuckled softly to himself, thinking, damned if that don't remind me of when I was a kid and used to cup my hands like that, pretending I was looking through binoculars.

From Chris' vantage point, it looked as though Ptecila was staring at a distant juncture where the valley grass met the treeline. Cupping his hands like his friend, Raven stared at the spot that the eagle had appeared to be hovering over. He saw absolutely nothing.

When Ptecila climbed down he dropped onto his pony's back and grinned at Raven. "It is them. *Hopo* (let's go)."

Chris reached out and stopped him from pulling ahead. Puzzled, he asked, "How do you know? It is too far away to see anyone."

Ptecila shrugged as he said, "I could not see them. I saw the dust of two or three horses. They were riding one behind the other. *Wasichus* do not ride in this manner, only Indians." He paused for a moment before continuing. Smiling, he said, "If they are Indian, they must be Lakota or Cheyenne. Our enemies, if only three in number, would not dare come this close to the big village."

Raven grinned and agreed. "Then let us go. You lead. If they turn out to be Crow or Shoshone, you can be the one to tell them we made a mistake."

Ptecila laughed and used his heels to goad his pony into a canter. They rode briskly down the gradient toward the valley below. Once they reached the foothills and found the tracks, Ptecila showed Raven that they were the same tracks as the ones they had found outside the village. He took the time to show Chris how he could tell that the tracks were fresh and not from the day before.

Squatting beside the spoor, Ptecila said, "Had the tracks been made in the night, or the day before, there would be tiny insect trails across the hoofprints." He also pointed out, "If the sides of the prints had started to crumble inward it would show us that the tracks are more than a couple hours old."

Raven was so impressed he was speechless. He shook his head and grinned. They mounted up and settled into their tracking routine, Ptecila leading with Raven bringing up the rear, while keeping an eye out for an ambush.

Scar's trail was easy to follow; the three Hunkpapas had made no effort to hide their tracks. This lack of caution by Scar brought a fresh patina of sweat to Chris' skin. He half expected to be bushwhacked at any moment. Ptecila needlessly reminded him to watch out for an ambush. In an effort to make up some time they recklessly rode at a ground-covering lope. Their dangerous gamble worked fine and covered a lot of ground until they were led back into heavy timber.

Because of the closeness of the trees, they were forced to drastically reduce the speed of their tracking. Once they were deep into the wild tract of forest they had no visible line of direction other than the tracks of the three Hunkpapa Sioux. When the sun slipped behind the mountains the diminishing light compelled them to stop tracking by sight. Ptecila got down from his pony and hunkered on his haunches but was still unable to see. Using the Oglala's sense of touch and an occasional educated guess, they were able to continue for a short period of time.

By true nightfall they had managed to put the 'sleeping cat' mountain behind them. Rather than look for a suitable place to camp, they decided to stop right where they were, in the middle of the Hunkpapa's trail.

When it started to drizzle, Raven wrapped himself in his new gray blanket that was a gift from Crazy Horse. Sitting down beside the trail, he checked the tether line that led from his wrist to The Black. The wrist tether was helpful in keeping Raven from sleeping too soundly as well as having his horse handy for an emergency. Pulling the blanket partially over his head, he brought his knees up under the cloth shelter. Along with an occasional tug on the wrist he could hear The Black and Ptecila's pony grazing nearby.

Ptecila looked unearthly as he crouched opposite Chris in the soft rain. He was perched on his heels. His blanket was pulled all the way over his head like a witch's shroud, and the pale light from the moon caused deep, eerie shadows within the folds. The only part of his face that was visible was the pale ring of paint around his right eye.

With Ptecila taking the first watch Raven allowed his mind to drift. The old wound in his leg began to throb in protest to its new position. Ignoring the petty discomforts he began to worry that they were too close to the trail. What if, he thought, the Hunkpapa decide to backtrack? Drowsiness began to make its presence felt and in no time at all, Chris' head dropped and his thoughts drifted away as his subconscious dreamily transported him to another time, far into the future.

CHAPTER 18

▲▲▲▲▲

The sound of muffled footsteps in the rain awakened him. Raven ever so slowly raised his head enough so that his line of sight cleared his arms. He was sitting with his arms resting across his raised knees on the very edge of a narrow trail. With only his eyes moving Chris quickly studied each of his men. Like himself, each had become a part of the darkness and the slanting rain. They were still in their positions and appeared to be sleeping. Wong and Joe he couldn't see but they had damn well better be awake, he thought.

He mentally cursed and quickly quieted his breathing when he saw the first NVA come up the trail. The rain bounced off his glistening pith helmet like water off a duck's back. The black Asian eyes never deviated from the path at his feet as he slogged by, not three feet from Raven's boots. He held his breath as other NVA filed past. Suddenly, his stomach did a flip-flop. One of his men, a Nung mercenary, had moved in his sleep and his hand had shifted and was lying partially exposed on the path.

Chris, mesmerized, stared at the Nung's hand. He expected discovery at any second. There seemed to be no end to the file of Vietnamese. They caused him to clench his silenced .22 automatic so tightly his hand cramped. For Christ's sake, Raven thought, there seemed to be a whole platoon of them. Heads down they marched on through the drizzle as though playing a military version of the game 'follow the leader.' Raven's nerves began screaming in his ear, willing him to do something ... anything. At any moment he expected one of his men to make a noise in his sleep. Or, he thought, one of these paddy humpin' bastards will step on the Nung's hand.

After what seemed like an eternity, Raven sensed that the end of the enemy file was at hand. The two soldiers bringing up the rear began a whispered conversation. Unexpectedly, they stopped almost directly opposite Chris' position. When he saw that one of their feet was right next to the hand on the trail he began to break out in a new sweat. Raven held his breath. At any moment he expected one of his men to suddenly awaken, see the gooks, and automatically 'pop a cap' on them. Softly releasing his breath, he waited and wondered what it would be like to die all alone in the jungle.

As the others disappeared up the trail, the two NVA began to talk in normal speaking voices. Raven could clearly hear them over the falling rain. Leave! Get the fuck out of here! His silent screams were ignored. At any moment he expected the worse to happen. When it didn't, he suddenly knew that it was going to be all right. He knew that his men had to be awake by now, so they must all be waiting for his command. His eyes dropped to the soldier's feet. The Nung's hand was gone! Almost giddy with relief, Chris silently gave thanks to the mercenaries' Buddah, or whoever it was they prayed too.

Suddenly, the closest of the two waved the other Viet away and stepped off the path. He stopped inches from Raven's legs. He hung his AK-47 from a bony shoulder and began fumbling with his fly. The NVA sighed and watched his comrade walk up the trail. The rain intensified as the yellow stream arced into the brush. Raven stared in disbelief as the man's urine struck his boots, splattering in all directions. He scarcely breathed.

The Viet shook himself off and looked down as he buttoned his fly. He stopped and stared. He was looking straight at Chris' boots. Bending from the waist he peered through the driving rain into the dense underbrush.

Recognition was just starting to show on the narrow face when Raven quickly extended his right arm and jammed the High Standard .22's suppressor against the man's forehead and pulled the trigger. There was a muffled 'pop' and the Viet's arms shot out from his sides. His mouth gaped with surprise as his eyes fixed straight ahead. His legs buckled and his assault rifle slid down his arm. Chris grabbed both man and gun before they hit the ground. He silently eased the body down beside him.

Before anyone had a chance to react, the dead man's friend returned. He stopped and was staring through the rain at the spot in the underbrush where Raven was crouched. A flesh and blood statue, Raven clutched the dead man's shirt front. It was as though he had been playing the child's game 'Simon Says' and controller said, 'Simon says, freeze!'

With his heart in his throat Chris waited. He knew that all it would take would be a single gunshot to kill him and his whole team. The NVA unit would be all over them before they had covered a hundred meters. Assault rifle aimed from the hip, the soldier cautiously stepped forward. His head abruptly turned, facing down trail.

Through the slanting rain, Raven saw an NVA coming up the narrow path. An apparent straggler, he was hunched over leaning into he incline. The pelting rain bounced off his pith helmet. The first Viet spat some Vietnamese over his shoulder at the straggler and took another step toward Raven.

Chris was petrified. He stared at the new arrival, and thought ... damn, but he's big for a Vietnamese. Suddenly, the straggler exploded into action. Before the first Viet could turn his head Joe Spotted Horse grabbed him from behind, his left hand clamped over the soldier's mouth as he smashed the rifle out of his hands. A huge knife was clenched in Joe's right fist. The slashing rain glanced off the knife's broad blade in splinters of silver light as he swiftly moved it from left to right, cutting the throat of the NVA from ear to ear. He cast the man's jerking body aside.

Before the body hit the ground Raven was hissing orders to his team. As his black-clad Nungs silently moved like shadows down the hill, Raven watched his friend sail the pith helmet into the brush like a giant frisbee. Joe snatched his pumpgun off his back and ripped off the constricting NVA uniform shirt. He grabbed his shotgun and faced Chris. His wet hair was plastered across his brown face in swooping curlicues that looked like black lace. He grinned at Raven as he whispered, "Do I have to do everything, *wasichu*?"

A hand roughly grabbed his shoulder. Raven automatically reached for his inverted fighting knife attached to his left canvas suspender. It was gone! A voice whispered in his ear, "Okute."

Chris' eyes sprang open. He recoiled from the brown, lined face only inches from his own. The painted circle around Ptecila's eye brought him back to the present with startling abruptness.

"Okute, you were dreaming."

Raven looked at his Oglala friend, but his mind drifted immediately back to Vietnam and once again he was running through the rain with Joe and the Nungs of his Insertion Team, trying desperately to shake the pack of NVA hounds off their scent. Ptecila's quiet voice brought him back to the moment.

"It is time."

Raven rose to his feet. The Black's tether tugged at his wrist and startled him. Still somewhat shaken from the dream, he waited a moment before moving again. Chris cradled the pumpgun in the crook of his arm and looked through the ghostly light of a false dawn. Ptecila was already huddled beneath his blanket. He looked up at the towering pine. The rain had stopped and the pine boughs were dripping noisily onto the leafy ground cover. Breathing deeply, Raven cleared his mind of all memories of Vietnam. When he was ready he began to think of what the new day would bring. Will it bring me more horrors, he wondered, or will it bring me Scar and his Hunkpapa? Perhaps, he thought, they are one and the same.

CHAPTER 19

▲▲▲▲▲

Shortly after first light they were hot on Scar's trail. Ptecila was ecstatic to find that the Hunkpapa tracks were fresh. At Raven's insistence, he estimated that they would catch them before the sun was directly overhead.

They rode with a renewed vigilance. At any moment Chris expected to hear the hiss of an arrow or the frightening hammer of a gunshot.

His ears attempted to sort through all the normal sounds of the forest and hear only the sound that didn't belong. He tuned out the singing of birds and the sweep of the morning breeze as it rustled the leaves. Raven watched with the same intensity that he listened and tried to watch everywhere at once.

Ptecila had taught him that he should be watchful for anything that is not normal with nature's order; especially when hunting man, always be on the lookout for anything not in harmony with nature. He recalled how the little Oglala's black cherry eyes had become animated as he gave Raven some examples: 'Watch the trees, but not at eye level. When an enemy uses a tree to hide behind, he will not look around it from where you would expect ... look above in the branches, or below near the base of the tree. Another thing to watch is the wind. If the wind is blowing, watch for any movement that does not flow in the same direction.'

They left the timber and walked their horses into a large meadow. A stream ran through the open area and a pond had been created by a colony of industrious beaver. Their lodges rimmed the pond's edges, looking like stick and mud dwellings of some lost pygmy tribe. The meadow was covered with an abundance of tall marsh grass, a scatter of stunted pine, and an occasional sprawling deadfall.

The tracks led to the right, following the edge of the clearing and staying close to the trees. Some sixth sense told Raven that something was about to happen. He felt the hackles begin to rise on the back of his neck. A quiet hovered over the clearing, unnatural in its absolute stillness. With a verbal query totally without reason, Chris said, "Ptecila?"

The Oglala tracker turned to look back at Raven. At that very instant, an arrow glanced off Ptecila's shoulder. His pony screamed! A feathered shaft had transfixed his chest.

"Ka-boom!"

Raven felt a hard tug on his blanket poncho that was simultaneous with the rifle shot. Instinctively, he cried out and fell from The Black into the boggy marsh grass. Barely moving, he readied the pump. Taking a quick peek above the grass, Chris saw the remnants of smoke drifting away from a spot at the edge of the woods about seventy-five feet to his front.

Ptecila's horse collapsed into the grass and began to scream.

Trying to ignore the horrible sound Raven waited and hoped that whoever had shot at him would think that Ptecila was either badly wounded or dead.

Finally, Chris could stand it no longer. Unable to see Ptecila anywhere, he belly-crawled to the mortally wounded pony. Avoiding the slashing hoofs, he used Bear's Foot's knife to put the suffering animal out of his misery.

Risking another peek, he saw The Black. He had run a short distance away, down their back trail.

"Okute."

Ptecila's hushed voice was just loud enough for Raven to hear. "I will stay in the trees and try to find the shooter with the gun."

Assuming that the Oglala could see him, Chris nodded. He quietly eared the hammer back on the pump and waited. He became something a little less than human: an inanimate object with the eyes of an eagle and ears of an elephant. He absently watched the tops of the marsh grass ripple and undulate in the soft breeze. A cloud of gnats hovered in front of his face. Deer flies and mosquitoes buzzed near his ears. Only his eyes showed life. He waited.

To his left the mounds of beaver lodges were stark against the blue-green background of the pond. On the right the meadow ended in a tangle of deadfalls and towering pines. The absence of bird calls and other forest sounds was a very loud reminder of the impending danger.

Where, he worried, are the other two? He didn't have the slightest idea. With the suddenness of the attack he had not even seen where the arrows had come from.

Taking care not to make the tops of the grass move, Raven carefully placed the pump ahead and began to inch himself forward. His goal was opposite the spot where he had seen the smoke. He may be gone now, he thought, but I have to start somewhere. He had shed his blanket, but the tension and humidity were still sucking the moisture from his body. He felt like he was drowning in his own sweat.

Where is Ptecila? The thought brought forth a feeling of guilt for having placed the tracker in such a perilous situation. As if in answer to Chris' question a sudden war whoop, followed by some enthusiastic, high-pitched yipping, brought Raven's head up and above the grass level.

At the far end of the clearing Ptecila was astride a galloping pony and leading two others. A jubilant Chris silently exclaimed, 'I don't fucking believe it. He's found their horses!'

"Ka-boom!"

Not more than fifty feet in front of Raven a Hunkpapa Sioux had stepped into the open and fired his rifle at Ptecila. He levered another round into the Spencer.

Before the Sioux was able to shoulder his rifle again, Chris was on his knees with the pump braced against his hip. The shotgun roared! The warrior staggered sideways. Raven blasted two more loads of buckshot into the Indian. The velocity sent the man's body smashing through the brittle branches of a deadfall.

Dropping back into the cover of the long grass, Raven thumbed more shells into the pump's magazine. Quickly, but quietly, he moved to a different spot.

Before he had dropped back into the grass, Chris had seen Ptecila disappear into the trees with the horses. Now, after the thunderous blasts of the pump, the silence was even more menacing. Why can't I hear Ptecila in the woods ... how can he keep three horses from making any noise? Raven's silent questions drifted away unanswered. A more frightening question was superimposed over the later. Where is Scar? Where is the other Hunkpapa? Rage was building inside. Come on you sonofabitch, he thought, let's get it over with.

A startled whinny from The Black brought Raven to his feet. An Indian had a hold on The Black's reins and was trying to get a foot in the stirrup! The Black screamed with rage! His long head whipped around; he was turning in a circle, while snapping at the Sioux like a wolf.

It wasn't until Raven felt the razor sharp grass cutting his bare hands and arms that he realized he was running. He was so focussed on the Hunkpapa stealing his horse, he barely felt the arrow graze his hip and rattle off into the trees.

The horse thief had just managed to get a leg over the saddle's cantle when The Black reared. He hung on as the stallion dropped to all fours. Chris was running flat-out when his feet left the ground. He hit the Indian like a linebacker blindsiding a quarterback! The force of his impact carried the two of them off The Black and into the boggy swamp grass.

With a final, twisting kick in the air, the black stallion pranced out of reach of the brawling pair.

The smell of the man's sweat and rancid grease was strong in Raven's nostrils. The Indian had both fists locked onto Raven's knife hand. He pushed harder on the knife, moving the broad blade closer to the Hunkpapa's thick chest. Suddenly, the man shifted to the side.

Raven knew that he was stronger than the Indian, but because of the grease he couldn't hold onto him.

With an abrupt, twisting move, the Sioux slipped out of his grasp, spun away, and pulled a war club out of his belt. Before he was able to raise it, Chris was on his feet. He feinted to the left, spun, kicked the warrior high on the chest. The Sioux staggered back. Not giving him a chance to recover Raven bore in. He punched him in the face with a straight, left-hand jab. When he raised his left arm to protect himself, Chris swiftly slammed the Randall knife in between his ribs. When the long blade slid in all the way to the hilt, a shrill cry erupted from the warrior's gaping mouth. There was a sucking sound as Raven pulled the blade free. The Hunkpapa's eyes bulged and he gagged, dropping to his hands and knees.

An arrow zipped by Chris' ear! He dove into the grass and frantically looked for the pumpgun. All at once, he remembered. In the frenzy of the moment when he thought he might lose The Black, he had left it behind in the grass. Pulling his revolver free of its holster, Raven glanced at the dying Hunkpapa.

Still on his hands and knees a gout of blood spilled from his mouth, staining the grass between his hands a dark red. His head dropped forward as he wobbled and fell headfirst into the trampled grass.

Ignoring the throbbing pain in his leg, Raven got into a squat position. Setting himself, he jumped up and ran. Without actually seeing it, he heard an arrow whir by his head. He ran straight toward where he had left the pumpgun. In doing so, he was probably running straight toward Scar, so he moved in a zig-zag manner. Stumbling over a bog Chris fell headlong into the grass as another arrow hummed by overhead. Raven's gun hand was sweaty. He wiped it on his jeans as he peered over the grass trying to catch a glimpse of Scar. Just as he was about to make the final dash to reach the pumpgun, he stopped. His hand gripping the pistol felt sticky. He looked and rocked back onto his heels. His hand was covered with blood! The arrow that had grazed his hip had taken a hunk of flesh with it.

Raven swore. He grabbed a handful of grass and wadded it over the shallow wound. The pressure from the waistband of his jeans should hold it in place, he thought. Another arrow whistled by overhead. Chris ignored it. A horse's scream came from behind him. His eyes whipped around to the rear. The Black was bucking and shaking his head. An arrow was sticking from his neck!

With a mighty roar of rage, Raven charged out of the tall grass. In spite of his fury he was thinking with absolute clarity. He knew exactly what he was going to do.

"Show yourself, you chicken-shit bastard! I'm going to cut your fuckin' heart out!" He punctuated his roar with the loud slam of his revolver. He shot at anything and everywhere. Suddenly, he stopped running. Just ahead of him, he could see the stock of the pump peeking out of the long grass. He continued to fire his gun until the hammer fell on the empty chamber.

Scar stepped away from the trees and into the open. He had an arrow notched and ready to let fly.

Raven smiled at him. You candy-ass sonofabitch, he thought, you finally show yourself, but you still make sure you're out of my pump's effective killing range.

"It is time for you to die, *Wasichu*!"

Scar began to slowly walk toward him. He raised his bow.

"*Hokahey*!"

Ptecila rode back into the clearing from the other side. Responding to the Oglala's pounding heels, his mount splashed into the shallows on the edge of the pond at a full gallop.

Chris dove into the grass. Scooping up the shotgun he rolled into an upright position as his eyes made a frenzied search for his target. Both warriors had already launched their arrows! Scar had his right fist pushed into his side. Raven brought the pump up and fired just as Scar leaped to the side avoiding another feathered shaft. For less than a second his eyes met Scar's. The splashing of Ptecila's horse's hoofs hammered in Chris' ears. Suddenly, the Hunkpapa slipped out of sight into the long marsh grass. The rattle of buckshot ripping through the weeds added impetus to Scar's retreat. Holding the trigger back Raven worked the slide twice more. The pump's booming reports echoed off the surrounding, solid wall of pine and cedar trunks.

Before the gunshots had stopped ringing in his ears, Raven was running through the grass toward the spot where Scar had dropped from sight. As he ran Chris' eyes never stopped moving. He knew deep inside that to find Scar lying in the grass was a very remote possibility.

Ten feet shy of the spot, he dropped down into the grass. He waited and listened. Behind him he could hear Ptecila's horse as it left the water. It had slowed to a walk and was slowly approaching him through the rustling marsh weeds and grass. Still, Raven waited.

Ptecila's horse had stopped. Soon, he heard the Oglala's sibilant voice.

"He is gone now, Okute."

Chris' head drooped. He muttered, "Shit." His head raised and he spoke again in an undertone. "Your ass is still going to be mine, Scar."

Standing, he looked back. The tracker was watching him from the back of his borrowed horse. Thank God, Chris thought, he's in one piece.

"Are you all right, Ptecila? You are not wounded?"

"I am well, Okute. The Black was not badly injured, a small wound."

Looking beyond Ptecila, Raven saw that The Black was standing, ears erect, staring at him. The arrow was dangling from a spot high on the neck, just below the mane.

Capturing his attention, Ptecila gestured for Raven to follow him. "Come, we will rest and I will tend to your wound."

Having forgotten about it, Chris stared in surprise. His jeans were soaked with drying blood. At least, he mused, the bleeding has stopped. Ptecila turned his horse and rode back toward The Black. Before following, Raven looked toward the north and quietly said, "I'm still coming, man. You had best be ready to rock 'n' roll."

CHAPTER 20

▲▲▲▲▲

Raven's voice was quiet but firm. Ptecila's wrinkled face was expressionless as he waited quietly for Raven to speak again.

They had returned to where The Black waited. Chris had removed the arrow and cleaned the wound. He then had tended to his own wounds. Besides his new one, there was the shallow burn across his ribs and the bullet hole in his calf. Raven was beginning to wonder if his leg would ever have the opportunity to heal. Afterwards he cleaned his weapons. The last thing he needed would be a weapon malfunction when he caught up with Scar.

Ptecila, having heard Chris' intent, was being stubborn about his wish to accompany him.

Raven was equally stubborn. "I must hunt this traitor down myself. It is a matter of honor. Not only did he try to kill Bear's Foot because of his hatred of me, he also attempted to murder The Black. Kola, I alone must do this thing. Do you understand?"

Ptecila pulled his gaze away from Raven and thought of what had been said. While Chris waited for his reply, he studied the profile of the wizened little tracker. He thought of how much he valued the man as friend and mentor.

"Okute, Scar is a bad man. He is also a formidable warrior. You are a *wasichu*, but you are also a great warrior. Because Scar has more knowledge of the woods

167

and nature, I think that I should continue to track for you. And it would be best not to hunt him when you are angry."

Raven smiled. "I fight better when I am angry. I have learned much from you, Ptecila. I think that I have learned enough to kill one wounded Hunkpapa."

He paused for a moment, thinking, how do I convince him not to join me? Already, I have lost one good friend and another lies badly wounded. He glanced again at Ptecila, who was absently making designs in the dirt with an arrow while he waited for Chris to continue.

"In the land that I came from we have a saying ...'A man has to do what a man has to do.' This is one of those things that I must do."

Ptecila fingered one of his long braids as he contemplated Raven's words.

Chris watched him. He couldn't help but recall how well the name, Ptecila (Small Buffalo) suited him. With his topknot of curly hair, dark skin and diminutive size, what name could be better. Could be a lot worse, he mused. He remembered meeting a Cheyenne whose name translated, was 'Buffalo Penis'.

Ptecila looked at Chris with a bright smile that lightened his dark and wizened face. "So be it. It will be as you say, *Kola*. I will wait here for two suns. If you do not return I will come for you."

They stood up and clasped hands. Raven replied, "No, my friend. If I do not come back by then I will not be coming back. If that happens I am counting on you to deliver The Black to Little Hawk."

Ptecila stared hard into the pale eyes before he slowly nodded. "As you wish, Okute. Your wound, it will not hamper you?"

Raven shook his head as he checked the pump, making sure it was fully loaded. Smiling, he said, "It is shallow, like the one I got in the big fight." He placed his hand on the pad of cloth, peeking above the waistband of his jeans. "It is nothing ... it just bled a lot."

Slinging the pump on his shoulder he loaded his revolver. Sunlight winked off the brass cartridges as he deftly slipped them one at a time into the cylinder. Finished, he gazed at Ptecila and quietly remarked, "Listen, my friend. If my medicine is bad and Scar kills me, he will then come for you and the horses."

"Do not worry, Okute. I will be ready."

Raven slung his prepared blanket-roll over his other shoulder. He met Ptecila's look with one of quiet intensity as he said, "I will return, *Kola*."

Turning abruptly, he walked north through the trampled marsh grass. Already at work studying the upcoming terrain, Raven murmured, "Here I come, ready or not ... you back shootin' sonofabitch."

CHAPTER 21

ΛΛΛΛΛ

Raven had been following Scar's spoor for more than an hour. When he had first picked up the tracks he had found traces of blood that made the tracking relatively easy. When the blood trail petered out, it told him that the Hunkpapa's wound was only superficial. His next concern was that Scar might lead him onto some rocky ground and lose him. After thinking about it, Chris decided that it would be smarter for Scar to leave a clear trail to follow. That way, he reasoned, he will always know my location.

Just knowing that Scar could be watching him at that very moment was scaring the hell out of him.

The trees began to thin out which pleased Raven because there would be less places for a man to hide in ambush. And, he mused, if there was one sure thing he knew about Scar, it was that the man was a back-shooter.

Raven stopped. Scar's footprints had disappeared.

As the trees thinned the ground became more firm and gradually evolved into a patch of rocky ground and Scar's tracks simply faded away. Looking beyond the stony area Chris saw that the trees gave way to some sort of open area. Blue sky was visible through the diminishing pillars and skeletal branches of pine and cedar.

With great care he approached the rocky patch. The stony ground led to several massive, moss-covered boulders. The huge rocks were situated right on the edge of the clearing.

170

Wasichu's Return

With mounting apprehension Raven tried to watch for tracks and be wary of an ambush at the same time. There. A tiny, round indentation showed between two rocks; it looked like the heel mark of a moccasined foot. Finally, he thought, his sign was back. His tracks led away from the boulders into the open area. Before moving into the clearing Raven scanned the sparsely foliaged terrain that encompassed Scar's footprints. All that was clearly evident was that after a short distance the open ground dropped off into a short cliff. Peeking above the ground level were the tops of several pine and some bright blue sky.

Cautiously Chris stepped into the open. As he moved his eyes were everywhere. He watched and listened, knowing that his life could depend on how attentive he was. Chris suddenly focussed on Scar's footprints. Something, he thought, is different about his tracks. He knew that the answer was in one of the clues that Ptecila had told him about. Faced with endless possibilities Raven's mind drew a blank.

Leaving the rocky soil the tracks became much clearer, but he still couldn't put his finger on what was wrong with the tracks. As he approached a domed outcrop the tracks vanished. Chris was completely stymied. Having come to the end of the open, solid ground he stood on the outcrop and looked beyond. Seventy to a hundred feet below him was the floor of a vast basin. It was while staring at the tops of towering pine trees that the realization hit him. He'd been suckered. Scar was behind him!

All at once it became clear what the Hunkpapa had done. Making sure that his tracks weren't visible he had left the stony ground, circled to the outcrop, then walked backwards returning to the rocky patch where Raven would be sure to see his trail.

Later, he would remember Ptecila's warning, 'If your prey suddenly is taking shorter strides and the heel print's indentation is deeper, then he is walking backwards.'

Feeling the short hairs on his neck stir, Raven instinctively continued to move and act as though he were still trying to figure out the tracks. With the tracks having ended he was running out of alternatives. A shiver of apprehension shot up his spine; he could almost feel the razor sharp arrowhead slice into his heart. Without any warning Chris took the offensive and gambled that Scar would be by the mossy boulders. Swiftly he spun around, dropped into a crouch, and pulled the trigger. The pumpgun roared! He only managed to get off the one wild shot before the arrow pierced his flesh.

The slender shaft glanced off his collar-bone and penetrated the muscle on top of his shoulder; its velocity had rocked him back a step and destroyed his equilibrium. With the white hot pain knifing at his shoulder, Raven lost his concentration and was unable to regain his balance. Teetering on the brink, he had a flash-frame image of Scar on top of the largest of the moss-backed boulders; falling backwards, another frame showed the Hunkpapa slotting another arrow onto his bowstring. Then he hit the tops of the tall pine and pain racked his body from every side. Chris felt like a pinball as he was buffeted and banged from one branch to another. Blinding agony exploded behind his eyes as the arrow in his flesh was snagged and hammered. Desperately, he tried to protect his head as he smashed through pine boughs. Raven plummeted through the smashing, scratching trees like a suicidal rock climber. At the final point of impact he hit the bed of pine needles flat on his back. He screamed as he heard something snap and pain probed with a red hot lance through his shoulder. His body bounced off the scaly trunk of a tree and came to a sliding, painful stop. Chris' last lucid thought was his fervent wish that the snap he heard wasn't a debilitating bone-break.

Raven gasped repeatedly and painfully sucked in as much air as he could. Savoring the oxygen, he concentrated on breathing normally. Opening his eyes he stared at the patches of blue far above him. His body pained him all over but one spot was a special agony. It felt like someone was pouring napalm onto the top of his left shoulder. Raven slowly, carefully raised his hand and with fingers, light as a feather, explored his wound.

About eight inches of arrow protruded from the muscle above his clavicle. As his mind cleared, he became aware of how fortunate he had been. Had he not dropped into a crouch when he spun around, the arrow would surely have transfixed his chest. With a slowly escalating horror he remembered the snapping noise. My God, he thought, am I crippled? Will I have to lie here helplessly and wait for Scar to come and finish me off? Fighting down his panic he tentatively moved his arms and legs. Except for the ripping pain above his shoulder everything was functioning normally. Carefully, with cautious movements of an old man, Raven got to his feet. He swayed like a sapling in a strong wind but kept his footing. He couldn't believe it; nothing was broken. Using the tree for support he gathered his senses. Relief coursed through his battered body as he realized what must have happened. His head was spinning, but with the exception of the arrow wound and a multitude of aches and pains, he was all right. Being careful not to bump the arrow, Raven reached across his chest and felt the shaft where it protruded behind his shoulder.

When his hand brushed against the blanket's fuzzy material, he became aware of how his blanket roll, slung across his back and chest, must have absorbed most of the impact.

His searching fingers found the bloody stub of the broken arrow's shaft. Thank God, he thought. The loud snap that he had heard was from when the arrowhead had snapped off.

Chris' thoughts turned to Scar and escape. Where is he, and where's my Winchester pump? Raven began a swift, but thorough, search of the pine needle-covered ground. He realized that the Hunkpapa was probably already searching for the fastest way down to the basin floor. Chris looked everywhere; his pumpgun was gone! He couldn't remember having dropped it, but he must have. He could almost feel the odds shift in Scar's favor.

Fighting off a rising tide of despair, the solid weight of the revolver tucked under his arm helped to bolster his confidence; the comforting length and heft of Bear's Foot's fighting knife tucked in its sheath, also helped. Knowing that he might black out if he tried to remove the arrow, Raven decided to leave it for the time being. Quickly getting his bearings, he hobbled away from the rocky escarpment and began to watch for a terrain that would help him hide his tracks.

CHAPTER 22

▲▲▲▲▲

Raven stared in awe at the desolation spread out before him. It's like watching a color movie, he thought, that suddenly switched to black and white

He had been moving gingerly through heavy timber for what had seemed like hours when he came to the dreary aftermath of a forest fire. A wide swath of blackened stumps and cindered logs dotted a predominately gray landscape that fanned out from his direct front like an abandoned beach from Hell. Raven moved to his right to circle around the ruined area, but something stopped him. Staring deep in thought at the blackened ground a wild idea began to take form.

Knowing that he needed rest and had to remove the agonizing arrow gave him an added impetus. He had to come up with a valid idea, or he would die. Far out into the gray wasted terrain Chris saw a cluster of lighter gray humps. Realizing what needed to be done, he walked in a straight line toward the distant shapes without making any attempt at hiding his tracks. Drawing near he saw that they were just what he had expected and hoped for: a jumble of mottled, gray boulders. Just beyond them and to the left was an exceptionally large pile of stumps and dead trees.

An unexpected wave of dizziness caused him to falter and take a staggered step. During his fall through the trees, Chris' head and hands had taken a beating. His other wounds had stopped bleeding, but he was getting weaker with each passing moment. Wearily, he stared at the boulders and charred logs and worked through the scenario one more time. When he had finished, a light of hope glimmered and danced in his eyes. Face all battered and scratched, Raven's sudden smile of anticipation appeared more a grimace than an expression of happiness. He quickened his pace and shuffled through the ashes toward the fire-blackened log jam. There is much to do, he thought, before Scar arrives.

Time became irrelevant as Raven awaited his prey. He remained absolutely motionless. Finally, his patience was rewarded. Scar's sudden appearance was almost ghost-like. The burly warrior soundlessly stepped away from the trees and into the open burnt area. Sweat ran into Raven's eyes. He ignored the mild discomfort and watched the Hunkpapa glide forward with the grace of a large cat. Scar's head was tipped forward in concentration as he followed Chris' tracks across the colorless terrain. With his face painted red and black and his body crisscrossed with the bogus bleeding scars, Chris thought he looked like the Devil inspecting one of his fields in Hell.

Within Raven's place of concealment the smell of ashes and smoke was nearly suffocating. In a facetious attempt to ignore his discomforts and pains, he thought of himself as seated in the world's largest ashtray waiting for some other butt to join him. Chris shelved his silly thought and focussed on doing whatever was necessary to stay alive.

The big warrior was so close that Raven could see his eyes. The black orbs seemed to be staring directly at him. Raven didn't breath. Scar looked away, and Chris was again able to breath. Staring angrily at the pumpgun held in Scar's right hand, dark, murderous thoughts tried to take control of his cautionary impulses.

He was very close. Chris breathed shallowly through his mouth. Surrounded as he was by dust and ash, he didn't want to risk the possibility of a sneeze.

Scar was almost directly between Raven and the log pile when suddenly he stopped and stared fixedly at the jumbled heap of dead trees. He crouched, bending forward from the waist as he gazed into the pile. Raven stared with hate at the man who had caused so much misery and pain.

From a distance of ten feet the warrior raised the pump and fired a blast of buckshot into the pile of charred, dead trees. Black chunks of charcoal exploded into the air like startled quail as Scar clumsily jacked another round into the smoking chamber and fired again. A gritty cloud of ash and dust rose into the air as he stared hard at his intended target. Eyes nailed to the log pile he stepped closer.

As Scar took his steps, Raven painfully stood up. The gray blanket that he had used to disguise himself as one of the boulders slid from his head and shoulders onto the ash covered ground. Standing sideways in a duelist's stance, he extended his arm and aimed his revolver at Scar's broad back. Raven pulled the hammer back. When the hammer snicked into full cock, Scar spun around and froze in place. His eyes widened and darted furtively.

"*Hohahe* (welcome) to hell." Raven pulled the trigger. The .44 bucked in his hand and the heavy bullet smashed into Scar's chest. He staggered backwards causing a small cloud of fine ash to rise about his ankles. There was another flat, loud report as the second bullet found Scar's heart, and he fell backward onto the burnt debris. A plume of gray ash rose as a final snarl escaped Scar's lips and he gasped his last breath. The dusty ash settled like a gray mist onto his open eyes and gaping mouth.

Chris lowered his smoking pistol. All at once he was consumed by a burning rage. He stumbled forward and knelt beside the body. Raven jerked Bear's Foot's combat knife free of its sheath. He paused. His eyes lifted to the tangle of burnt, twisted trees into which Scar had fired with the pump. Within the hodge-podge of shattered browns and grays there was a clearly visible, bright red spot. It was the corner of Raven's red silk scarf.

CHAPTER 23

ᴧᴧᴧᴧᴧ

Raven awoke to a throbbing pain and the twitter of birds welcoming a new day. He hated to move but knew that he must. Ptecila would be waiting. Flitting thoughts of Blue Feather and Little Hawk added to his motivation.

Mustering his will and depleted strength, he sat up. Waves of pain and an undulating sea of alternating dizziness and clarity took turns at controlling his body. He braced himself on his hands. A sharp pain pierced his upper shoulder when he moved his left arm. Flies buzzed around the bloody area on his hip. He stared blankly at the water in the bubbling creek at his side and remembered.

The night before he had been following the narrow stream hoping that it would take him to the pond and Ptecila. Because of the pain and the failing light, he had stopped and prepared for what he knew had to be done.

Just thinking of last night brought on a patina of cold sweat.

When the moment came he had quickly pulled the arrow out of his shoulder. There was a sudden gush of blood; the pain was so severe that he fainted and fell into the shallow waters of the creek. Shortly thereafter the icy water of the creek revived him. He had stayed in the water regaining his strength, as the cold water slowed the bleeding of his wound. While he lay there he had watched twilight slowly fade into night and witnessed the multitudes of stars as they brought the blackness of the heavens to life. He had also thought of the irony of dying alone in a Montana mountain stream after living through the hell of Vietnam.

When he was able, he crawled out of the creek and collapsed among the rushes. His final awareness had been when he pulled his blanket over his wet shoulders to help fight off the violent tremors that racked his body and to discourage the swarm of mosquitoes that were determined to eat him alive.

Raven's right hand passed through a ray of new sunlight and tentatively explored his shoulder wound. The bleeding had stopped but the flesh around the hole was hot to his touch.

"Shit!" he exclaimed. He knew that it was probably infected and Ptecila's help was needed more than ever.

Moving slowly he used the pumpgun as a cane and rose shakily to his feet. Using only his right hand he managed to swing the shotgun across his back. He then pushed his left hand through the sling to immobilize it. With any sudden move of his left hand, the pain was so intense that he feared losing consciousness. The shallow wound above his hip began to ache and throb, adding to his discomfort.

Chris began to follow the creek in what he thought was a southerly direction. With the denseness of the tall pine and cedar and the added complication of a partially overcast sky, Raven wasn't certain of his directions. Foolishly he continued to follow the stream. It became more and more difficult for him to hold onto a rational thought.

Time passed as quickly as Raven's endurance. Much to his chagrin the stream had gotten smaller instead of bigger, as it would have if he had been drawing closer to the pond. To make things worse, he hadn't the slightest idea where he was in relation to Ptecila. His worry was multiplied by the realization that at times he would think he was back in

Vietnam and would catch himself talking to Joe Spotted Horse, or one of his Nung mercenaries.

Chris stumbled, lost his balance, and fell to his knees. He shook his head in a futile attempt to shake off his dizziness. I'm burning up, he thought, this fever is eating me alive just as quickly as the mosquitoes and flies. He crawled on his hands and knees the short distance to the creek and drank thirstily. He took off his bandana and soaked it in the icy water. It took a while for the silk to absorb the moisture. Deer flies buzzed around his head and hip as he watched the bright red slowly darken until fully saturated. Ignoring the pain that bit into his shoulder, Raven tied the sodden scarf back onto his head. He relished the soothing coolness on his fevered brow. Still on his hands and knees, Chris raised his head and looked into the yellow eyes of a very large dog. The huge animal was less than ten feet away and was staring right at him.

Raven blinked and shook his head, hoping the image would disappear. He was certain that the dog was a part of his fever. He looked again. If the image changed at all it had become clearer. Dog, my ass, he mused, that's a wolf. He swallowed and fought down his sudden fear. Keeping his gaze locked on the wolf, Chris tried to get up. The wolf, standing near an opening in the underbrush and trees, continued to watch him. Raven got one leg under him and tried to stand. He lost his balance and crumpled to his knees. Excruciating pain knifed into his shoulder and hip. By the time the pain ebbed, suicidal flies were trying their best to enter any of his available orifices. Eyes tightly shut, Chris tried his best to convince himself that the wolf was a hallucinatory image brought on by his fever.

He was on his knees and elbows. His face was in his hands as he rubbed briskly trying to clear his head and vision. A cloud of gnats joined the other insects and swarmed around his head and hands. Suddenly, he was aware of moist breath on his cheek. His heart seemed to stop beating. He held his breath and waited for the fangs to rip into his throat. There were a couple of snuffling sounds, and then Raven felt a wet tongue caress his cheek. He jerked; pain from his wounds knifed through his body. Only fear's vise-like grip on his throat had kept him from crying out. When the hot breath again brushed his ear and cheek, Chris did his best to turn into stone.

After what seemed like an eternity of silence he risked a quick peek. The animal had returned to his spot near the open area. Once again he was sitting and staring at Raven, looking as though prepared to wait there all day. The wolf unexpectedly stood up and moved into the opening in the trees where he stopped and looked back at Raven.

Still on his elbows and knees Chris didn't move. He returned the wolf's stare. Still holding Raven's gaze the wolf rushed toward him. Raven's heart was in his throat as the wolf abruptly stopped and trotted back to the open area. He stopped and looked over his shoulder at Chris.

Raven stared at the wolf in total disbelief. His pulse was hammering so hard in his throat he nearly retched. Am I delirious, he wondered? He closed his eyes and tried to ignore the pain in his shoulder. Chris once again shook his head hoping to rid himself of the obvious illusory image of the wolf. When he opened them, he half expected him to be gone. He was still there. The wolf was standing quietly, tongue lolling, watching him with his penetrating yellow eyes. Peering through the ever present cloud of insects, Raven returned his stare.

Am I going insane, he wondered, or is he waiting for me? Their eyes locked. Raven shook his head again. This time the head shake was a derisive one, aimed at his own damned foolishness. The yellow-eyed son of a bitch, he thought, is probably just waiting for me to die. He got up onto his hands and feet and, with a helpful rush of adrenalin, rose shakily to an upright position. His eyes quickly darted toward the wolf. He expected to see his furry backside disappearing into the trees, but the wolf hadn't moved so much as an inch. Chris made a half-hearted swipe at the swarming gnats and thought, what the hell, hallucinating or not, I'm going for it.

After several wobbly attempts, Raven was able to retrieve his pumpgun and take a couple of unsteady steps toward the ever watchful wolf. The big animal turned and loped into the clearing behind the opening in the underbrush. Halfway across, he stopped and looked back at Raven. Staring at the wolf, his mind flip-flopped back and forth between what he thought was illusion and what he knew was reality. Having no other agreeable alternative he stumbled forward and followed the wolf into the forest.

He couldn't recall how long he had been struggling to keep up with the wolf, but he remembered having fallen only once; when that happened the wolf had waited patiently for him to claw his way to his feet.

Raven was staggering and stumbling, barely remaining upright. His view had become like a kaleidoscope, a scene of constantly changing patterns, pictures, and shapes. Trees, tall grass, stones, and still water blended together until they were obliterated by a familiar brown face that was smiling at him and growing larger with each heartbeat. He closed his eyes and felt himself begin to drift away into the darkness.

He opened his eyes. Yellow light pierced the night shadows and glanced off towering pines that were pointing, reaching for the blanket of stars. A shower of sparks climbed toward the pointed tops of the pine trees. A dull pain gnawed at his shoulder as Raven raised his head. Ptecila was poking at a fire with a green stick. Strips of meat, suspended from other pointed sticks, were dripping sizzling fat into a small campfire. All of a sudden he was famished.

"*Washtay*, Ptecila."

The Oglala's head popped up at Raven's greeting and he grinned.

"Greetings, Okute. You have been 'walking in darkness' for a long time."

Chris smiled weakly.

"Did you see my wolf?" he said.

Ptecila stared at him for a quiet moment. His eyes dropped and he said, "I did not see him, Okute. When you came to me you spoke of a wolf. Before Wi had completed his journey and made the world dark again I looked for his tracks. There are no tracks, Kola."

Raven's ears did a doubletake. He couldn't believe it. There has to be tracks! They have to be there, he thought, He led me straight to the pond.

Ptecila's soft voice interrupted his thoughts. "You have raved of how your wolf led you here. I believe you, Okute. But it was not just a wolf. It was the spirit of our friend. He is watching over you."

Ptecila looked away and began to rearrange the sizzling meat on their sticks.

Raven stared into the night thinking, Dear God, could it be? With his mind's eye he could see a young warrior on a big black stallion charge recklessly into a milling group of Bluecoats. He could clearly see him joyously striking left and right with his heavy bow and smiling in wild abandon.

Tears welled momentarily as he whispered softly, "Wolf's Spirit."

CHAPTER 24

ΛΛΛΛΛ

Raven felt suspended. His legs vibrated from a strange, lurching, backward movement. An unusual, yet familiar, sound was grating on his nerves and was connected to his odd, swaying motion. A childhood memory came to him ... the abrasive noise a stick made when dragged forcefully through the dirt. The recollection was interrupted by a sudden waft of the acrid scent of horse sweat and the irritating buzz of an inquisitive fly. He opened his eyes. A blue sky, covered with mountains of gray, cumulus clouds, hovered overhead. An unexpected jolt brought with it a stab of pain on top of his left shoulder. The debilitating pang was brief but savage. When it passed, Chris raised his head and tried to get his bearings. He was surprised to discover that he was on an Indian travois being pulled backwards by a powerful looking gray horse.

The grating sound that had touched his memory was caused by the ends of the two long travois poles that bore his weight as they were dragged across the earth's surface. A new, unidentifiable sound drew his attention off to his right. Ptecila was there. He was riding a strange pony and leading The Black and another horse. Raven watched him quietly. The Oglala must have felt his eyes and looked back at him.

A wide grin added more wrinkles to Ptecila's brown face as he shouted happily, "*Washtay*! Okute, you have returned!"

Wasichu's Return

Chris returned his grin and gave a weak hand wave. He raised his hand to his face and was shocked to feel several days growth of beard. Damn, he thought, that fever must have really knocked me on my ass. He carefully pushed himself up onto his elbows and looked around. They were crossing a vast, arid plain. His last remembrance was of rolling hills and pine trees. The only hills to be seen now were a faint blue smudge on the horizon.

Raven's thoughts suddenly turned to Blue Feather and Little Hawk, and a smile tugged at his lean, whiskered cheeks as pleasant memories began to take form. The smile lost its form as he remembered the last time he'd seen his friend, Bear's Foot. The image of the powerful warrior, lying unconscious and weakened by his terrible wound, saddened and infuriated him. He prayed that his ministrations were enough to pull him through.

Chris thought briefly of the sprawled form of Scar's body as it lay among the gray of the ashes. Rage returned and simmered for an instant until it was replaced by an unexpected remorse for what he had done to the Hunkpapa. He closed his eyes and thought of happier times. The constant sway and pitch of the litter was lulling him to sleep. I must be healing, he thought, I'm not hurting nearly as much. He had noticed that there was no pain unless he were to make a sudden move or the travois poles hit something solid. Eyes still closed he began to drift. A vision of his wife, a smile lighting her ebony eyes, dissolved as he slipped into peaceful oblivion.

Raven awakened to the sting of wind-blown sand striking his face. An undulating blanket of black clouds were in the southwest and were rolling toward them at an unbelievable rate of speed. Chris' helplessness sent a chill up his spine. Suddenly, Ptecila was there. He threw a rawhide loop over the travois horse's head and viciously lashed his quirt across the broad rump. The animal surged forward and forced Raven to hang on as the travois' splayed poles bucked and heaved. He grit his teeth against the jolts of pain that pierced his shoulder like arrows of fire. They raced the approaching storm at full gallop. It didn't take long for Raven to realize that he was in for the wildest ride of his life. All at once it became dark as night. Driving winds caught them; then the wind turned into sheets of rain and punishing hail. In less time than it takes to tell it, Chris was soaked, drenched to the bone. The wind and rain stopped. An eerie quiet prevailed.

Raven could hear Ptecila up ahead yiping and yelling encouragement to the gasping horses as they thundered across the prairie. The ride had become a nightmare of pain and fear. Suddenly, a wall of terrifying noise descended on them like the wrath of God, drowning out all other sounds. It grew louder with each passing second. A flash of lightning briefly illuminated the prairie. Within that tiny interval of time, Raven clearly saw two, wild-riding riders out on their left flank. They were lashing their ponies and relentlessly driving them in the same direction that he and Ptecila were moving. In an instant they were swallowed by the return of the dark, murky dusk. Another flare of lightning revealed a ceiling of greenish-black clouds hanging low to the ground and coming up swiftly behind them. The sky beyond the dark mass was the color of agitated muddy water. The strange threatening sight was quickly extinguished by a return of the encompassing darkness. Fear reigned as the thud of the pony's hoofs could only be felt and not heard because of the roar of the escalating, swirling wind.

Wasichu's Return

With the suddenness of a curtain being raised, the darkness lifted once more. Raven stared with a horror that only the helpless can feel and understand. A coal black funnel was on the ground and was rushing toward them with the speed of a runaway locomotive. The tornado was cutting a swath of destruction that was several hundred feet wide. Trees, brush, and other debris were rising from the base of the vortex as it slashed its way across the open prairie. It was less than a mile away and still coming straight at them! Chris was terrified. Here was an enemy he couldn't fight. All at once the travois became airborne! He hung on and braced himself. There was a jarring impact! Excruciating pain exploded in his shoulder as he clung to the leather and wood frame. The litter skidded sideways like a race car turning a sharp corner and came to a sliding, bumpy stop. They were in a sunken drywash. Like magic Ptecila appeared beside him. He helped Raven upright and they stumbled through the buffeting, violent wind. The little Oglala hurried Chris to the bank closest to the oncoming horror. Weak as he was, Raven allowed Ptecila to wedge him in between two massive boulders. The fever from his wounds had taken so much out of Raven that he was forced into the role of spectator. Through the grit and the whipping, swirling gloom he watched his friend's struggle with their terrified horses. Finally, Ptecila managed to lead their rearing and twisting mounts down the arroyo toward a place of safety. Helplessly, Chris watched as the laboring Ptecila disappeared in a spinning cloud of dust and dirt.

The noise of the approaching twister hammered in his ears like a thousand trains that rhythmically chugged and roared as they converged from all sides; the clamor drove out all reason and thought.

Eventually the cacophony quieted to a mere roar and Chris allowed his exhausted body to relax for a moment. His relief that the funnel had apparently missed them was monumental. Just the same, he kept his eyes shut as the wind-driven grit continued to sting his face and hands. When he did open his eyes his stomach muscles involuntarily tightened. An Indian was standing a few feet away pointing a rifle at him.

Raven was lying on his right side, his arm pinned beneath him. He didn't know the whereabouts of the pump, and his revolver was out of reach underneath his left arm. Knowing that there wasn't a chance in hell that he could reach his weapon in time, he tried to become a nonentity. He didn't even breath.

The Indian was having difficulty standing still. Although it had diminished, the wind was still a violent force. It was blowing the man's long, unbound hair straight out to the side so that it was parallel with the sandy ground. Two small braids fashioned in the Crow hair style whipped back and forth across his angry face like frenzied sidewinders. The Indian's black eyes were locked onto Raven's with undisguised hatred.

Chris watched as the warrior fought the buffeting wind and stepped closer. He cocked his rifle. Suddenly, another Indian was there between Raven and his potential murderer. The new Indian's back was to him but his meaning was clear. He was stopping the killing. Raven let out his breath and stared as the first Indian jerked away and staggered into the wind up the rocky draw. His rescuer turned and faced him. As their eyes met, Chris' breath caught in his throat. Without saying a word the young Indian turned away, lowered his head against the gritty wind, and followed in the wake of his murderous friend.

Raven's eyes followed him until he disappeared into the blowing sand. He let out his breath and muttered, "I am one lucky sonuvabitch."

To protect them from the blowing sand, Chris narrowed his eyes to mere slits and watched the Crow youth until he vanished into an opaque cloud of dust and grit. He gave his head a slight shake and thought, who would believe it?

Raven's awe derived from the unlikelihood that after sparing a blue-eyed Crow's life at the Little Big Horn, that same Indian would, less than two weeks later, save his life in return ... and do so in the middle of a tornado. Long after the boy was gone, Raven thought about him. There was something curiously familiar about the youth.

The wind continued until it was replaced by a deluge of rain and hail. The new onslaught lasted but a few short moments. The quiet that followed the storm was almost as eerie as the strange color of the sky. Raven rose slowly to his feet. He swayed unsteadily in the relentless wind and looked around for Ptecila. The clatter of hoofs striking rock drew his attention to the other end of the draw. His quick glance was just in time to see the two Crow ride up out of the wash and disappear over the edge.

"*Hau*, Okute!"

Ptecila's voice pulled Raven around. The tracker was walking toward him leading The Black and their other horses.

"Are you all right, Ptecila?"

Ptecila grinned and waved a weathered hand in the direction where the two Crow had departed .He said, "Our friends have left? It is well that they have gone. I was very close to putting an arrow into the tall one's liver."

Too tired to be surprised by Ptecila's ability to be aware of everything around him, Raven didn't ask how he knew. He looked up at the changing sky. Sunlight had broken through the still turbulent clouds. Unable to quell his curiosity he slowly turned and faced his mentor and friend. His legs felt too weak for any sudden moves.

"You saw them ... the one with the rifle?"

Ptecila nodded. His lined, brown face twisted into a wide, elfin grin as he said, "*Han* (Yes). The tall one looked as though he were planning to take your hair. I wonder why the other one stopped him."

Strangely reluctant to tell his Lakota friend the whole story, Raven slowly turned and stared at the spot where he had last seen the pale-eyed Crow. Softly he said, "I do not know. Perhaps if we meet again, I will ask him."

BLACK HILLS

PART 4

EXCERPT FROM THE JOURNAL OF CETAN CHIKALA (LITTLE HAWK)

▲▲▲▲▲▲▲▲

It had been many suns since I had last seen Okute and Ptecila. Both my mother and I had been worried because they had not returned. Our hearts were on the ground from wishing to see Okute again. It had been too long.

Perhaps he did not know that we joined Crazy Horse's band of Oglala and had been moving east toward Paha Sapa (Black Hills). I knew that I need not worry, Ptecila was with him and would find us.

We were camped east of the Rosebud. I was soon anxious for us to move on. We were camped not far from the place where grandfather was killed and where I was captured by the renegade Indians. There were too many wanagi (spirits) nearby; I thought we should leave. My friend, Bear's Foot, was anxious to leave also. But I think he would just like to go anywhere that my grandmother, White Star, was not. My mother had been caring for Bear's wound and my grandmother was helping her. Bear's Foot has said that he does not want her help. He said she is like the wind that blows across the southern prairie, '... if the strength of her wind does not blow you over, you may be certain that her hot air will at least blow irritating sand into all your private body openings.'

White Star laughed at Bear's complaining and teased him mercilessly. Once I heard her tell my friend, '... your

195

mother must have had a vision when she had named you. Look at those big feet! It must take a whole deer hide to make you one pair of moccasins!'

I think that their teasing and complaining really meant that they liked each other, but each would rather be buried in an anthill by murderous Apaches than admit it.

The day I am going to write about was very special. I can remember the excitement that coursed through my veins as though it happened yesterday ...

It is nearly time! I waited impatiently for Wi to rise above the far away hills. Wakan Tanka has truly smiled on me. Crazy Horse has invited me to join him and other warriors at first light. My chief said that I no longer need to guard the pony herd. I am about to ride with my first war party!

The tipi flap lifted and Gray Weasel came out. He quickly looked to see if Wi had shown himself yet.

Gray Weasel is one winter older than me. Since joining Crazy Horse's band he and I have shared the same lodge.

He looked at me and grinned, saying, "Oo-oohey (It is time)."

I looked quickly to the east. Wi was peeking over a hill! To my ears, my heart began to thump as loud as a grouse's wings when he's courting on his drumming log.

"Hopo (Let us go)." I said.

We raced to the pony herd. After finding our mounts we trotted them to the gathering place. Of course we were the first to arrive. Soon everyone was there except our leader. When Wi's mighty light began to spill across the prairie, like water from a broken beaver dam, Crazy Horse appeared. Just the sight of him prepared for war caused my breath to catch in my throat and my heart to swell with pride.

Wasichu's Return

Raising his rifle overhead our chief led us away from the village. We rode one behind the other in a long line. First in line was the leader. The others would follow behind him according to their importance in the warrior society. Since Gray Weasel had already been on two war parties I was the last in line.

My pony, Hawk's Wing, did not like eating the dust of the others. When I told him that we were finally going to become warriors, he quickly accepted his place among the other horses.

Hawk's Wing is a very smart horse, but he is still just a horse. Before Wi has completed his day's journey one of our party will be convinced that Hawk's Wing has the heart and mind of a chief.

Paha Sapa was a blue smear in the distance when our scout returned. I did not know what the scout had seen, but Crazy Horse had us urge our ponies into a faster pace. As we rode, the news finally drifted back to me that the scout had seen the dust of some wasichus.

After swinging south we rode hard. We would gallop our ponies and then slow to a trot, then a walk. When they were rested enough we would again run before the wind.

Soon we came to a place with trees and rocky hills. A scout was sent out again while we rested our ponies and waited for his return. I was so excited it became difficult to keep the others from noticing. Crazy Horse came and joked with Gray Weasel, then put his arm around my shoulders as he spoke to us. By the time he left us, I was so proud that I thought I would puff up like a toad until I burst.

The scout returned. He came riding in so fast that I looked beyond the dust expecting to see Bluecoats chasing him. He spoke quickly to our chief who swiftly shouted orders to several warriors. There was much excitement as everyone scattered up into the rocks and trees. We were going to surprise the wasichus! Gray Weasel and I grabbed the warrior's ponies and led them into the mouth of a gully that was out of the way. It became very quiet. Even the birds had stopped their singing.

After the longest wait of my life I heard the bang and clatter of one of the white men's travois. My ears also told me that it was one that Okute said was called a 'wagon'. I heard a wasichu shout and then make a loud whistle. Other white voices were shouting as well. I did not understand their words but Gray Weasel and I could tell that they were getting very close. We stared into each other's eyes and listened as we waited for the trap to be sprung.

A loud scream made us both jump to our feet. Loud, war cries, followed by gunfire, erupted all around us. Many wasichus were screaming and shouting in pain and anger. Because we could not see, gunshots, the screech of a dying horse, war cries, and angry voices all sounded unnaturally loud to our ears. It was deafening. We were flinching at every noise. If only, I thought, we could see what was happening it would not be so frightening.

Suddenly, there was a gunshot close by followed by a rattling in the bushes. I tightened my grip on my bow and reached for an arrow just as a wild-eyed wasichu burst through the bushes and slid to a stop right in front of us. For less than three heartbeats we stared at each other. Then the white man shouted something and pointed at me. I saw the sun glance off the metal of a two-barrel, tiny pistol clutched in his hand. Hawk's Wing gave a savage whinny and lunged toward the man who swung his gun toward the sudden movement. My bow whistled as I swung it with both hands! It struck the wasichu solidly catching him just above the eye. He fell as if the bow had struck his legs instead of his head. He did not move. I did not move. Blood ran over his brow and into his eye. I looked at Gray Weasel who had not moved either. He was staring open-mouthed at the unconscious white man. I noticed that Hawk's Wing's lead rope was wrapped around his fist. It explained why Hawk was unable to reach the man. In the back of my mind I noticed that the sounds of fighting were not as great now.

Another noise from the bushes had me quickly notch an arrow. Fiercely painted, He Dog abruptly slipped into the ravine. His eyes glittered as they absorbed the situation with a glance. The wasichu moaned and moved his legs. He Dog stepped forward and placed the muzzle of his rifle on the man's chest and pulled the trigger. At the sound of the shot both Gray Weasel and I jumped, and Hawk's Wing nearly pulled Weasel off his feet.

The white man's body jerked, his legs stiffened, and then he was still. After the loudness of the rifle it became very quiet. It wasn't until that moment we realized Crazy Horse's trap had closed, and the fight with the wasichus was over.

A loud sound of escaping air drew both He Dog's and my gaze toward Gray Weasel. He must have been holding his breath. I caught a glimpse of the tiniest of smiles on He Dog's lips as he looked away from Weasel's sickly expression. He stepped up and used the barrel of his rifle to flip the dead man's coat open. He was wearing a vest that looked like it was covered with shiny wildflowers. He Dog grunted when he saw the hard pieces of paper that had fallen out of the man's coat. The hard paper had different shapes painted on them in red or black.

He Dog looked at me with his strange, wolf-shaped eyes and said, "This one and several of the others were men that gamble, living off the misfortune of others."

He poked at the hard papers with his rifle muzzle. "They use these papers with the marks on them to gamble with instead of the plum pit that we use."

Bending over, He Dog picked something shiny out of the grass. He turned to me and grinned. "You have counted first coup, Warrior. This is yours."

He placed the wasichu's small pistol in my hand. My heart lifted and soared upwards, gliding like an eagle. My first thought was how pleased Okute would be when he sees my pistol with two barrels. I quickly knelt and went through the man's pockets until I had found all the bullets for the strange little gun.

While He Dog was taking the wasichu's scalp, Weasel and I led the ponies out into the open. The first thing I saw was a wagon and some dead mules. Clothing and bodies were scattered here and there. Lying closeby were five scalped bodies. Some of them were dressed like the man He Dog had shot. When my eyes had sought out the remaining faces, I was happy to see that we Lakota were still seven in number.

A loud noise startled me. Two warriors in the wasichu wagon were throwing unusual-shaped objects out onto the ground. I saw something round like our sacred circle. It had red and black shapes side by side on its shiny surface. There were many other discarded things that I cannot describe.

After leading all the warriors' horses out into the open, Gray Weasel and I swung up on our pony's backs and rode around the area where the fight took place. This was done so that when we were needed to help strip a body or to carry some loot we would be there. Soon all the Lakota had reclaimed their ponies and had finished gathering their new possessions.

Wasichu's Return

As Crazy Horse began rallying his warriors, Gray Weasel unexpectedly turned to me and said, "I will give you both my ponies for Hawk's Wing."

I stared at him in disbelief. Weasel stared back, impassively. My head whirled with the sudden offer.

"Why do you wish to make this trade?"

I asked the foolish question to give myself time to think. Why a trade? Suddenly it made sense. Gray Weasel must have thought that Hawk's Wing had lunged at the wasichu to protect me.

"I have simply taken a liking to Hawk's Wing," he said.

Ignoring Weasel's phony reason for a trade, I met his gaze and tried not to laugh as I interrupted him. "I do not wish to trade him."

My friend looked at Hawk's Wing and then back at me. Angry, he stuck out his chest and boasted, "Someday, Little Hawk, that horse will belong to me. One day soon I will be a famous warrior with many horses and you will want this trade."

Weasel dug his heels in and his pony lunged forward to take his place behind the line of warriors moving west.

We moved slowly in behind Weasel's mount and I leaned forward and whispered into my pony's ear. "Should I tell Gray Weasel that you are not as smart as he thinks?"

Hawk's Wing twitched his ears as though he was truly listening and understanding my words.

"Perhaps I should tell him that it was your hatred of the wasichu scent that made you attack."

He turned his long head and rolled a bloodshot dark eye my way. Shaking his head to rid himself of a pesty fly, he looked forward again as though destined to follow Gray Weasel's pony forever.

Barry Brierley

Feeling the heft of my little gun in my pouch reminded me of Okute. I remembered how Hawk's Wing used to try to bite him every chance he got. After Okute had been with us awhile he had stopped the biting. I wonder if it is possible to stop smelling like a wasichu.

CHAPTER 25

▲▲▲▲▲

A wave of dizziness caused Raven to reel in the saddle. Ptecila covertly watched as his friend struggled with his balance. He moved his pony closer to The Black. He had grown attached to the spotted pony he had acquired from Scar. Being sentimental, he had given it the same name as his last horse, 'Windbreaker'.

"All is well, Okute?"

Raven clenched his teeth as a sharp pain bit into his shoulder while he readjusted his posture in the saddle. He forced a smile and replied, "All is well, my friend. My head still spins a bit but it passes."

The Oglala tracker smiled as he said, "Your wounds have healed on the surface ..." He brought his fist to his left chest. "... now, the rest of your healing will be done by Wakan Tanka. And you need meat; perhaps buffalo heart or tongue will help return your strength."

Raven grinned and slapped the neck of The Black. "Perhaps my head spins because I had become used to traveling at the same level as the coyote. Now, on The Black, I feel like I am flying with the eagles."

The big stallion turned his head and stared at Chris with apparent disdain.

Ptecila laughed, pointing at The Black with his thumb. "See, Okute, what a wise horse you have? He has the look in his eye of a chief that must tolerate the actions of a *heyoka* (clown)."

Raven joined his laughter and urged The Black into a canter. Not being encumbered with the extra horses Ptecila felt that it would be best for Chris to ride out front. At the moment, except for an occasional giddiness, Raven felt well enough to handle just about anything.

With the passing of time, rest, and inactivity most of Chris' strength had returned. A dizzy spell like the last one was becoming pretty rare. This last one, he thought, was probably from pushing himself too hard too soon.

Enjoying The Black's easy gait Raven let his thoughts drift back to the days he was fighting the fever. He had been unconscious during the time that Ptecila had built the travois, and they had left the mountains. Raven was still trying to figure out how tiny Ptecila had managed to get his 185 pounds of dead weight onto the travois' platform.

Chris' daydreaming was interrupted by the noticeable change in the terrain. The gently rolling prairie had unexpectedly changed into larger hills adorned with an occasional rocky outcrop. He worried that he might have made a wrong turn. Glancing back at Ptecila, Raven saw that he was slowly following along. He didn't see Raven's look; he was busy watching their back trail and flanks. Relieved by the Oglala's lack of concern Chris resumed his musing. Ptecila had told him that while Raven was 'walking in darkness' they had met a small hunting party of Hunkpapa Sioux at the northeast part of the Greasy Grass. Ptecila had known one of the warriors. He had told the tracker that Crazy Horse's band had moved east toward Paha Sapa. He had not known the whereabouts of Blue Feather and Little Hawk, but he had heard that the great Bear's Foot was with the Oglala chief. Raven and Ptecila had later agreed that Blue Feather and Hawk would definitely stay with their wounded friend.

Riding up a gradual incline he stopped short of the top so he could see beyond without exposing himself on the skyline. Raven smiled and decided to wait for his friend to catch up. While he waited he stared in awe at the dark mass that loomed on the horizon. He knew what it was but he wanted Ptecila to confirm it.

The tracker pulled up beside Raven. His eyes immediately fastened onto the distant blue hills. Their short string of horses swung in behind them unnoticed.

"*Paha Sapa* (Black Hills), Okute."

Chris nodded and said, "I hope it will be as you have said ... that Crazy Horse will be camped nearby."

Ptecila dipped his wavy topknot toward the Black Hills as he replied, "He will be there; you will see. Paha Sapa is *wakan* (holy). Our chief will be there to chase away the wasichus who tear at the Earth Mother's skin searching for the yellow metal."

Raven felt a rising excitement. Blue Feather will be waiting. I wonder, he thought, if she is as anxious as I am. He grinned at Ptecila. "Well, what are we waiting for?"

Chris let out a loud yell and dug his heels into The Black's ribs. Being almost as startled as Ptecila, The Black lunged forward and raced down the long slope. His leaping start had all the appearance of having been initiated by a rude cattle prod.

The Oglala tracker stared for a moment at Raven's dust. He slowly shook his head and spoke softly to his pony. "Windbreaker, I think Okute is feeling much better. He seems anxious to return to his wife's blanket." He paused for a moment and stroked his pony's spotted neck. "Wasichus are a strange people ... yet, at times, they are much like the Lakota. Sometimes it is very confusing."

Since his pony had no comment, Ptecila heel-tapped him into starting down the long, grassy slope. Raven was no longer in sight as the little Oglala followed slowly in The Black's hoofprints.

Chris let him run. The big horse seemed to thrive on the sudden activity. We both need to burn off some dormant energy, he thought. After several minutes at full gallop Raven felt a sudden pain in his arrow wound. He slowed The Black to a lope, then a walk. Chris relaxed and noted that, except for some throbbing, the pain in his shoulder had stopped. All of his other nicks and abrasions, even the hole in his leg, had healed. He rationalized that his shoulder was taking longer because of the infection.

Coming out of a deep gully, Raven steered the stallion onto a strange, meandering path. It climbed a slope that led to the crest of an unusual looking, rocky hill. The Black Hills again appeared and he moved The Black over the top. When Chris was beyond a rocky prominence that rose like a wart on the prairie backside he stopped to wait for Ptecila.

Raven's anticipation of seeing Blue Feather again was growing with each passing moment. He waited impatiently. Exasperated by the inactivity he decided to move over to the next hill and wait for him there.

He started The Black down the rocky hillside. Before his view was gone Chris stole a final glance to the rear. Still no sign of Ptecila. He moved slowly down the steep gradient through tall grass and rocky ground.

With the suddenness of a surprised grouse, a bear reared up out of a hole directly in front of them. The Black braced his forelegs and dug in. Snorting loudly, he fought the bit and shied away. Jerking hard on the reins, Chris turned him back and looked again. The 'bear' was pointing a rifle at him!

"Hold it right thar, ye claim jumpin' sonuvabitch!"

Tightening his grip on the reins, Raven stared in absolute disbelief. A wildly bearded mountain of a man who was wearing a tattered bearskin coat crawled out of a hole and stood up. He was huge!

The man, taller than Bear's Foot, was at least twice his size in girth. He was bearded almost to his beady eyes. His head was topped with a filthy mop of ratty hair that was nearly a perfect match in color and lack of cleanliness with the ankle length bearskin coat that was buttoned to the neck.

By God, Chris thought, if he had a black nose and bigger ears I'd swear to Christ he was a bear.

Making a threatening gesture with his rifle, Bear Man growled, "Don' ye be movin' none! I'll blow a hole in yer hide thet'll ..." Without turning his shaggy head, he bellowed, "Clem! Git yer scrawny ass out here!"

Raven held The Black perfectly still. He didn't want Yogi to misunderstand his stallion's nervous movement for an escape attempt. This guy might be smarter than your everyday run-of-the-mill fence post, he thought, but I doubt it.

"Clem? ... right now! It be hot out here!"

The man's face glistened with sweat. He had to keep blinking to keep it from running into his eyes.

I don't believe this shit, he mused, it has to be eighty degrees in the shade and this bozo's wearing a fur coat and bitching about the heat.

Further down the hill a filthy, rail-thin scarecrow of a man stepped into the open. Behind him, Raven could see the opening to what must be a mine shaft.

Clem was wearing an idiot's grin and a set of mud-caked clothing that was held together by a ragged pair of flannel suspenders. He was also wearing a scuffed holster that was carrying an old cap'n'ball revolver high on his bony hip. Still wearing his tell-tale smile he began clawing his way through the tall grass up the stony hill.

Without looking at it, Chris thought of the pumpgun hanging by its thong from the saddle. He knew he'd never reach it in time, but he knew he was going to have to do something. Where in the hell is Ptecila? Raven began to sweat.

Pig eyes still clamped on Raven, Bear Man shouted, "Clem!?"

Without raising his head, Clem answered, "Ahm comin'."

Ready to try just about anything, Raven smiled. "Listen Mister, I'm just passing through. I don't want any trouble."

Bear Man scowled. Baring a set of horrible looking teeth, he snarled, "Ye shut yer yap an' climb down off'n thet hoss."

Having no immediate alternative, Chris stepped down.

"Clem ... we got us a claim jumpin' bastard, here! We needs ta kill em. We can throw his carcass down thet ol' mine shaft over yonder."

Without preamble, the fear pierced Raven's body and took his breath away as surely as a solid punch to the solar plexus. The fat giant had spoken of killing him in the same tone of voice he would have used to announce that he had to go take a shit. Raven's breath returned and with it came the beginnings of a towering rage.

Raven grinned like a wolf licking his chops before ripping the throat out of his next meal. There is no way, he thought, that I'm going to die at the hands of a pair of clowns like these.

Bear Man didn't see the smile; he had glanced at Clem as he stumbled up to them. Clem saw the smile but he just grinned foolishly in return. He stopped next to his partner and stared blank-eyed at Chris. Drool oozed out of the corner of his mouth, and he sucked it back up and grinned even wider.

"God help me," Raven whispered.

Knowing that his fate was in the hands of the demented, icy fingers of apprehension ran up his spine and tickled the back of his neck, raising the hackles and bringing back the fear. He glanced at Bear Man; the giant was rocking back and forth from one foot to the other. While maintaining the see-saw motion his eyes would momentarily leave Raven and beseech the heavens for help as he muttered, "What ta do ... what ta do?"

As before Chris' rising anger took control and obliterated his personal fear. He was now worried that before his fate was resolved Ptecila would come riding over the crest. He knew that if he did the Oglala was a dead man.

Having somehow reached a decision without divine assistance, Bear Man gestured angrily for Raven to throw him The Black's reins and to step back.

When he flipped the reins Raven was conscious of the weight of his revolver tucked under his left armpit. He knew that the pistol could not be seen because of his long vest, but he had to figure a way to stay alive long enough to reach it. If I don't make a move soon, he thought, I'm dead meat. He moved back a couple steps.

The huge man, rivers of sweat running down his face, stepped forward and scooped the pumpgun off the saddle. Clem just stared, grinned, and didn't bother to suck up his drool.

Trying not to let the anger show in his voice, Chris said, "You're making a big mistake. We can talk this out."

The fat man's eyes flared with anger as he growled, "I tol' ye ta shut yer yap. Now ye keep it shut 'til I tell ye ta open it!"

Fixing Raven with a menacing stare Bear Man edged his way back to Clem. The scrawny miner was staring with empty eyes and his mouth hanging open.

Bear Man cocked the hammer on the pump and asked, "What kind o'gun is this'n?"

As the giant handed his rifle to Clem, Raven's heart began to pound against his ribs. He knew that all the idiot had to do was point, pull the trigger, and he was a dead man.

Clem handled the rifle as though it were a shovel. Bear Man cuffed the smaller man along side of the head.

"Point it at 'em, ye dumb bastard!"

Sulking and flinching at the same time Clem poked the rifle toward Chris.

Inside, Raven's guts churned and twisted as the big man examined the pump. Dear God, he worried, where is Ptecila? A gust of wind swept up from the rocky draw. Nausea gnawed at Raven's stomach as the breeze brought with it the stench of unwashed bodies.

Suddenly, Bear Man pointed the pump right at him and said, "I axed ye b'fore, now ye best tell me true ... what kind o' gun be this?"

Fighting down his futile rage, Raven stalled for time as he said, "It's a Winchester model 97 twelve-gauge pump shotgun. It's a repeater."

The snub-nosed shotgun looked like a toy in the fat man's huge hands. He looked sharply at Raven and replied, "It be a scattergun thet shoots mor'n twice?" Something in his eyes told Raven that his time was running out. His muscles tightened and a spasm of pain skewered the wound in his left shoulder. A wave of dizziness made him pray ... not now, God. Please, not now. His head cleared.

Bear Man's eyes darted toward Clem who was staring as though in a trance.

"Stop thet!"

The huge man's elbow jarred a spark of life into Clem's vacant gaze. His pig eyes raked Raven as he growled, "How's this here repeatin' scattergun work?"

Chris could only stare, because at that very instant he knew what he was going to do. Later he would swear to himself that he had felt the adrenalin seeping into his bloodstream.

"You see the wooden grip near the end of the barrel? You have to jerk back real hard on it."

Bear Man's huge paw wrapped around the grooved wooden forearm. He grinned viciously, baring his awful teeth.

Ejecting a shell from the chamber of a Winchester 97 can be a very painful experience. When the slide is pulled back it exposes the bolt as it slides over the hammer to cock it. Unless he is careful a novice could very easily peel the flesh off the back of the hand grasping the pistol-grip or wrist of the stock.

Bear Man was not the careful type. He slammed the slide-action back. He screamed as the bolt ripped the skin of the back of his hand. Blood flowed instantly. He dropped the pump and cradled his bloody hand as he screeched, "Kill 'em! Now!"

Raven was already moving.

Clem's eyes got big as he thrust the big rifle toward Raven and pulled the trigger. He was too late.

With Bear Man's scream of pain, Chris' right hand was already tugging his Colt free of its holster beneath the vest. He slid to his right just as the rifle roared. The resulting gout of gunsmoke partially hid Clem causing Raven's first shot to be high, hitting the miner in the upper chest. Clem staggered back and fell to his hands and knees.

The Black whinnied and backed away, pulling his reins free of the anchoring rock.

Raven's second shot struck Bear Man in the belly as he reached for the pumpgun. A puff of dust from the bearskin coat marked the point of impact. The heavy bullet merely caused the giant to pause and grunt before reaching again for the pump. Raven stared wide-eyed as Bear Man wobbled, steadied himself, snatched the shotgun, and straightened up. His eyes gleamed with malevolence as he slammed the chamber shut and pointed it at Chris.

A loud hiss and buzz zipped by Raven's ear followed by a meaty thud. The fur-coated giant dropped the pumpgun and clawed frantically at the feathered shaft protruding from his throat. Blood began to spill over his lower lip and into his bushy beard.

"Kaboom!"

Chris felt the heat of the bullet as it snapped by his face.

Clem was on his knees using both hands to realign his four pound cap'n'ball revolver. The whole front of his filthy shirt was red with his blood.

With his whole focus centered on Clem, Raven ignored the hiss and buzz of another arrow. Before the scrawny miner could fire again Chris shot him in the chest. This time the bullet found the heart and Clem collapsed onto the trampled grass like a discarded doll.

Bear Man was still standing! Because of the arrow in his throat, his snarl and roar gurgled as he ineffectively plucked at the second arrow buried in his vast chest. The huge miner teetered as he tugged at the reed shaft that was sticking from his bearskin coat like an aberrant branch of a shaggy barked tree. His fur coat was matted and slick with blood. Roaring with rage he grasped the shaft with bloody hands and tried to wrench it from his body.

Raising his revolver to finish him, Raven hesitated when he heard the hurried whisper of leather on grass. He looked. Ptecila was running hard down the steep, grassy slope. He was on a collision course with the swaying giant. The little Oglala didn't even slow down. He swung his bow with both hands. With a sickening thud, the heavy, elk horn bow flattened Bear Man's fleshy nose. More blood spurted as the man's eyes rolled back and he toppled backwards, crashing to the ground and sliding down the hill.

"*Anho!*"

Ptecila's coup shout echoed the loud thump of the fallen giant's body hitting the ground. The small warrior stared quietly at Bear Man's motionless form.

Nauseated by all the spilled blood, Raven sat down. He was exhausted. The life and death tensions of the last few moments was too much for his weakened body. He looked again at Ptecila who was still staring at the miner's huge body. He was wearing a strange expression on his seamed and weathered face.

"What is wrong, Ptecila?"

He glanced at Chris, smiling pensively. "It is nothing. It is just that I have never counted coup on a bear before."

Raven didn't know whether to laugh or cry. The men they had killed would certainly have done the same to them. In fact, they were planning on doing so. Still it bothered him. He wasn't so sure that the pair were capable of determining the difference between right and wrong.

Barry Brierley

"*Hokahey!*"

Ptecila's war cry startled a snort and whinny out of The Black and brought Chris stumbling to his feet. Following the Oglala's line of sight Raven stared with joy-filled eyes. What he saw blew away any thoughts of guilt or remorse. Lining the ridge on the other side of the draw was a rank of horseback Indians. Near the middle of the feathered row one man drew all of Raven's attention. The warrior's body was adorned with painted hail spots. His unbound hair whipped in the wind and partially covered the blue lightning bolt painted on his cheek. Crazy Horse, he thought; I've come home at last.

CHAPTER 26

ᐱ ᐱ ᐱ ᐱ ᐱ

Raven cradled Blue Feather in his arms and tried not to let his worry interfere with his reacquired happiness. Little Hawk had recently been complaining of a pain in his pelvic region below the navel. Not wanting to alarm his mother, Chris had laughed it off as indigestion. Hell, he mused, maybe that's all it is, too many berries.

Blue Feather stirred in her sleep and tightened her arms around Raven's chest. A slight breeze slipped in through the tipi's smoke hole. Being still damp with perspiration from their recent lovemaking the cool air raised goose-flesh on his naked arms and legs. He pulled a blanket up over his wife's supine body.

Raven's fingers absently stroked her silken hair as he thought of the weeks since his homecoming. Much to his relief Bear's Foot had completely recovered from his gunshot wound and was as full of mischief and good humor as ever. All Chris had to do was lay his head back and close his eyes and he could see again the look on Bear's Foot's face when he and Ptecila had ridden into camp. He saw again the spark of respect and gratitude in his eyes when Raven had returned the fighting knife to him along with its newly designed sheath.

Taking the sheathed knife the huge warrior had carefully, almost reverently, run his fingers through the long, glossy black hair of Scar's scalp.

215

Chris had felt nothing but disgust for the self-labeled 'trophy hunters' of Vietnam. The taking of ears and other parts of the enemies' anatomy sickened him. He rationalized that his taking of Scar's scalp had accomplished two very important things. First of all, it proved to Bear's Foot that he had been avenged so that he didn't have to cut a bloody swath through the Hunkpapa Sioux looking for Scar. Secondly, it strengthened the people's belief that Raven was now one of them.

With Ptecila's help Chris had been able to cure the scalp and to fasten it to Bear's sheath in a decorative manner. It wasn't the best job, but the great warrior acted like it had been done by a master craftsman. He remembered how Bear's Foot had admired the sheath for a long moment. When he had glanced up at Raven, tears were in his eyes. He spoke softly.

"You are a friend like no other, Okute. I will cherish this gift like our friendship, forever."

Blue Feather opened her eyes and ended his reminiscing. The starlight that filtered through the smoke hole cast a blue light over her beautiful face. Sleepily she reached up and pulled Raven's face down and kissed him. The sweetness of her kiss awakened his sleeping desire. His hand slipped under the blanket and found the warmth and smoothness of her skin. Her lips parted, pulling away from his. Blue Feather moaned softly as Raven's hand followed the soft contours and explored the hidden valleys and sloping hills of her body. She pushed the blanket aside and gasped as he found a secret secluded spot that welcomed his touch. Her searching fingers found him easily. Clenching him with a firm fist she pulled him to her. They made love slowly and with great tenderness. When their needs had been satiated they remained entwined until the morning's first light. The sun turned the lodge-skins amber and brought butter-colored rays of sunlight slanting into the tipi's cozy interior.

Slowly, so as not to wake her, Raven carefully unraveled his arms and legs from his wife's. From the moment he had opened his eyes his thoughts were focussed on Little Hawk. He quickly dressed and slipped outside. The bright sky made him squint as his gaze swept the village. After the great encampment on the Little Big Horn, Crazy Horse's village had seemed tiny at first. It didn't take long, however, before it felt like home to him.

The camp was just beginning to stir with its usual daily activities; children were everywhere but no sign of Little Hawk. Then he remembered. Having recently gone on his first raid with Crazy Horse, Little Hawk would no longer be considered a child. He would probably rather die, he thought, than be caught playing with the other children. The hackles stirred on the back of his neck as he realized what he had said. Here I am, he chided, worrying about Hawk's health and at the same time talking facetiously about his death.

He hurried through the camp. He saw several boys Little Hawk's age, but his son was nowhere to be seen. All at once he spied Hawk's friend and lodge-mate, Gray Weasel. The boy greeted Raven with great respect. Chris covertly smiled, thinking, Little Hawk must have been telling his friend some exaggerated tales about his new father. The words Gray Weasel shared with Raven about Little Hawk weren't very encouraging. He had said that Little Hawk wasn't feeling well and had decided to stay in the lodge.

Chris left the boy and rushed through the camp toward Little Hawk's lodge. His concentration was so centered that he didn't hear several greetings that were thrown his way. Apprehension was at its peak by the time Raven neared the boy's tipi.

A pretty, young girl was hovering near the tipi's door flap. When she saw Raven coming she quickly ducked behind the lodge. Chris stopped for a second. He'd seen her before. Her name was Deer, he mused, or is it Doe? He shrugged it off and stepped toward the tipi. Just as he arrived he saw her peek around an adjoining tipi and then she was gone. Suddenly, Raven stopped in his tracks. Damn, he thought, that's almost deja vu. The first time I saw Little Hawk, he was peering at me from behind the lodges ... just like Doe was doing. No it's not Doe, he realized, her name is Fawn.

Stepping up to the tipi Raven threw protocol aside, along with the door flap, and slipped inside. He stood in the comparative gloom for a few seconds as his eyes adjusted. His heart lurched as he spied the boy's still form lying on some robes. Relief flooded through him as he saw the rise and fall of Little Hawk's narrow chest. Moving swiftly to his side Raven placed his palm on the boy's high forehead. The heat he felt beneath his hand justified his increased anxiety. He noticed that the Derringer he had earned on his first war party was clutched in his right hand. When he looked up, a pair of large black eyes were fastened onto his face. Little Hawk smiled and said, "*Hohahe* (Welcome), Okute."

"*Washtay*, Hawk. How are you feeling?"

"I am just tired, Okute. I thought I might rest this morning. Later, Gray Weasel and I are going on a scout."

Raven studied Little Hawk's face and tried to see beyond the boy's pride to determine how he really felt.

"Do you still have the pain?"

"It is nothing. Sometimes I forget that it is there."

As he spoke Chris noticed that his hand had moved down until it rested near his abdomen in a protective gesture.

Speaking softly, Raven suggested, "Perhaps I should look at the place that hurts. Your mother is worried and allowing me to examine it will make her happy."

He noticed the protective hand relax and drop to his side. Little Hawk stared at Raven impassively, then slowly nodded.

Releasing the boy's thong that held his loin-cloth in place, Chris carefully pushed and prodded in various spots near his stomach. There was no reaction.

"If I hurt you in any way, please tell me."

Raven held his breath as he pushed in on the lower right side of his abdomen. Little Hawk frowned but said nothing. When Chris released the pressure, Little Hawk instantly grimaced and exclaimed, "*Dho!*" His hand quickly grabbed Raven's, stopping any further exploration. Raven didn't need to explore any further. He felt light-headed with dread. He rocked back on his heels and forced a smile.

"I think it will be best if you and Weasel call off that scout you have planned."

Little Hawk stared at him. "What is wrong, Okute?"

Raven's mind galloped through all the possible answers he could give. His mind blanked. How in the hell, he thought, do you tell a twelve year old Indian boy that he has an infected appendix ... and then, tell him that if it ruptures he's going to die? Chris knew that he would have to lie to him ... and his mother.

How could I possibly explain, he wondered, that if it ruptures he will die because there are no medical facilities or doctors in the nineteenth century with the capability to save his life?

219

CHAPTER 27

⋀ ⋀ ⋀ ⋀ ⋀

Raven's breath caught in his throat at his first sight of Bear Butte looming in the distance. He glanced behind at the smiling face of Bear's Foot. He returned his gaze to the butte and wondered again if he were crazy to think that his plan might work. He heard a laugh come from Little Hawk, riding on the travois. Bear was leaning down talking to him, trying to keep him at ease. I wish he'd come up here, Chris thought, I could use some kind of tranquilizer.

The day before, it was necessary to tell Blue Feather the big lie. He had no alternative, just as he had none when he answered Little Hawk's question by being evasive. He did tell him that he was going to take him to a special Medicine Man that could cure him.

With his wife he had to be much more creative. How do you explain to a mother, he asked himself, who has never heard of surgery or an appendix, that a stranger is going to cut her son open and remove a portion of his intestines? Chris shook his head in vexation. And then, he thought, convince her that he will fine afterwards.

In his mind Raven went through the story he told Blue Feather one more time. He could vividly remember the dazed expression on her face when he told his fabrication.

Unexpectedly, The Black shied to his left. Chris heard the tell-tale buzz before he saw its tan and gray coils underneath a clump of prickly-pear cactus. Seeing the stallion skip to the left, Bear's Foot heard the rattle and guided the travois in a wide swing around the spot.

Bear Butte was closer now. Raven noticed that the sky was just as blue, the clouds as white. Everything is just as I remember it, he thought, if only everything else will be the same when I need it to be. A vision of Blue Feather's stunned expression brought back the memory of his lie.

He had told her that a bad spirit had made a home in her son's body. Before she had a chance to react, Chris had rushed on telling her of the cure and what must be done.

He said that he only knew of one Medicine Man with the power to cure him. The holy man's name was 'Doctor' and he lived far away in the land that Raven came from and that the people there are very warlike and kill all strangers. He also told her that the 'Doctor' owed his life to him. Because of the debt Raven will be able to take Little Hawk safely to the 'Doctor' to be cured. He further embellished his tale by telling her that he had to leave with Little Hawk as soon as possible before the demon takes over his whole body, killing him.

Bear's Foot, having heard the story from Blue Feather, had followed them. When discovered, he had insisted upon coming along as far as was possible without endangering Little Hawk. Chris was secretly delighted because he would need someone to watch over Hawk later while he took care of some necessary business.

When the butte began to loom over them Raven's guilt disappeared and was replaced by worry. The responsibility and fret settled over his shoulders like a leaden shroud. They approached the small lake on the western approach to the butte.

This is where my life began with the Lakota, he thought, let's hope that this isn't where it will end. He looked toward the summit of the towering monolith and shuddered. The lightning, the thunder, and wind: it all came back to him in a frightening rush of remembrance. Can I do it again? His silent query remained unanswered. He stared at the butte, wishing he was able to unveil its many mysteries. I must do it again ... if I fail, Little Hawk will die. It's as simple as that.

Uncharacteristically, they made their camp in the trees away from the water and out of sight of any wandering Indians or whites. After they had settled in, Raven told Bear's Foot that he needed to visit the wasichu village up in the Paha Sapa.

Concern showed on the warrior's face as he warned, "There are many bad men in the camp of the dead wood, Okute. Men that no longer care if they are human beings. Truly, there are more weasels in that camp than men."

Chris grinned at Bear's worried expression. "If I need any help I'll just whistle," he said.

Not understanding Raven's humor, Bear scowled and replied, "If I am to stay with Little Hawk, I will be too far away to hear. You must promise to be wary at all times, *Kola*."

Suddenly serious, Chris slapped the broad shoulder and lowered his voice so that Little Hawk could not hear, as he said, "I promise. And you must promise that you will not allow Little Hawk to move around. He must remain as still as possible."

"It will be as you say, Okute," Bear's Foot rumbled.

Moving to Little Hawk's side, Raven knelt beside him. He was still on the travois litter, minus the pony, and was propped up on one elbow. His face was drawn and pale underlined by a subtle sadness.

Raven's heart reached out for him, wishing there was something he could do to make him feel better. At that moment Little Hawk smiled. He stared into Chris' eyes and said, "Come back, Okute. I will be waiting for our journey to begin."

Being careful not to bump him, Raven hugged him and moved quickly to The Black. On his way he made eye contact with Bear's Foot. The Minneconjou's tiny nod told him that he need not worry about anything but himself. Pulling himself up onto The Black, Chris spun him around and urged him into a ground eating lope.

While skirting the lake he looked back but was unable to see any sign of the camp. Good, he thought, if I can't, neither can anybody else. Throwing a final glance at Bear Butte to his left, Raven pushed his stallion into a ground eating gallop and headed toward the dark mass that was the edge of the Black Hills. A light rain began to fall. He lifted his head and let the rain pelt his face with its cold, wet kisses. Seeing the shifting clouds, Chris was reminded of the Lakota gods, Sky Father and the Thunder Beings. Just then a small barrage of distant thunder rumbled overhead. While looking for a trail moving south into the hills, he wondered if it was a good sign or bad. He knew instantly that it was a silly thought and totally dismissed it. He thought of Blue Feather and of the trust she had put in him. Raven felt a confidence growing inside of him that was unlike anything he had ever experienced before. He just knew that he was going to succeed. But first, he mused, I need to do a little shopping.

"I wonder," he mused aloud, "if Deadwood is as wild and hairy as the historian's claim it was."

CHAPTER 28

ΛΛΛΛΛ

Caleb Starr left the dubious shelter of the clapboard dry goods store and stepped into the clinging mud of Deadwood Gulch's main thoroughfare. The rain had finally stopped and the sun was trying to peek around a towering, cumulus cloud.

He was a lean, hard-looking man of indeterminate age. From the crown of his gray, wide-brimmed hat to the soles of his muddy, stove-pipe boots, Caleb Starr gave the impression of independence and strength of character.

Shifting his chew to the other cheek, Starr spat an amber stream into the mud. He moved up alongside his buckskin gelding and set a sack of flour up behind the saddle's cantle. The big horse snorted at the sudden weight and shifted from a three leg stance to four. Starr tied the flour sack on behind the cantle then looped a smaller bag of coffee beans over the pommel. While lengthening the loop on the coffee bag, Caleb noticed that there was an unusual number of townsmen crowding the main street.

Some of the men in the street were horseback, while others were in the back of mule-drawn wagons. The majority of those on the thoroughfare were on foot, slogging their way through the clinging mud.

Caleb's snort of disgust was very similar to the one made by his horse. "Only a damn fool or a soft-brain would be dumb enough to come to town when the rock pounders and Chinamen are up and about," he quietly muttered. He threw a glance at his horse, raised his voice, and asked, "Which one am I, hoss ... fool or soft-brain?"

Starr tightened the saddle girth. "Probably both," he grumbled,. "if I'm askin' my hoss questions and expectin' a reply."

He stopped deriding himself long enough to gather the reins and haul himself up onto the saddle. Hesitant to join the muddy flow of people and animals, Caleb waited. Curious, he wondered why so many of the riff-raff, and even miners, were out sloshin' through the mud. He also thought it peculiar that so many were headin' west.

The sun broke clear of the clouds. Eyes narrowed against the sudden sun glare, Starr stood in his stirrups and looked beyond the long line of makeshift shacks and countless tents that bordered the narrow street. Unable to see anything that could be causing a ruckus, he sat down again. He did notice that every one of the two-story buildings lining the street had at least one fancy woman hangin' out her window with her goods on display. Reluctantly, Caleb lowered his gaze to street level and speculated on the destination of the crowd. His first thought had been that people were rushin' to a fire. But there ain't no smoke.

"Well," he murmured, "must be a shootin' or a hangin'. I can't feature any of these geezers gittin' their feet muddy for any other reason."

Turning the rangy buckskin, Starr joined the throng of people. They moved up the narrow, muddy street like a herd of mindless lemmings. He shook his head in wonder. It always amazed him how people will willingly join a crowd and wade through mud-covered streets just to see where everyone else is goin'.

Barry Brierley

Ignoring his fellow travelers Starr busied himself with wavin' at the fancy gals and letting his gaze scan the rooftops and canvas-covered establishments of the sprawling, mining town.

The town of Deadwood Gulch consisted of a long, cramped strip of hastily erected tents and shanties with a few two-story buildings thrown in to make it look like a real community. The inhabitants were about as permanent as their places of business. These denizens included miners, gamblers, prostitutes, plainsmen, and Chinese laborers and launderers. The town's location was smack in the middle of the Black Hills in Dakota Territory. The whole town was surrounded by steep hills. In many instances, the hills tapered down into the very backyards of the businesses that lined the busy, main street. Except for a few solitary pine trees the town was treeless. The surrounding hills were completely devoid of flora. A forest fire had left in its wake a legacy of thousands of burned, charred, and blackened trees scattered across the steep, naked slopes.

Starr's gaze had moved to the razed hills and a familiar memory encroached upon his thoughts. On the rare times that Caleb came to town, he was always reminded of the War Between The States. Twelve years earlier, in 1864, he had been involved in a major battle. It had taken place in a heavily wooded area somewhere back East and the big fight had been dubbed 'The Wilderness'. Thousands had died in both armies, but his most horrible recollection of the battle was the many fires that had swept through both armies. Hundreds of wounded had been trapped by the raging fires and were killed by either the flames or the suffocating smoke before their comrades could rescue them.

Shaking off the lurid memory Starr's attention returned to the crowded street. Near the top of the street's gradient he could see a gathering of people and horses. One horse and rider looked disturbingly familiar.

"Damnation!"

Starr's curse was followed by a blur of motion as he snatched his heavy Sharps rifle out of its scabbard as though it were a pistol.

The man he had recognized was the last person he expected to see on the streets of Deadwood. Caleb had left him camped on the far side of the encompassing hills in a grove of aspen next to a lively stream called Whitewater Creek. His name's Billy and he's Starr's best friend, partner and wrangler all rolled into one copper-colored package. His real name is, He-Who-Talks-With-Horses. Billy is a full-blooded Crow Indian and the younger brother of Starr's wife, who had died a few years previous.

That morning Caleb had insisted that Billy wait for him in camp. Although the Crow and whites had been friends and allies for many years, Starr knew that it wouldn't make a bit of difference to the residents of Deadwood; to them an Indian's an Indian and they lived by the creed, 'the only good Indian's a dead one.' On his own, Caleb thought, Billy won't last in this town any longer than a fly on a frog's lip.

Keeping his gaze fixed on Billy, Starr spurred his gelding into increasing his pace. He had just remembered that, since Custer had got all his men killed up on the Little Big Horn River, there was a standing reward of $250 for the scalp of any Indian, dead or alive. He made a mental note to remind his two boys to stay away from town. They bein' half Crow, he thought, best not take any chances.

Starr cursed under his breath. He noticed that Billy's hands were tied behind his back. Eyes riveted on the cluster of horsemen, Caleb allowed his buckskin to pick his way through the refuse-cluttered mire of the street. Lowering the big Sharps, he let it rest across his thighs. He changed his mind about letting his horse pick his own way and steered him around a slow-moving threesome. "Too many deaf mud-stompers in the way," he murmured.

One of Billy's captors was a large man on a gray horse. The man was waving a rope and making a lot of noise trying to exhort the crowd. Caleb grunted in disgust, thinking to himself, only a damn idiot would wave a hangin' rope around in a town that ain't got a tree big enough to swing a man from.

Starr felt some pride in how Billy was handling the situation. The young Crow was quietly sitting his horse acting as though he wasn't even a part of all the goin's on. From a distance, Starr noticed, a person couldn't even tell Billy was Indian. He didn't look much different from anyone else. He was wearing a white man's cotton shirt and homespun pants. His long hair was tied into a knot at the back of his head and he was wearing a blue calico bandana on his head, pirate style. Some of the miners wore their handkerchiefs that same way to keep the sun off their head and the sweat out of their eyes.

The buckskin, hoofs plopping and sucking in and out of the mud, was moving a little faster. Caleb figured he was only a spur tickle away from breaking into a trot. Several of the gamblers and miners, curious about the crowd, braved the street's mud and puddles of horse urine and rainwater to get a better look up the street. Eyes narrowed with concentration, Starr didn't pay anymore attention to the group of men stumbling out of Saloon No. 10, than he did to the rest of the crowd.

Just as the buckskin came up behind the group from the saloon, the man with the rope swung the coiled hemp back-handed into Billy's defenseless face. The brutal act triggered a reflex from Starr; he eared the hammer back on his Sharps rifle.and it settled into its niche with a crisp, double 'click'.

With the sound of the hammer locking into place, Caleb's side vision picked up a flicker of movement. He looked and immediately froze, stopping his horse in midstep. He was staring into the muzzle of a very large revolver!

I must be gettin' old, Caleb agonized, I barely saw the jasper move.

The pistol was held in the rock steady grip of a tall man with piercing gray eyes. Beyond the cannon-sized muzzle and the killer eyes, Starr caught a glimpse of long, chestnut brown hair spilling out from under a flat-crowned, wide-brimmed, black hat. The man's aim hadn't wavered so much as a fraction. The pistol's large black eye was staring directly between Caleb's blue ones. He didn't dare move a muscle. He waited.

The snapping pale eyes darted here and there as they evaluated Starr's intent and located his rifle. He also made note of its readiness to fire and that it was pointed away from him.

Sweat began to trickle down Caleb's chest. Without taking his gaze off the stranger's eyes he slowly turned his head aside and spit.

Apparently satisfied that Starr hadn't intended to back-shoot him, the man gave him an abrupt nod and slipped the long revolver back under his coat, then coolly turned away as if nothing had happened.

As soon as the gun was put away those townsfolk, who had stopped to watch the action, resumed their walk up the street's incline.

Touching the gelding with his spurs Starr trotted him past the long-haired stranger and turned his attention back to Billy's predicament. Seeing that the man with the rope was still talking, he knew that his friend wasn't in any immediate danger. Instantly, his thoughts returned to the pistolero. One thing for sure, he thought, I was but a trigger-squeeze away from meetin' my maker.

His first impression of the stranger had been that he was just another tin-horn gambler. Then he had second thoughts. When the man had put his pistol away Starr had caught a glimpse of another revolver. Both pistols had matching ivory grips and were stuck behind a scarlet sash. Two-bit gamblers, he thought, just don't tote around a pair of fancy, heavy revolvers.

All at once, Starr swore and dug his heels into the buckskin's flanks. He was close enough to see the blood on his friend's face. All thoughts of the man with the fancy guns left his mind. The gelding's hard canter and Caleb's stern expression opened a lane through the crowded street. People scattered, avoiding the mud splattering hoofs, as Starr closed with the men that appeared determined to see his friend die.

CHAPTER 29

ΛΛΛΛΛ

When Starr stopped his mount at the edge of the crowd, the big loud-mouth with the rope was still talking.

"Since the sheriff ain't in town, I say, string 'em up an' put his red ass on ice 'til he gits back."

Overlaying a restless murmur that swept through the crowd, several voices were raised in agreement. One raucous voice shouted, "Let's jus' kill the red belly an' take his hair!"

Billy quietly sat his horse, impassively listening and watching. He was battered and bruised, but had a quiet demeanor that looked out of place among the loud voices and angry faces.

A ferret-faced little man muscled his horse in between Billy and the man with the rope. Narrow face flushed with drink and excitement, he whipped out a Bowie knife and flourished it overhead. Spittle flew from the wide mouth as he shouted, "I say we lop off his ears an' skin 'em alive!"

"And I say, you let him be!"

Starr's voice cracked with whip-like authority. A hush settled over the mixed mob of spectators and rabble rousers. Those among the gathering who were between Starr and Billy's captors began to shove and push. Frightened, they slipped and slid in their frantic effort to get out of the line of fire. The mob parted like the Red Sea had for Moses and left behind them an open lane of muddy street.

A hum of conversation rose from the crowd, punctuated by several loud jeers and angry, threatening remarks.

Caleb ignored them all. His attention was fixed on the three horsemen that were flanking his friend. During the brief lull he had quickly sized them up.

The man on the left was the fella with the rope, a big red-faced jasper wearin' miner duds. Between him and Billy was the ferret-faced soft-brain with the knife. On the right, a man cut from a different piece of leather was quietly sitting his horse. Starr had immediately sensed that this was the fella that needed the closest watchin'. Average height and lean as a wolf his hard eyes peered at Starr from under his narrow-brimmed hat. He carried two-guns; one rode low on his right hip while the other was tucked behind his waistband.

It was the big, loud-mouthed miner that was the first to react to Caleb's intervention.

"Who'n the hell are you to be stickin' yer nose in?"

A garbled drone of voices rose from the onlookers. One was clearly heard above the others. "Injun lover!"

Other hecklers joined in. They continued until they saw a wide grin split Starr's cropped, salt and pepper beard. The shouted insults dwindled away as the mob awaited Starr's response.

"Name's Caleb Starr. Me 'n Tom are of a mind you should let," nodding to his friend "Billy go free."

"Why should we?"

The quiet words came from the hard-eyed horseman on the right.

"An' who'n the hell is Tom?" shouted the over-sized loud-mouth with the rope.

During the verbal exchange Starr's eyes, partially concealed by the brim of his hat, were constantly assessing the strength of the opposition.

The adle-minded one was worrying him. He just sat his horse, his wild-eyed gaze jumping from one speaker to the next. The glitter in his eyes reminded Starr of a wolverine he had once seen caught in a steel trap. The animal had that same crazy look just before the foam showed on his jaws and he attacked with a mindless fury.

With a casualness that was both calculated and deceptive, Starr answered, "Well, first of all, Billy there," again nodding toward his tied and beaten friend, "he's an Absaroky, Crow Indian. I've known him neigh on to twelve year. Not once durin' that time had he ever raised a hand against a white man."

Caleb paused to spit and, hopefully, for his words to sink into their thick skulls.

"To answer your second question, Tom is sittin' right here on my lap." To make his meaning clear, Starr gave his cocked rifle a gentle pat.

An uneasy quiet settled over the gathering; Starr decided to help move things along a mite quicker. He smiled again and said, "Yessir, Ol' Tom's only got one eye but he's got one hell of a long reach ... if you get my drift."

When Caleb had confronted the three men, he had positioned his buckskin sideways, allowing the muzzle of his Sharps to be pointed in their general direction.

Without taking his eyes off Billy's three captors Caleb turned his head and spat into the muddy street.

The miner, his face twisted with anger, had turned a turkey-wattle red. He dropped the coil of rope and his gray horse skittered sideways. He jerked hard on the reins as his other hand hovered near his holstered revolver.

Starr's experienced eyes saw and evaluated all three men in a flash. His darting glance dismissed the miner as a bully, mostly a talker. He expected the dance to be started by the pistolero on the right. He was far and away the most dangerous of the three. Ferret Face, in the middle, was quiet but his crazy eyes were jumpin' all over the place. The big knife was out of sight but his left hand was hidden on the off side of his horse.

Chancing a quick peek at Billy, he was rewarded with a swift glance of his friend's eyes toward Ferret Face's hidden hand. The instant Billy's gaze again met Starr's, he gave a tiny, barely discernible nod. This confirmed Caleb's belief that the man's hand held a hidden weapon.

Unable to restrain himself any longer the big miner surprised Starr by shouting, "Injun lover! Yer a dead ... "

His angry words drifted away like smoke caught in a sudden gust of wind.

Starr stared spellbound. The man's coloring faded from red to pink to pasty white. Even Ferret Face changed; he appeared to shrivel into an even smaller package. The normally shifty eyes were wide and staring. The gunman on the right, who had seemed pretty relaxed with the situation, had suddenly turned into a flesh and blood statue. Starr didn't understand what was happening.

The crowd had begun to buzz with whispers when the loud-mouth had shut up, but not anymore. It was so quiet the mob reminded Starr of a tin-type he had seen of a Denver hangin' crowd. Except for a few rollin' eyeballs, he thought, they look just like that picture.

It was the quiet gunman on the right who broke the spell. Caleb wasn't surprised. What did confound him was the fact that his word's weren't directed toward him. The question the man asked tolled inside Starr's ear like a bell.

"You takin' a hand in this game, Hickok?"

The famous name sizzled in Starr's brain as though it had been branded there with a red-hot, running iron. Following the gunman's line of sight, Caleb risked a glance over his right shoulder. A space had miraculously opened up around the famous shootist.

Starr felt a jolt in his stomach as he choked back a grunt of surprise. Incredulous, he recognized the gambler who had braced him in the street. He felt his stomach twist as nausea set in and the realization hit him. He had come damn close, he thought, to having a bullet planted in his brain-pan by Wild Bill Hickok!

While keeping a close watch on the three men, Caleb tried to get a grasp on the reality of the situation. He hadn't even known that the famous gunman was in the territory, not to mention Deadwood. The last he had heard, he was in Cheyenne, or maybe Denver.

Caleb's quick peek had given him a good look at Hickok. The tall man had a calm, steady look about him. Women would call him handsome, with his long, curly brown hair and sweeping moustache. His strong jaw and frosty gray eyes were his most striking features.

Having taken his time to answer the man's question, Hickok's voice was loud in the unnaturally quiet street.

"It seems to me, Mr. Varnes, that Mr. Starr has the deck stacked against him."

Starr was befuddled. Why would a complete stranger, especially Wild Bill, stick his nose into such a dangerous situation? He stared at Billy as if he might find the answer there, but he knew it was a wasted thought. How would Hickok know his friend, Billy?

The loud-mouthed miner began speaking to Hickok. This time there were no threats or bluster; it was mostly whine. Caleb blocked out most of what was said and concentrated on watching the other two jaspers. He did hear him say something about 'Hickok not wearin' a badge' before he stopped his wheedlin'.

Before Hickok could respond to the whiner's voice, Starr interceded.

"I'm through listenin' to talk. I'm cuttin' Billy loose!"

He touched his spurs to the gelding's ribs and the buckskin carried Starr toward the group at a sedate walk. The tension that hung in the air was a threatening, tangible presence. A liquid plop and squish of the horse's hoofs was the only lucid sound to be heard.

Caleb ignored the loud-mouth. He sensed that the man's fear of Hickok would keep him from making the first move. His right hand was on the pistol-grip of the rifle. He watched the other two and waited.

If any gun-play were to start, Caleb had no intention of using the cumbersome, single-shot rifle but wanted them to think that he would. He knew that in the time it would take him to unlimber the big rifle, it would give one of them ample time to put a bullet in him. The hickory grip of his revolver was only inches away from the hand on the rifle. The pistol's well-oiled, six-inch barrel was tucked away in a holster of smooth, slick leather. Set up for a fast cross-draw, it rested just below Starr's left hipbone with the butt turned outward.

The gelding's mud-sucking hoofs stopped directly in front of Billy and the half-wit. Caleb didn't look straight at Ferret Face, he kept his head turned just enough so that he could watch the one on the right, also.

Starr kept his voice quiet so that only those close by could hear, as he asked, "What's it goin' to be, boy? You fixin' to die right here in the street, or are you movin' out of the way?'"

The man's narrow face twitched with indecision and his beady eyes jumped to the left and right as he looked in vain for some immediate help.

Going with his instincts Starr decided to gamble. He would momentarily ignore Varnes and the miner and concentrate on the least stable of the three. He knew that on the off-side of his horse, Ferret Face had a white-knuckle grip on some kind of weapon.

Within a span of a few seconds several things happened so fast that, later, witnesses would argue about what actually did happened.

Caleb drove his spurs into his gelding's flanks! The buckskin lunged forward and Starr forcefully stopped him, sliding to a halt alongside the narrow-faced man's startled horse. Ferret Face's shifty eyes widened in surprise and fear. Suddenly, Billy's moccasined foot streaked upwards! His muscular, horseman's leg gave impetus to the callused foot as it struck the little man's hidden arm, kicking it up and into the open. A large cap 'n' ball revolver was clutched in his hand.

In a blur of shiny steel, the barrel of Caleb's colt slammed into the side of the man's head. The beady eyes rolled back in his head and his fingers released their grip, letting the pistol fall into the wet mud. His slight form crumpled and slowly followed in the pistol's wake. Before the unconscious man's body was clear of his saddle, Starr's revolver was cocked and aimed at Varnes, the gunman on the right.

Varnes, his hand on his holstered revolver, froze. His eyes glittered with animosity, but he didn't move.

Without taking his eyes off the lean gunman, Starr said, "Billy, watch the big miner on the gray behind me."

From the corner of his eye he saw the white of his friend's smile light up his brown and bloody face.

"I will watch him, Long-Eye."

Billy's halting English and his use of Starr's Crow name forced him to give an answering smile.

"Him, the one with the white, twisted face that look like him trying to break wind?"

Caleb chuckled as he replied, "Yeah, that's him all right."

The crowd, who had been stunned into silence by the sudden turn of events, began to stir. An indefinable murmur rose from the onlookers then drifted away into an uneasy silence.

Keeping his arm extended and his gun leveled dead center on Varnes' chest, Starr backed the buckskin until he was able to watch both of the would-be lynchers. He threw a glance at the pistol-whipped soft-brain, but it was a wasted effort. The man hadn't moved; he was still lying in his bed of mud. Starr was half-way expecting some type of interference from the mob but couldn't take the time to worry about it. Leastwise, he thought, they're bein' quiet. Hope that don't mean they're up to somethin', he mused.

"Billy, come on over here."

As the young Crow, using his knees to guide him, walked his horse through the mud to Starr, the crowd began to buzz once more. A few shouts rose above the drone of whispered words. Caleb and Billy both ignored them. Billy, stopping his pony with a single word in Crow, grinned at Starr as he waited for him to unlimber his knife.

In a voice so low that only Billy could hear, Caleb whispered in Crow, "When we leave stay close beside me, no matter what happens."

A new, louder hum of muttering came from the shifting, uneasy gathering. Ignoring the crowd noise, Starr cut Billy loose. Not once did his eyes leave the sneering Varnes. The crowd noise stopped as Caleb's voice lashed out at the gunman. "What's it gonna be, Varnes? My arm's gettin' a mite tired. You never can tell, I might get a twitch in my trigger finger."

With his gaze still locked in on the glaring shootist, Starr turned his head and casually spit an amber stream into the street.

Without a backward glance, Varnes swung his horse around and kicked him into a gallop. A splatter of mud flew in wet clumps from the horse's hoofs as the gunman rode away.

Caleb lowered the heavy pistol and switched hands momentarily so that he could work the start of a cramp out of his arm. He looked at the miner, shifted his chew and spat again. Although he couldn't see him, Starr could feel Billy quietly sitting his pony on his opposite side. He stared at the miner until he began to fidget. Other than taking his hand away from his holstered gun the man hadn't moved.

Putting a little snarl into his voice, Caleb said, "I think it's 'bout time for you to git!"

Color flooded the miner's fleshy face as quickly as water poured into a bucket.

"Could be I might ask Billy here to help you git started. I ain't asked him, but there's a good chance that he didn't take kindly to your puttin' those rope marks on his face."

Sensing that the miner wasn't going to fight, the mob began to mutter and growl like wild animals being denied their meals. The crowd began to slowly move out of the street. A voice shouted, "Injun lover!" Others joined in with assorted racial slurs and insults. Starr remained completely unruffled, staying focussed on the miner.

"Well!?"

Caleb's demanding query quieted the jeering voices. Only a few of the more blood-thirsty were still hanging around. The red-faced miner was not one of them. He jerked on his reins, turned his gray mount, and spurred him into motion. In a flurry of curses and flying mud the miner rode away.

Glancing at the motionless form in the mud, Starr holstered his pistol and lowered the hammer on the Sharps. Turning to Billy, he told his grinning friend to fetch their pack-horse. The horse's lead rope was lying in the mud where Varnes had dropped it. The docile animal hadn't moved; he was just waiting to be taken home.

As Billy eased his horse away, Starr's quiet voice followed him. "It's best we take leave of this hell-hole and do so, pronto."

The man that Starr's pistol had slapped into the muddy street began to stir. Caleb watched him like a wolf would watch a wounded wolverine ... very closely.

Hearing the sound of sucking mud, Starr's hand automatically darted for his pistol as his head swiveled toward the noise. Hickok stood a few feet away. When he had arrived, or how, Starr had no idea. Just like Caleb, Hickok wasn't taking any chances. He also was watching Ferret Face. The man was now trying to get up and was having a problem with his balance on the slippery mud.

Taking advantage of the opportunity Starr covertly took a good look at the 'Prince of the Pistoleers.' Hickok looked to be over six feet tall, broad shoulders settin' on a solid frame that was poured into a pair of black stove-pipe boots. Behind the open flaps of a long black coat, Caleb saw a buckskin vest and the scarlet sash. His guns were out of sight.

Lifting his gaze Starr found Hickok's cold gray eyes staring at him. Somewhere, he knew, he had seen a pair of penetrating eyes like those. Brushing the thought away he said, "I'm obliged to you for backin' my play."

Hickok's gaze drifted back to the struggling little man in the mud, as he said, "It looked to me, Mr. Starr ... "

"Name's Caleb," Starr interrupted.

Hickok's eyes flicked toward Starr as he continued. "It looked to me, Caleb, like you didn't need any help. But I decided to make myself available in case the situation were to take a sudden change."

Hickok turned away from the pathetic sight of the muddy scarecrow. As Wild Bill faced Starr, once again he transfixed him with his penetrating eyes. He said, "Back by the saloon I nearly made a terrible mistake. I came within an eye-blink of killing you."

Caleb thought he saw a shadow of sadness darken the pale eyes. Before he could be sure, the shootist had looked away and resumed speaking. "It wasn't the first time I have made a mistake like that." Hickok's gaze returned to meet Caleb's. "I hope that this was the last time. I like to pay my debts, Caleb. After my mistake, earlier, I felt like I owed you something. Now we're even."

With a final glance toward the struggling half-wit, the famous gunfighter nodded, turned, and sloshed away in the direction of the nearest saloon.

Watching him leave, Starr thought of Hickok's final words. He remembered hearin' about Wild Bill's havin' accidently shot and killed a good friend of his. Accordin' to the story, the man had come runnin' up behind him when he was in the middle of a shoot-out. Hickok, thinkin' he was one of the badmen, had spun around and shot him dead.

Hearing something Starr looked and saw Billy walking his horse over to Ferret Face. The man had managed to drape himself over his mount's saddle but was unable to pull himself the rest of the way. He saw fear enter the man's eyes as Billy reined in beside him. The crowd was gone now, but the young Crow decided to be careful. He looked all around, checking to see if anyone was showing any special interest. Satisfied that no one was, he reached out and put his hand on the muddy face and shoved. The little man who had wanted to 'skin 'em alive' slid off the saddle, landing flat on his back in the slimy mud. He lay there in the sucking gumbo, waving his arms and legs like an overturned turtle.

Starr grinned at Billy and asked, "Now, can we get out of here?"

Billy answered his smile and they reined their horses west and spurred them into a canter. With pack-horse in tow they moved up main street toward the twisting road that led up the hill and out of Deadwood Gulch.

In the street behind them the muddy, cursing figure was trying to find enough leverage to make it up onto his hands and knees. Several men had come out of a store and were standing on the boardwalk watching his hapless struggle. A man in a seedy looking suit was trying to make a wager on, 'how long it would take the adle-brained fool to get on his horse.'

There were no takers nor did anyone offer to help him. One of the men watching called out, "What's the matter, Ears, can't ya ride that bronco?" Everyone laughed. Ferret Face ignored the taunting and tried to get up.

Help didn't arrive until the little man had managed to pull himself up onto his knees by using his saddle's stirrup. A tall man wearing a ripped and holed blanket poncho stopped his big black horse beside him and offered his hand.

The men on the boardwalk continued to laugh and heckle as the stranger helped the 'adle-brained' one onto his horse. They stopped when the stranger stared hard at them for a moment.

When the man turned his stallion to move back down the street, the mud-caked scarecrow stared incredulously at the man's boots. He watched carefully as the man rode away. His horse had a white spotted rump and notched ears like an Indian pony.

Ferret Face, known in Deadwood as Ears Riley, smiled muttering softly, "Big John ain't gonna believe this shit."

Caleb and Billy were halfway up the long hill leading out of town when the plainsman looked back. He unexpectedly jerked the gelding to a stop and stared. He saw the tall rider wearing the red blanket help the soft-brain onto his horse. When the rider turned his horse around to move back down the street, Starr spied the stallion's spotted rump and said aloud, "Damn my eyes, if that ain't who I think it is."

Caleb turned to Billy and said, "Take the supplies back to the ranch. I just seen me a ghost. Reckon I'd best be takin' a closer looksee."

Billy quietly sat his horse and stared at Starr. His expression showed definite disapproval.

"Don't you be starin' at me like that, hear? I'll be careful. You head on home. I'll be along, shortly."

Billy gave him a lazy smile and reined his horse back up the hill. Over his shoulder he remarked, "Long-Eye, keep a close watch on the white man's firewater. It has quick feet and will slip around behind you with its war club. Remember, we have a new corral to build tomorrow."

Billy pushed his horse into a lope, and he and the trailing pack-horse slipped around a bend. Caleb grinned at his friend's receding back and grumbled, "Gawddamned, wet nurse."

He moved his gelding back down the hill toward the muddy streets of Deadwood.

CHAPTER 30

ᴧ ᴧ ᴧ ᴧ ᴧ

Raven's senses couldn't begin to absorb all the sights, smells, and the incessant clamor. It was as new and wondrous as his first days among the Lakota. Deadwood was a whole new world for him; strange yet familiar scenes met his wide-eyed, roving gaze. Animated people and animals were everywhere. A hodge-podge of bizarre faces and figures, their bodies clothed in a variety of fashions, crowded the occasional boardwalk and muddy thoroughfare. After the quiet of the prairie, the town noise was overwhelming; teamsters screamed obscenities at their mules; whips cracked with violent authority; horses whinnied; mules brayed; men shouted and swore. In spite of his fascination with it all, Chris felt crowded and out of his element.

Disheveled women shouted from the few second story windows as they teased and flaunted their wares. A group of Chinese in uniform dress, a long, single braid hanging down each of their backs, slogged by through the clinging mud. Raven absorbed it all with relish. If bicycles, cars, and scooters could be added to the scene, he thought, I'd feel as though I were back in Saigon.

Having walked The Black nearly the entire length of the crowded street, he was about to turn the stallion and traverse the street one last time when, all at once, he stopped. A short distance up the street, a little man covered in mud was trying futilely to climb up on his horse. People in the street were slogging by him as though he wasn't even there. A group of men on the opposite side of the boardwalk were laughing, pointing, and heckling. Feeling sorry for the man who obviously wasn't a horseman, Chris moved The Black in close and gave him a boost up onto his saddle. In lieu of a thank you, Raven received a wild-eyed glare. In spite of the mud-splashed hair he noticed a bloody welt that had risen alongside of the small man's head. While turning The Black, the bunch on the boardwalk continued to guffaw and point until Raven's pale-eyed gaze drifted their way. Their laughter stopped as suddenly as a snapped cassette tape. He continued to stare at them until The Black carried him past them.

Above the normal street noise Raven could hear singing and laughter coming from an establishment that was obviously a saloon. *NUTTALL & MANN'S NO. 10* was painted in bold letters above the doorway. He remembered seeing a group of men crowding into the place during his initial ride up the street. Ignoring the shouts of a jaded-looking whore calling to him from across the street, Chris moved The Black up to the bar's hitching rail. As he stepped out of the saddle the big stallion gave him a look. Ignoring The Black's accusing eye as surely as he had the whore's imploring shouts Raven removed his soggy poncho. He threw the blanket over his saddle and spread it out to dry, then loosened the girth on the saddle. After looping the reins over the rail he checked the straps that were holding his new blanket where it was rolled behind the cantle.

He had bought the blanket at Farnum's Grocery and Dry Goods Store; it was the main reason for his coming to Deadwood. A new blanket was as necessary a part of his ceremony as Little Hawk's carved horse. He had left another important part of the ritual for Bear's Foot, finding a cherry tree and making four cherrywood stakes.

Having fastened the pumpgun underneath the stirrup fender Raven checked to be certain that it was secure and that its outline was still concealed. He gave the gun's elk-hide case a final tug, avoided the muddy puddles of horse urine, and stepped up onto the boardwalk. Chris stomped the mud off his hiking boots and absorbed the familiar bar room smells of stale beer, smoke, and spilled whiskey. He stepped through the door and walked into a hectic scene that could easily have been created in Hollywood. The saloon in the classic film Shane came to mind immediately.

Raven squeezed into a space at the bar between a hunter who reeked of old blood and a long-haired dude who could have come from Universal Pictures' central casting. With his flowered vest and striped pants he looked dressed for a role as a Western gambler.

Being completely ignorant of the current money exchange Raven pulled out several coins and slapped them on the bar. He thought briefly of the dead men of whom the money had once belonged and shrugged away any lingering guilt. Any grief over a pack of blood-thirsty scalp-hunters, he thought, was wasted effort.

A burly bartender with oiled hair parted down the middle and a big handle-bar mustache took his order for a beer.

"Sure ya wouldn't want pink gin, instead? We got us a big supply o' the stuff."

Suppressing a shudder, Chris shook his head. "Beer's fine."

Who in hell would've imagined, he mused, a rough-tough Westerner bellying up to a bar and asking for a shot of 'pink gin'?

The turmoil and volume of sound reminded him of the bars in Saigon. The most notable thing that was missing was the roaring blast of rock 'n' roll and the mixture of shrill Vietnamese and shouts of American profanity. He saw two ugly whores fighting on the stairway while another was drunkenly trying to sing from the balcony. Raven made a face and muttered to himself, "Some things are the same no matter where you are."

His beer came. He leaned back against the bar so that he could watch everybody. As his eyes swept the crowded room he half expected to see Jack Palance lolling at a poker table, dressed in black, and wearing two guns as he had in Shane. That's one thing everyone here has in common, he thought, they're all packing a weapon.

Chris sensed that someone was watching him. The hairs on the back of his neck raised. His eyes automatically went toward the door. The little man he had helped out of the mud was standing in the doorway. Even as Raven looked, the mud was drying and falling off him in clumps. Beside him stood another man, a very big man. They both stared at him as though they'd seen a ghost. The big one's mean yellow eyes appeared to be focussed on Chris' feet. The other man stood on tip-toe and said something in the bigger man's ear. Because of the bar noise Raven couldn't hear what was said, but he saw the man nod and raise his eyes. He met the man's gaze and didn't like what he saw. There was anger, plus a crazy desperation, in his hot-eyed look. Chris looked away as he thought, damn, this I don't need. I can't afford any trouble. I have to get back to Little Hawk. "This bar scene was a dumb idea," he grumbled.

He took a sip of beer and almost spit it out. It was warm! Jesus H. Christ, he thought, no wonder they drink a lot of gin.

Suddenly, Raven forgot all about his warm beer. He felt their presence as surely as if one had reached out and touched him. He looked up. Deadwood's version of Mutt and Jeff were standing right in front of him. For the first time Chris noticed that the little man he had helped out of the mud wasn't acting too normal. His beady eyes were shifting, jumping all over the place. Not again, he thought, not another nut case ... I don't need this shit, especially now. With an unexpected sudden move, the bigger man was right in Raven's face.

He was wearing filthy, ripped and torn clothing. His large right hand was hidden inside his jacket's pocket. He poked Chris with whatever object he had hidden there as he sneered and said, "You better move your ass outside, motherfucker. We got some questions for you."

Raven, his mind whirling with confusion, pushed away from the bar and moved slowly through the crowd. The smell of unwashed bodies was almost overpowering as he moved to the door. Outside, the sun slashed at his eyes, causing him to duck his head and squint. The boardwalk and street were still crowded, but Chris felt frighteningly alone. The hidden object, obviously a gun, prodded him hard in the back. The larger man's voice rasped in his ear, "Move to the back of the building."

He stepped out of the sun onto the shaded narrow path that separated the saloon and adjoining building. Raven's anxiety level was rising in leaps and bounds. A vivid picture of Little Hawk flashed through his mind. He pictured his son writhing in agony as he waited in vain for Chris' return. Nearing the back of the building he became more desperate with each step away from the crowded street.

A push from behind catapulted Raven into the open area behind the saloon. Eyes slit to keep out the sun he mindlessly noted how the fire-blackened hills came right down to the back doors of the buildings. A sharp blow to the back sent him stumbling forward and released a bolt of white-hot fury that swiftly began to take control. His rage almost pushed him into attempting some reckless retaliation. Chris spun around. Yellow Eyes was pointing a revolver at his head. He forced himself to calm down. The smaller man was hopping from one foot to the other and waving a rusty Bowie knife in the air. Spit flew as he said, "Let me cut him, Big John. Then he'll tell us what ... "

Raven's anger was a battering ram butting against his crumbling wall of self-restraint.

"Tell you what? I don't know what you're talking ... "

His thoughts abruptly tumbled together as his mind stretched beyond the limits of chance and reality. Raven stared aghast at Big John's brawny forearm. The man's sleeve had been pulled back exposing a tattoo. It was the tangled anchor and globe of the United States Marine Corps! Raven's mind felt as though it was doing flip-flops. Etched within a pair of sweeping ribbons was the inscription '3rd Marine Div. Southeast Asia, 1970'.

While Chris felt his equilibrium rapidly losing its stability the muddy knife wielder screamed in his face, "Where'd ya get them boots?"

Reflexively, he answered, "They're mine."

Big John jabbed the pistol into Raven's chest as he shouted, "You came here from that goddamn butte, didn't you?"

A vortex of whirling images spun through Raven's head as he struggled to keep a sane perspective. He thought again of Little Hawk and how the boy's life was dependent on him staying alive. The thought calmed him. He emptied his mind and forced himself to relax.

The smaller man lunged forward with the knife extended. Big John caught him and held him back. While holding his struggling comrade with one arm, he pushed Chris back a step with the barrel of his revolver. Furiously, he thrust his friend aside and yelled, "Goddammit, Ears! Kill him an' we'll never find out how to leave this fuckin' place!"

"What happened, how did you get here?"

Raven's quiet query seemed to calm them both. They looked at each other. The one John had called 'Ears' started to fidget. His eyes began to dart here and there. Suddenly, they settled on Chris. He lunged forward, waving the big knife like a sword! Big John's foot lashed out catching the much smaller man in the side and knocking him to the ground. John, yellow eyes blazing, loomed over the little man and screamed, "If you ruin this for me, I swear I'll kill you, you crazy sonuvabitch!"

Ears cowered on the ground, holding his ribs. An incredible sadness cooled and softened the big man's gaze as he turned to Raven and quietly said, "We didn't mean to do anything wrong. Shit, we were stoned, man ... "

As he continued speaking, Big John's eyes glazed, and he began to speak in a monotone as he relived his harrowing experience all over again.

"... we were up on that goddamned butte just screwin' around. You know how rowdy a bunch of guys can get. Shit, some of us had just got back from the Nam. An old Indian was there at the top; he was chantin' and holdin' this old Injun pipe up toward the sky ... "

He stopped and jerked his thumb at his partner. "... old, dumb ass Riley, he grabs the pipe from the old man. When he grabbed it, the stone part fell off and hit some rock and broke in two pieces. That old Indian ... he flipped out, man.

He started screamin' and yellin' at us in Indian ... next thing we know, we got lightnin' jabbin' us in the ass."

With a sudden, unexpected move Big John extended his gun hand so that the revolver's muzzle was almost touching Raven's forehead.

Ears Riley scrambled to his feet, his wild eyes darting back and forth between the two men.

"And I think you know all about that lightnin'," John said, "Am I right, motherfucker?" He nodded toward Chris' feet. "Those hikin' boots of yours were really a hot fuckin' item a couple a years ago, ain't that right?"

The pistol barrel never wavered as Big John's wolf eyes stared hard into Raven's pale gray ones. "We've been goin' fuckin' nuts livin' in this cruddy dump for almost a year." He grinned viciously. "I noticed that before I came along an' put this cannon in your belly, you looked like you were havin' a good time. Well, mister, we ain't been havin' a good time. Too bad Larry an' Cruiser are up at the mine, they'd enjoy talkin' to ya ..." John's sneer turned into a leering smile. "... or listenin' to you scream."

Chris' mind seemed to contract and expand, not from a fear of Larry and Cruiser, but of the realization that there were still more time-travelers out there.

Suddenly animated, Ears began to hop back and forth from one foot to the other as he beseeched Big John, "Kill 'em. Shoot 'em. Blow 'em away!"

"Shut up, Ears ... you dumb shit!" The big man's snarl momentarily quieted the smaller man.

Through it all Raven managed to maintain an outward calm. He was fairly certain that Big John would keep him alive as long as he thought that Raven could help him get out of the nineteenth century.

"The thing that's got me all excited is that you're so content ... you must have some idea how to get the fuck out of ... whatever it is that we're in ..." John put the pistol's muzzle directly on Raven's forehead and moved his leering face in close. "I'm right, ain't I?"

The shock of discovering that he's not the only twentieth century man in Deadwood was beginning to wear off. Raven was getting tired of having a gun stuck in his face and a knife whistling by his ear.

"If'n you so much as break wind I'm puttin' a bullet in your brain-pan!"

Raven's eyes shot to his right. Caleb Starr was standing less than ten feet away! The pistol in his right hand was extended at arm's length and was pointed straight at Big John's head. For less than a heartbeat, nobody moved. In a soft voice Chris said, "Don't even think about it ... don't move. I've seen him shoot."

Big John looked deep into Raven's eyes, sneered, and said, "Fuck you."

With impressive speed the big man ducked, pivoted, and shifted his aim. Before he could squeeze the trigger his head snapped back. The flat hard report of the gunshot crashed against Chris' eardrums like a thunderclap. A black hole, suddenly rimmed with red, was stark on Big John's pale forehead as he fell backwards through the gunsmoke.

Even before Big John's body had stopped jerking, the narrow-faced Riley was off and running.

"Let him go!"

Caleb's pistol was already tracking him when Raven's shout caused him to lower his revolver. They watched as the little man scuttled around the far corner of the saloon and was gone.

Before Raven or Caleb was able to exchange a word the back door of the saloon flew open, and the mustached bartender was standing there with a double-barreled, ten gauge leveled and ready to let fly.

"You all right, Caleb?"

Not waiting for a response the bartender's roving eye settled on the body sprawled at Raven's feet.

"Peers like Big John ain't." He watched Starr tuck his big revolver away in its holster and nod at him.

"I'm obliged, Mike ... for you comin' on out here."

Mike, the bartender, bobbed his oily head and replied, "Weren't no trouble, Caleb."

Faces suddenly appeared in the doorway behind Mike. The bartender shooed them away before turning back to Starr and saying, "Shoot, I still got my eye on that little filly you were gonna sell me."

He grinned a gap-toothed smile that reminded Chris of the movie actor, Ernest Borgnine, as he added, "Ya could say, I'm protectin' my interests."

Raven fought down the nausea caused by the shock of John's revelations and his sudden death. He proffered his hand and forced a smile.

"Once again you've saved my ass, Caleb Starr."

Starr grinned and took his hand. He gave it a brief shake as he said, "Well Christopher, it weren't no big thing. You'd have done the same for me."

Caleb turned away and spat an amber stream onto the body lying in the muddy grass.

For some reason, Chris felt obligated to explain what happened. He glanced at Mike and said, "Those two douche-bags brought me out here at gunpoint and were..."

Raven paused. He couldn't think what to tell them. "They, uh, were going to kill me."

Mike was staring at him, looking puzzled. Oh shit, Chris thought, he doesn't believe me.

The bartender's eyes narrowed. They looked like two hard, blue marbles as he leaned forward and asked, "What in the hell're doosh-bags?"

Raven's mouth fell open and he stammered, "It's a, ah ... robbers."

Mike gave his toothy smile again, leaned back, and nodded. "When Caleb here asked me if'n I'd seen someone lookin' like you, I told him I seen ya leave. Didn't take note 'o the other two though. But then, I been used to seein' them jaspers."

Mike glanced at Chris' hands. Raven looked down and saw that he still had the mug of beer. He dumped it out and handed the mug to Mike.

Caleb spat again. Gesturing toward Big John's body he asked, "What's the name of the weasel-faced runt who was a friend of this'n.?"

Mike replied, "That'd be Ears Riley. He's a bit soft-brained." He smiled. Welcoming the chance to gossip he added, "Got the name 'Ears' 'cause he killed a Chinaman and cut his ears off. Some say he wears 'em around his neck on a string."

While Mike and Starr continued to talk, Raven felt a chill move up his spine. His thoughts turned inward as he remembered again the horror of Vietnam, the ear collectors and other ghouls among his comrades and enemies. He shuddered and shook off his haunting memories.

He interrupted Caleb. "I'm sorry, my friend, I have to go. My son is very sick and needs me."

Caleb's dark eyes studied Raven's gray ones. Turning to the bartender he said, "Mike, set me up a shot of gin. I'll be in shortly to settle up."

With a nod and wave for the bartender, Raven moved into the gloom of the lane separating the buildings. He glanced at Starr who was following close behind. He felt like hell leaving the plainsman so soon, but the longer he stayed would be unnecessarily risking Little Hawk's health, and maybe his life.

It wasn't until he stepped back into the sunshine and saw the busy street full of animated people and animals that the thought hit him. Except for the handful from the bar, not one person came to investigate the gunshot. Even as he was thinking of it another gunshot came from up the street. The flow of pedestrians and horsemen were unaffected by the sound of gunfire. Must be a pretty normal happening around here, he thought.

"I see you still have the stud," Caleb said. "That's one fine lookin' animal."

Chris nodded and smiled as he said, "Don't say it too loud; he'll hear you."

Caleb grinned and spat into the muddy street as they approached the hitching rail. Starr's gelding was tied next to The Black. Raven freed his reins and looked at Starr as he said, "I feel bad about this, Caleb. I've only been in town long enough for you to save my neck."

Caleb slapped him on the shoulder and replied, "Shoot, Christopher, don't let that worry you none, I understand. That boy who's sick ... would that be Little Hawk?"

Trying not to let the concern show, Raven nodded and said, "He'll be all right. But he needs me to be with him as soon as possible."

Caleb turned aside and spat into the street. "I know how ya feel. You feel 'bout as useless as teats on a boar hog. With younguns, sometimes there just ain't a thing a body can do."

Caleb paused for a moment lost in thought. He threw a quick glance at Raven before continuing, "I recollect tellin' you that I had me a Crow woman I had taken as a wife; she died a few years back. I'll never forget the look in her eyes when she held our young 'uns for the first time. That was somethin', that was ... 'twas a good number of winters ago, before I went off to war."

A faraway look appeared in Starr's eyes as he absently stared up the street. He looked back at Chris before continuing, "I got me a pair of sons, twins, they be. One boy, he took to ranchin' real natural like. The other ... well, he's different than his brother. We don't see many things eye to eye ... but shoot, he'll come 'round."

Chris stepped into the stirrup and mounted The Black. His gaze noticed the curious brand burned onto Starr's buckskin, a five pointed star encircled by a larger 'C'.

Caleb smiled, stepped forward, and casually grasped the stallion's bridle.

Raven asked, "How old are your boys, Caleb?"

Starr's head lowered as he calculated the years. His eyes glistened as his gaze met Raven's.

"Damnation, they must be 'bout fifteen, sixteen years old. Before he showed up at the spread a couple a days ago, I hadn't seen Nathaniel for nearly a year and a half."

When Caleb began talking about his son, his posture diminished and he actually looked vulnerable. Knowing his strength, Chris was surprised.

Starr glanced aside and absently watched the people slogging by in the mud before continuing, "Peers he's a bit mixed up, can't seem to make up his mind if'n he's red or white ... sorta acts like he don't want to try bein' both. I'm thinkin' maybe I'll tell him 'bout you and your boy and how we met."

Squaring his shoulders Caleb met Raven's gaze and held it as he spat into the street and said, "He's got it in his craw that I'm the only white here that'll treat an Indian fair. Except for you, I reckon he 'bout called it right."

There was an awkward silence until Chris stuck his hand out and the two friends shook hands again.

"He'll come around, Caleb."

Raven's quiet assurance appeared to lift the plainsman's sagging spirits. He grinned as he replied, "I reckon you're right, Christopher."

They said their goodbyes in the awkward way that men have, and Raven assured Caleb that he would stop by his ranch as soon as Little Hawk recovered.

Giving Starr a small salute, Chris reined The Black away from the railing. The big stallion dug his hoofs into the mud and broke into a canter, scattering a group of Chinamen and causing a handful of cussing miners to make room on the busy thoroughfare. Raven looked back, but Caleb Starr had disappeared into Saloon No. 10. Chris stared wistfully for a moment. Soon, he thought, I hope to vanish from the top of Bear Butte and the nineteenth century just as easily.

WASICHU'S RETURN

PART 5

Wasichu's Return

EXCERPT FROM THE JOURNAL OF CETAN CHIKALA (LITTLE HAWK)

▲▲▲▲▲▲▲▲

Silently I watched Wi's orange light illuminate the towering butte sacred to my people. Captured within the day's fading sunlight, Bear Butte stood tall and proud while I lay among my blankets like the weak and helpless.

Where is Okute? The sun moved so much slower when I was forced to be still. I felt like the mouse that was being hunted by the hawk. I dare not move. Okute had told me that if I did not lie still, the demon inside my stomach would burst and spread his poison all through my body.

A large shadow passed over me, and Bear's Foot's quiet rumble interrupted my thoughts.

"He comes."

Since my new father's return from the west, Bear has treated him in much the same way that he treats our chief, Crazy Horse. If one were to listen for it, as I have, hidden within his voice there was a new respect and love.

Okute slowly walked The Black into our camp. Before dismounting, he stared at his backtrail and our sacred hills. He and Bear spoke for a moment, but their words were too soft for me to hear. I knew that something was bothering Okute, but he did not speak of it with me. He did ask of my well being and even placed his hands on my face and throat. Perhaps, I thought, by doing so he was able to tell if the demon was asleep or awake.

261

Later, after speaking some more to Bear's Foot, Okute took his knife and began cutting on the cloth bag that he called a backpack. It was the same travois-like bundle he was wearing when I had first seen him walking on the prairie several moons ago.

I watched carefully as he cut two holes in the bottom corners of the bag. He also arranged some leather straps that would loop around the openings. Not knowing what his efforts were for, I soon tired of watching and felt weariness pull my eyes shut. My mouth was full of a cloying sweetness caused by the honey flavored rocks that Okute had brought me from the wasichu's village high up in the Paha Sappa. The candy, as Okute called it, was a comfort for me as I rested. Soon the candy was gone and I began to doze. I awakened when the demon began to bite and chew. I did my best to ignore him and encouraged the drone of Okute and Bear's Foot's voices to soothe and blunt the pain. In time, I could not fight the pain any longer, and I felt the claws of the demon pull me down to 'walk in darkness' along an unknown, fearful path.

I heard a breathing other than my own. My body felt like a moth enclosed within his cocoon; yet, I felt my legs swinging free. I opened my eyes to an eagle's view of the land far below. Wi's closing light bathed the prairie in its special colors. The darkening, cloudless sky appeared more vast, than ever before. Where, I wondered, was the surface of the lake where we had camped? It was at that moment that I realized where I was. I was nearing the top of Paha Mato, and I was being carried on Okute's back like an infant in its cradle-board. The trail twists and turns so that the campsite is on the other side of the butte. Okute had me positioned in such a manner that I was facing away from him with my legs dangling through the holes I had watched him cut into his backpack.

I felt the demon stir when my cocoon shifted and I slid, as Okute maneuvered his way through a more difficult portion of the trail. I squeezed my eyes shut and clenched my teeth to keep from crying out. I felt myself begin to drift away as Okute's soft words helped to dull the gnawing edges of my pain.

"Brave up, Hawk. We are almost at the top."

My eyes opened to the realization that I must have walked in darkness again. We were on top of the butte. I was lying within what had to be one of our sacred circles, of the type used in holy ceremonies. The circle was made with four cherrywood sticks pushed into the ground to indicate the four directions. Tied to each of the stakes were four strips of colored cloth; each of the four colors represented one of the major races of people in the world. Inside the circle was Okute's gun-with-no-barrel and my family's spotted horse carving. Okute was standing near the eastern stake. Except for a new blue blanket wrapped around his waist he was naked. His arms were raised and he was chanting a prayer to Sky Father. As he finished and moved to the next stake I noticed that clouds had formed in the dark sky and had begun to act in a strange manner; they were moving in different directions. As I puzzled over this weird phenomena a strong gust of wind swept the top of the butte. Thunder simultaneously assailed my ears and caused me to jump and awaken the sleeping demon within me. I grasped my stomach and listened as Okute chanted louder so that Sky Father could hear him over the loud voices of the Thunder Beings. Lightning began to light up the sky like a flaring council fire. I glanced at Okute and saw him stagger from a sudden gust of wind that nearly swept his blanket away.

My heart began beating as hard as a boy would strike his first drum. I was terrified! Lightning was now striking all around the butte. I pressed my hands to my ears to keep out the loud anger of the Thunder Beings as they cast their lightning lances everywhere. The noise was becoming as loud as the Bluecoats' wagon guns.

Okute finished his prayer and allowed the wind to push him toward me. As he stumbled toward me, I stared. I couldn't believe what I was seeing. Okute was smiling. No, that is not right ... Okute was grinning! The grin was as large as what would be on a wolf's face after he had pulled down his first deer. Had the storm frightened him so badly, I wondered, that his mind had blown away with the wind?

Okute hovered above me. The wind made him sway as though he were weightless; it whipped his hair and blanket in completely different directions like the clouds. As powerful as the wind was, it couldn't remove Okute's strange smile. I saw his lips move as he spoke. Because of the wind and Thunder Beings, I was not able to hear all of his words. I did hear him say, "It is happening, you will see and hear many strange things that will frighten you, Hawk. Try not to be afraid. I will always be nearby watching over you."

Okute said some other words but they were blown away. The lightning bolts were striking close at the bottom of the butte. Shivers of fear climbed my spine as Okute dropped to the ground beside me and put his strong arm across my chest. I grabbed his arm and held on tight. Knives pierced my ears with blades of sound as lightning struck the top of the butte. My breath was sucked from my mouth as I felt Okute's body, as well as my own, raise into *the air. Pain sliced through my stomach as our bodies were slammed back to the butte's surface. Grit was in my teeth and eyes as a wavery, swirling darkness snatched away my last conscious thought and I began my journey of walking in darkness.*

CHAPTER 31

ΛΛΛΛΛ

A familiar, yet strange, sound was invading Raven's psyche. Although a distant sound it roared and thundered enough so that he opened his eyes. A generous scattering of stars spread across the dark sky like sequins glittering on a black velvet stole. When the sound came again Raven started to rise. He stopped when he became aware of the pressure of Little Hawk's head on his arm. Carefully, so as not to wake him, he lifted the boy's head just enough to free his arm. Little Hawk's skin felt hot and dry. Chris got to his feet and stared down at the young Sioux who had become such an important part of his life. Little anxiety alarms began to send signals that raised the hairs on his arms. He didn't know for sure, but Raven suspected that it wasn't normal to run a high fever with appendicitis.

Pausing only long enough to pull on a long-sleeved shirt underneath his vest, Raven quickly began to collect his gear. The snarl of sound came again. He hurried to the western lip of the summit and looked down. A shudder, followed by a jolt of surprise, raced through his lean frame. In his concern for Little Hawk's health he had momentarily forgotten. I'm back, he exclaimed, we made it back to the future!

Far below were a half dozen dipping, weaving, yellow lights. They illuminated the gray ribbon of the county road that slashed its way past Bear Butte. Because of the perspective of his view Raven was puzzled by the strange sight. When he realized what he was watching a brief smile touched his lips. Motorcycles, he thought. I'm staring at a bunch of bikers playing in the road like a group of wayward kids. That's one confrontation I think I'll pass on, he mused. At least for the moment.

Swiftly turning away from the edge Raven finished collecting his belongings and moved back to Little Hawk. Along with the awareness that he'd made it back to 1976 came the urgency that had brought them there. He knew that he needed to find a doctor, and he had to do so right away. While he prepared to leave his eyes lifted and looked to the south where a few lights were visible. To the right, in the southwest, there was a subtle glow about five or six miles away. Hidden by foothills and the encompassing trees was the small town of Sturgis, South Dakota. Chris' attention was drawn back to the south where the closer lights winked invitingly at him. He knew that beneath the few lights was Fort Meade, a remnant from the old cavalry days. It had been partially converted into a Veteran's Administrative Hospital. It was there, about four miles away, that Raven hoped to find medical assistance for Little Hawk.

When Raven began to put his gear together panic set in. The pipestone horse carving was gone! Calming himself he tried to think rational thoughts. After he had borrowed it from Little Hawk, Chris had used the horse in the ceremony, just as he had when he went back in time and the carving had disappeared then, also. Later, it had resurfaced in the possession of the rightful owner. Confused as to who should have the carving, Chris moved again to the spot where he had left it. When he squatted to sift through the rock and debris he felt a hard lump in his jean's pocket. Puzzled, Raven got to his feet and pulled the object out. His head spun as reality disappeared and the impossible made its presence felt. The pipestone artifact glowed softly in the palm of his hand. It was while staring at the horse carving that the thought hit him. If I had this stone horse in the spring, he reasoned, it would be a safe assumption that I would still have it now in the late summer. Raven shook his head in frustration and pocketed the artifact. If I continue to try to make sense of it all, he mused, I will go nuts.

With Little Hawk still rigged into the confines of the backpack, Chris sat down and propped the boy up. He maneuvered himself around so that he was in a position to hoist him onto his back. When Raven straightened and adjusted the weight on his back a low moan came from the young Minneconjou.

"Okute."

The weakness in Little Hawk's voice frightened Raven. His own ignorance of the ailment only added to his fears.

A sudden increase in the motor noise from the county road below momentarily diverted Raven's attention. He wondered what the young Lakota could possibly imagine would be making such a clamorous racket.

Gently he said, "All is well, Hawk. Rest. Soon you will be well again and we can go home."

Glancing over his shoulder Chris saw that he had again drifted off into sleep. With pumpgun in hand he carefully moved across the starlit summit and started down the trail that would lead him back to the twentieth century and all that he had chosen to relinquish.

Nearing the bottom, Raven moved swiftly past the dark shape of the A-frame building that was the Bear Butte Park information center. He moved rapidly down the hill and crossed the road that led to the center and eventually came to a fence. Climbing the fence he felt Little Hawk stir as his weight shifted inside the pack.

A sudden acceleration of the roar of motorcycles drew his attention to the right where he saw the six bikes race south on the county road that led to the two-lane highway. The road ran east and west and passed in front of Fort Meade on its way into town. He absently wondered if Sturgis' annual motorcycle rally was in progress.

The stars gave him enough light to see that he was crossing a large field. Here and there among the grass were patches that appeared lighter in color than the grass. When he moved close enough to identify the patches, he was surprised; it was dried cattle manure. Raven didn't remember any cattle grazing near the butte. A loud snort from an obviously large animal stopped him in his tracks. For a frightening second he thought his heart had stopped along with his feet. When he thought he could breath again, Chris began to look for the guilty party. The sound had come from the treeline which was a dark smudge directly in front of them. While he squinted in an attempt to see form within the colorless smear of trees, a large, blacker portion of the mass began to move. It began to grow in size, informing Raven that it was moving toward them. As his eyes tried to penetrate the weak light he willed his heart to keep beating. The threatening mass abruptly left the hazy shadows of the treeline and stepped into the open pasture where its size grew until it loomed. Chris' swallow sounded loud. The pallid light from the stars was enough to clearly show the upswept horns and the thick, curly tangle of his immense head.

"*Tatonka*."

Raven's whispered exclamation was half relief and half apprehension. The huge, bull buffalo was standing less than thirty feet away.

Slowly, he began to move to the bison's left. The large shaggy head turned with him every step of the way.

"*Tatonka?*"

Little Hawk's soft query was so unexpected it startled Raven. He had been so focussed on the buffalo that he had almost forgotten his piggy-back passenger.

"Yes, Hawk. He is probably trying to figure out what type of two-headed animal we are and if he should bother to chase us away."

Chris continued to move. The bull watched but made no sudden, threatening move in their direction. After he was past the trees and the bull was out of sight, Raven remembered having seen the penned buffalo last spring. Fine time to think of it now, he mused. Climbing the fence to take leave of the pasture, he looked back for a final time to assure himself that the big animal hadn't changed his mind and had somehow managed to sneak up on him.

Climbing a gentle slope he shifted Little Hawk higher on his back and said, "*Tatonka* is behind us now, Hawk. Soon you will meet the medicine man that will remove your demon."

Although Raven held his breath so that he could hear the boy's reply, all he heard was the swish of the knee-high grass against his jeans.

After a few eventless miles Raven was relieved to see the lights of a car in the distance as it passed by, right to left. Beyond the road he could see the yellow glitter of the street lights scattered throughout the grounds at Fort Meade. When he approached the paved road Raven looked both ways for cars. As soon as he reached the safe shadows

of the trees on the other side of the road, Chris grabbed
hold of the backpack and pulled while he twisted around so
that he could see as far back as possible.

"Hawk?"

From the corner of his eye he could see Little Hawk's
head slumped forward, chin on chest. He didn't move.

CHAPTER 32

∧∧∧∧∧

Raven breathed a sigh of relief and looked toward the double doors that Little Hawk had just been hustled through. His roving eye saw the framed prints on the walls and the fake plants next to the plastic chairs and sofa. The receptionist was an older woman with a blue rinse in her white hair. Raven mentally shook his head and wondered if there was anything in the room that was real.

His worry for Little Hawk wouldn't allow him to relax, so he killed time with pacing. Just as he noticed that Blue Hair was keeping a wary eye on him, the double doors swung open and a man wearing green cotton scrubs and a bad hair piece entered the room.

Under his breath, Raven muttered, "Jesus H. Christ."

Although Chris was the only person in the waiting room, Hair Piece had to have the receptionist point him out. With clipboard in hand the man breezed over to him. He gave Raven a brittle smile and readied his pen and said, "Name?"

Raven scowled and asked, "How's the boy?"

"I'm sorry but I can't give out that information."

"Who can?"

Not liking the look in Raven's eye the man swallowed and replied, "Doctor Harris."

"Get him."

"Well ... he's on call."

Raven's rage began to simmer.

"You mean to tell me that you haven't called him yet?"

"Well ... I ..."

"I phoned the doctor. What's the problem?"

The voice came from behind him. Raven turned to find a dark-haired, attractive, middle-aged woman standing a few feet away. She was staring at him with a bemused expression on her face.

The woman was dressed the same as Hair Piece, but the similarities ended there. This lady, he mused, knows what's going on. Raven's anger subsided and he felt less alarmed.

Before answering her question, he glanced at her name tag, 'Wendy Perot, R.N.'

Chris spoke quietly as he replied, "Nurse, a while ago I brought a young Lakota boy in here for treatment. I'm not a doctor but he appears to be suffering from appendicitis"

"It just so happens you may be right ..."

The woman's calm, pleasant manner had a soothing effect on Raven's anxiety. Her brown eyes searched his face as she continued, "Are you the boy's father?"

"Yes. I'm his step-father. Is he going to be all right?"

Her direct gaze fixed on Raven's face as she replied, "Yes, I believe so. Would I be correct in assuming that you, Mr. ...?"

"Raven. My name's Christopher Raven."

As he gave his name, Chris looked at Hair Piece. The man looked miffed but wrote it down before he stalked away. Wendy Perot smiled and continued, "Mr. Raven, have you had some medical training?"

"Just in the army. I was in Special Forces."

"Then I feel you will understand. I took some blood tests from your son and his white count is very high. There is some major infection at work. Instead of contacting the doctor on call, I phoned a surgeon, Doctor Jones; he should be here at any moment. He will examine him and determine what the next step will be."

Seeing the worried look on Raven's face, the nurse tenderly added, "If I recall correctly, wasn't the expression 'hang loose, it don't mean nothing' used a lot in Vietnam in situations like this."

Raven grinned at the woman's clumsy, if heartfelt, attempt to calm his fear. "Thanks. It shows, huh?"

Wendy Perot returned his grin then looked momentarily puzzled as she asked, "May I ask why he wasn't brought in sooner? Surely his symptoms were evident long before now."

Having been prepared for the question, Chris replied, "Little Hawk ... ah, I mean Bobby ... and I were camping up in the hills. We had hiked and climbed a long time so that we could be alone. Turned out not to be the smartest thing I could have done."

The sound of a door closing somewhere out of sight animated Wendy. As she turned to leave she said, "The doctor's here, Mr. Raven. Would you give the receptionist your name and whatever else is needed? I'll be right back."

Without waiting for his reply the nurse hurried out of the room. Raven stood in the middle of the empty waiting room and thought of Blue Feather. He wondered how he would be able to face her if his worst fears came true. The shadows from the cheerless, poorly lit room seemed to close in on him as he slowly moved toward the lady with the blue hair.

CHAPTER 33

ΛΛΛΛΛ

Raven couldn't stand sitting any longer. While he paced he recalled how after signing papers to give the surgeon permission to operate, he had to lie. He gave the receptionist Joe Spotted Horse's widow's home address and phone number as his own.

It was fortunate that he still had it written down and stored away in his billfold. He had forgotten that she now lived in Pine Ridge rather than up north at Eagle Butte. With Joe's wife, Suella, being Oglala, it was only natural for her to be near her parents while Joe was at war, and especially now, after Joe's death.

He glanced for the umpteenth time at the swinging doors where they had wheeled Little Hawk into surgery and thought of the nurse, Wendy, and of the lies he was forced to tell her. His fabrications were major ones but were necessary to get help for Little Hawk.

Raven had asked her to look after his son, because he would need special attention when he comes out of anesthesia. He told her that he'll be terrified. Chris went on to explain that his son was raised by his wife's mother who was a fanatical, traditional Lakota. Her influence was so domineering, Chris lied, that Little Hawk speaks nothing but Lakota and knows very little of modern ways. His grandmother insists that there is a *wanagi* (spirit) in the boy's head that keeps him from accepting modern ways.

275

Raven's musing was interrupted by the throaty roar of a pair of motorcycles as they pulled into the parking area. Judging by the motor rumble, he thought, they have to be Harley-Davidson bikes. When the motors were shut off the quiet returned as though its serenity had never been interrupted. Raven peeked out the window. Two burly, outlaw biker types were coming up the sidewalk supporting a third man between them. Before moving from the window Chris noticed that one of the Harleys had a side-car.

"This is just great," he muttered to himself.

Not having a reputation for showing great patience with macho bikers, Raven sat down out of the way and tried to become invisible.

The biker trio stomped noisily through the door. The engineer boots and their assorted chains and leather made a lot of racket in the quiet room. The one in the middle was whimpering and cradling his right arm as he limped into the room. His jeans were ripped and bloody along the length of his right leg. The biggest of the three, a bearded giant, seemed to take pride in being the filthiest as well. Raven was at least ten feet away, and if asked, he would have sworn that he could smell him.

The third biker wasn't as tall as the other two but was twice as wide.

Staring at the older woman behind the desk Bearded Giant bellowed, "Where in the fuck's the doc?"

Raven saw the blood leave the receptionist's face as she stammered and tried to regain her composure.

For the first time since leaving it there, Chris thought of the pumpgun hidden inside a hollow oak just outside the gate. He struggled for composure as he watched the biker bully the poor woman.

"Where the fuck is he? We got us one injured son-of-a-bitch here!"

Blue Hair managed to calm herself enough to reply, "He ... he is in surgery."

She turned her head in Raven's direction as she added, "... he has an emergency appendectomy."

All three heads swiveled and six hostile eyes were aimed at Raven where he sat against the far wall.

He couldn't resist a patronizing wave and a cheerful, "Hi, fellas."

The bearded one's eyes narrowed and just as he was about to say something, one of the adjoining doors burst open and Hair Piece entered the room.

He apparently had come from the operating room, because he was in scrubs from head to toe; the top of his head was covered and a mask hung from his neck.

All attention had instantly fallen on him. The only sound was the injured biker's incessant whining.

Raven silently got to his feet; his gaze was riveted onto the pale face of the new arrival. Before he was able to ask if Little Hawk was all right, Bearded Giant got in the man's face and asked, "Are you the doc?"

Intimidated, the man mumbled, "No, no ... I'm just the resident."

The wide biker's brow furrowed as he asked, "Ya mean ya live here?"

Bearded Giant elbowed him aside with a snarling, "Shut the fuck up! I'll ask the questions 'round here."

He stared hard at the sniveling, injured man and added, "You shut-up, too!"

"Hey, Resident!"

Raven's shout brought a blanketing silence with it.

The bearded one roared, "Who the fuck are you!?"

277

Patience gone, Chris' anxiety over Little Hawk's welfare over-shadowed his good sense. He had to shut the man up and look after his son. Raven gave in to his mounting fury and pulled the long-barreled Colt free of its shoulder rig. He cocked and aimed the pistol at arm's length at Bearded Giant.

"I'm the man that's going to put a new hole in your fat face if you don't ... may I quote you? ... shut the fuck up!"

It became very quiet. He caught a glimpse of a round, white face topped with a swirl of blue hair. Chris made eye contact with the resident and asked, "How's my son?"

The resident, his face glistening with sweat, replied, "He's doing fine. The problem was appendicitis as diagnosed. Dr. Jones has just removed the infected appendix."

"Good. Now unless you're needed back in surgery, how about taking care of the injured man? Looks like he's got a broken arm."

The resident's pale face dipped and he gestured for the man to accompany him down the hall.

Raven's gaze flicked over the two bikers, and he gestured to a pair of plastic chairs that looked capable of supporting their weight.

"Have a seat, boys. It may take him a while. Right now he's probably on the phone talking to the cops."

Bearded Giant's eyes hadn't left Chris' face since he'd pulled the gun. They were burning with hate. He growled, "I'm goin' to get you, motherfucker, and you goin' to wish you were dead."

Raven moved closer to the door. Keeping the revolver pointed in the outlaw bikers' general direction he took a peek out the window. Nothing.

"I'm leaving now. If I see either of your ugly faces so much as peek out the window, I'm going to put a bullet hole in both those shiny bikes of yours."

The other biker grabbed Bearded Giant's arm as he implored, "Don't let him hurt my Harley, Big Lou!"

Big Lou continued to glare as Raven silently slipped out the door and was gone. Without giving his friend a glance, Big Lou replied, "Shut the fuck up."

CHAPTER 34

▲▲▲▲▲

With all the lights and the occasional vehicle passing by on the county road, the darkness had lost its density. Raven leaned back against the cool metal of the railing that encircled the playground and looked up at the brightly lit golden arches. He crumpled the Big Mac wrapper and listened to the quiet hum of voices coming from McDonalds. His thoughts drifted and returned to Little Hawk. He gave a small sigh of relief as he remembered what had happened earlier.

He had hidden outside in the trees near the parking lot. He watched the police arrive with their lights flashing. Their doors burst open and with guns in hand they had rushed into the building. One of them had even come outside and made a token but futile search of the area. It wasn't too long after that the cops left. Raven knew that he was now a marked man. Every cop within a hundred mile radius had his description and knew that he was 'armed and dangerous.'

A short time after the police left, the trio of bikers came out and went on their merry way. The one with the broken arm in a sling was still whining, and Big Lou was still telling him to 'shut the fuck up.'

It wasn't more than an hour later that the nurse, Wendy Perot, came out and moved briskly toward a 1971 brown Ford. She was putting her key in the lock when Raven's voice stopped her.

"Don't be frightened, it's me, Raven."

Chris saw the nurse jump and slowly straighten. He could have sworn he saw her face pale. But in the weak light it was impossible to tell.

"How's the boy?"

"He's fine. You were right, he was terrified when he came out of anesthetics. But he calmed down."

Raven noticed a quaver in her voice. She's frightened, he thought. Why?

Wendy Perot turned the key and opened her car door. Her eyes strained to see into the shadows, but try as she would she couldn't see Raven. "We're going to have to be honest with each other," she said.

She thought at first he wasn't going to answer, then his voice startled her when it came from an entirely different place than before.

"Why do you say that?"

"Because you didn't tell me you had a gun, nor that the boy's name really is Little Hawk and that he doesn't understand English. You said that he doesn't speak it."

Raven paused. He sensed that her fear was gone. I like this woman, he thought. She doesn't scare easily and she doesn't run to someone else when she doesn't understand something ... or, at least, I don't think she does.

"You're right. I should have told you more ... about Little Hawk. I'm sorry."

"I didn't tell you that just to wrangle an apology out of you. What I meant was ... I wasn't entirely on the level with you either. I speak Lakota. I'm a quarter blood Hunkpapa, and I was married to an Oglala."

Raven stepped out of the shadows. Wendy Perot held her ground and it was obvious she wasn't afraid of him.

"Thank you for what you've done."

"My pleasure. Now get in the car, I'll give you a lift into town."

"Thanks, but how ..."

Wendy grinned impishly and her arm swept out indicating the two other cars in the lot, as she said, "Well, since I know who those cars belong to ..."

Raven grinned and shook his head in self derision, as he replied, "Had I completed it, that would have been a stupid question."

Wendy laughed and slid behind the wheel and unlocked the passenger door. As Raven climbed inside, she softly said, "*Hohahe* (Welcome), Okute."

Raven grinned and before he could catch himself, he replied with, "*Palomo* (Thanks)." The smile slowly left his face as he realized that she had tricked him.

"I'm sorry. I had to know if you were Okute. You are all that boy talks about. I know that there's something strange about this whole situation, but ..."

Raven held out his hand in a supplicating manner and was about to speak, but Wendy quickly raised her hand to stop his words, and said, "I don't want to know, okay?"

The quaver is back in her voice, he thought.

"It's enough for me to know that this boy worships you. He mentioned some things that scared me to death ... I don't want to know anything about you or where you're from, all right?"

Somewhat shaken by the nurse's revelations, Raven nodded and turned away. Wendy started the car and drove away from Fort Meade.

The police car eased around the corner. Its lights brushed across the windows of McDonalds. The multiple reflections interrupted Raven's thoughts. He watched the car from the shadows as it slowly accelerated and disappeared around another corner. His thoughts returned to his conversation with Nurse Perot.

Luckily, she had left the subject of he and Little Hawk's strangeness and had told him more of the boy's prognosis. It wasn't until she had dropped him off at the small park near the high school football field that she became frightened again. Raven thanked her for everything and commented, "What an unusual site for a football field." He was staring at the rock cliff that hovered over the whole length of the northern side of the field. Suddenly, her pale face was peering up at him. She stared at him with wide, scared eyes and said, "Before the surgery Little Hawk awoke for a moment. He asked me if Dr. Jones was the medicine man who was going to remove the demon from his belly." She stared at him, then asked, "Can you explain that?"

Going with his instincts, Raven chose not to tell another elaborate lie. He shook his head and looked back toward the unusual ball field. He didn't even look when he heard her car pull away.

Another car turned the corner near where he was standing and its bright lights brought Chris back to the present. He was beginning to get a little nervous as he watched the car disappear around the corner. All the McDonald customers were gone now. Feeling somewhat conspicuous, Raven moved deeper into the building's shadows and suffered the assorted aromas associated with fast food establishments. Another car moved down the deserted street. It was moving slowly, and it was the right color but there was a major dent in one of the fenders. Why hadn't she mentioned that?

Chris moved out into the open and watched as the old model Buick pulled over to the curb. He peered through the window at the attractive Lakota woman behind the wheel. She looked frightened.

"Get in. Please hurry."

Her eyes were looking, watching everywhere as Raven opened the door and slid in next to her.

"Hello, Suella."

Suella Spotted Horse turned and looked at him with frightened eyes as she whispered, "Hello Christopher."

CHAPTER 35

⋏⋏⋏⋏⋏

Raven waited until they were on I-90 moving east before breaking the painful silence.

"I'm sorry I haven't been to see you sooner."

Suella kept her eyes on the road and shrugged a shoulder as she said, "It's all right Christopher. I know you were going through some rough times, just like me."

Her black eyes touched Chris with heartfelt compassion. He felt a tightening in his throat as he looked at her. The depth of her scarcely hidden sorrow consumed him. Her gaze left him and returned to the road. He felt both relief and a sense of loss.

The light from the dash played across her striking features. Her beautiful face was beginning to show some of the strain of reservation life. It had to be tough raising a son without his father. And Raven knew that with her great beauty and pleasant personality, Suella had her pick of the lot.

"How's Marlon?"

"Marlon's fine. He misses his father, but who doesn't."

Chris cringed inwardly at the subtle bitterness in Suella's voice. He scrunched down in his seat and tried to relax.

"I apologize for my phone call. Maybe I shouldn't have dragged you into this mess. At the time it seemed the thing to do. I hadn't planned on becoming a wanted man. The bikers, along with my temper, put a crimp in my plans."

Suella glanced at Raven. Her smile brought a new brightness to the car's gloomy interior. Her voice had some of her old fire behind it when she said, "Joe used to laugh and tell me about the trouble you two would get into. He would say it was because of your 'inability to take a backward step'."

Thinking of Joe, he felt the old familiar tug in his chest and catch in his throat.

"We had great times together, Suella. Too bad it had to be in the middle of such a shitty little war."

"I know you did. We had some great times, too."

Raven glanced her way and saw a tear slide down her cheek. She didn't bother to wipe it away; both hands stayed on the wheel and her eyes on the road. Knowing it was best to not say anymore, Chris shut his eyes and let the drone of the motor lull him to sleep.

The sudden lurch as the big Buick hit gravel and bounced over a pothole, caused Raven to bolt upright in his seat. Suella swerved back onto the blacktop. Her brief smile brightened the front seat's interior as she said, "I just wanted to see if you were faking sleep, so you wouldn't have to talk."

Chris grinned and rubbed his hands over his face in an effort to wake up.

"You haven't changed, Suella. Still a little bit *witke* (crazy)."

"I'm sorry for my sad face earlier. You deserve better than that, Christopher," she said with a dazzling smile.

Shaking his head, Raven replied, "I'm the last person who you should ever feel a need to apologize."

Suddenly, he sat up straight. He saw a building up ahead lit up like a Christmas tree. An adjoining field served as a parking lot; old cars and pickups were parked every which way.

"What in hell is that?"

"That's Carlos' Place. It's right on the edge of the res. It's an old-time roadside tavern. It's the only place I could talk Aaron into agreeing to meet you."

Suella wheeled the Buick into the gravel turnaround and stopped the car. Carlos' looked like it was the only building for miles, but Raven knew it was just an illusion. There are probably several hundred Sioux within a couple square miles, he thought.

"Are you sure you wouldn't rather take the chance that the sheriff won't check my house."

Suella's words startled him. He'd been thinking of Joe's brother, Aaron. He'd never been able to figure out why the man didn't like him. He smiled and shook his head.

"Aaron said that he would hide you for two days, no more. Has he ever told you why he doesn't like you?"

Raven glanced her way and shrugged. "I was just wondering about that, myself."

Raven opened the door to get out and stopped. He noticed the dome light didn't come on. He looked on the frame for the button and saw that it was taped down so that the light wouldn't be activated. He looked at Suella and she quickly looked away.

The year before, the traditional Lakota and those in support of the chairman of the Oglala, Dick White, had been fighting constantly. Murder reigned, while death and terror followed in the wake of White's roving teams of muscle men who were nicknamed goon patrols.

The instant Raven felt the tape on the door's switch, he had remembered its purpose. The year previous there had been many murders after dark when the victims were exposed by the dome light either getting in or out of a car.

"You mean to tell me that the 'goon patrol' bullshit is still going on?" Chris' question bristled with anger.

Suella's shoulders drooped with resignation as she nodded and said, "Sorry, Christopher. I didn't tell you because I didn't want you to worry. It's our problem and we are handling it. Please. I don't want you to get involved."

Raven was quiet for a moment then slowly nodded and gave her a small smile. "You are one tough lady."

Seeing the opportunity to lighten the mood, Suella made a fist and shook it at Raven as she proclaimed, "And don't you forget it, *Wasichu*."

When Chris started to get out of the car, she grabbed his hand. He stared into her midnight eyes as she continued, "You come back, Christopher. When you do, I want to hear the truth about what happened at the hospital and why you were there. Okay?"

"You've got my word, Suella. It won't be soon. I may have to wait until I'm back in this area again, to tell you. And you might not believe it when you hear it, but I will tell you."

She released his hand and Raven stepped out into the warmth of the night and shut the door. Suella treated him to one last smile before accelerating and pulling out of the parking lot.

He stood there and stared at the tavern. He could hear music, raucous laughter, and shouts, the usual bar noises. It was probably the last place he would have picked for a meet such as this. Hell, for all he knew the sheriff's department stopped by every hour on the hour. Once again, he thought, *Aaron Spotted Horse is showing his disdain toward me and my friendship with his brother.*

With a disappointed shrug Raven wove between a couple of cars. They were so pitiful he stopped and looked closer. The two Indian cars were so dented and rusted out they looked like a pair of battered prize fighters facing each other for a final, painful round. He stepped around another car that had a few more rounds left, and approached Carlos' noisy doorway. He made his approach with the same caution that he would if he were walking into a lion's den.

Raven stepped through the doorway and stopped. Heads turned, smiles disappeared, eyes became hooded and suspicious. The smell of smoke and stale beer hit him in the face like a fist. The place was packed and his was the only visible white face. The sound level diminished rapidly, as though a hand was steadily turning down the volume. Every dark face in the joint was pointed at him. The hostility was so thick in the air, Raven would have sworn he could smell it mixed with the spilled liquor and smoke.

"*Washtay.*"

Raven's greeting seemed to hang in the air and then bounce from corner to corner with more echoes than you hear at the Grand Canyon. Of course, this was in his mind. The reality was that you could actually have heard the proverbial pin drop.

"*Washtay.*"

Hearing Aaron Spotted Horse's reply encouraged Raven's heart to begin beating again. Aaron's chunky frame pushed away from the bar and ambled toward him.

Joe's older brother stopped beside Raven. His unsmiling face was only inches away as he slowly reached up and rested his heavy arm across Chris' shoulder and faced the throng of seated and standing Lakota. His husky voice sounded loud in the quiet. "You remember my brother, Joe?"

289

Heads bobbed their concur and voices were raised in assent as Aaron raised his hand to quiet them. His hand fell heavily on Raven's shoulder.

"This wasichu was also Joe's brother."

A hum of quiet, animated conversation moved through the room. Several were nodding agreeably.

"They were together in Vietnam, for a long, long time. Joe told me this man saved his life; not once or twice, many times. I never liked this man. It wasn't until my brother was dead and on his final journey that I realized something."

Here and there a voice would query, in both Lakota and English, just what was it he realized?

"I was jealous. In my whole adult life, I never met a wasichu that wanted me to be his friend. Now for the first time, I am asking a white man for his friendship."

Raven was stunned. Aaron Spotted Horse turned and offered his hand, as he said, "*Wonumayin* (A mistake has been made)."

Raven grasped the older man's hand and embraced him. As the room returned to its normal chaos and the noise level began a rapid ascent, hands came from everywhere grasping him and giving a friendly squeeze.

Aaron steered him to the crowded bar and a space appeared like magic. For the first time since returning to the 20th Century, Raven didn't feel like a displaced person.

CHAPTER 36

∧∧∧∧∧

The Lakota who made the announcement had been looking out the window.

"Two cars. Both are carrying apples," he proclaimed.

While trying to understand the man's meaning, Raven noticed that the sound level lowered drastically. It was then he remembered that traditional Lakota referred to Dick White supporters as apples; they are red on the outside but white on the inside.

The front door opened with a bang. Two very large, very drunk, middle-aged Lakota stumbled into the bar. They preceded a short, chunky Lakota who sported horn-rim glasses, a crew-cut and a sneering smirk. The crew-cut and the smirk could only belong to one person, Dick White. Raven grinned inwardly as he thought of the traditional nickname for him, 'Little White Dick.'

While the first pair cut a swath through the tables for their boss, three more bigger than life Indians crowded into the place. The big boys commandeered a table occupied by a couple of old drunks. The table was right next to the back door so the big, brave warriors bodily threw the two hapless old men outside. Raven felt rage begin to kindle a small flame in his belly. He forced himself to ignore the incident and picked up his talk with Aaron. The Lakota had been telling Chris about his and Joe's early years on the res. Raven listened with one ear; his other noticed how the noise level had picked up again. He also noticed that the 'party' atmosphere had disappeared; very few smiles were evident and the sound of laughter was clearly missing. A subtle tension had entered the bar along with White and his goon guards. Chris tried to forget it and enjoy himself ... he agreed with something Aaron said and laughed at an anecdote about Joe, but his heart wasn't in it. He glanced in the mirror behind the bar and saw that one of the goons was staring at him with a drunken leer. Raven looked away and tried to stay cool by thinking of Little Hawk and Blue Feather. He looked back and saw the pudgy Dick White laugh heartily at something one of his bodyguards had said. The drunken goon was still staring at him. Chris' simmering anger began to boil.

"Let's get out of here. I'm pretty well beat."

Raven's request seemed to take Aaron by surprise.

"Why's that?"

He grinned and said, "Aaron, if I were to tell you how far I've traveled in the past twenty-four hours, you would not believe me. All I'd like to do now is hole up for a couple of days and give the cops time to forget about me."

Aaron somberly studied him for a moment then smiled and nodded. "Sure thing, Christopher. I got just the place for you to stay. *Hopo* (Let's go)."

Aaron pushed away from the bar. Chris finished his beer and turned to follow. He stopped. Aaron was moving toward the back door. He saw Raven hesitate and said, "Come on, my car's out back."

Knowing he'd have to move past the goons, Raven cursed under his breath. He sensed that something bad was about to happen. Following Aaron, he kept his gaze straight ahead. As he was about to squeeze by Dick White's table, a hand clasped his wrist in a vice-like grip and stopped him.

Raven tried to ignore the heat that was rising from within and looked into the drunken face of the huge goon who had ahold of him.

"*Miye yuska* (Release me)."

The big Indian was having a problem focusing as he tried to peer into Chris' eyes.

"What the fuck kinda Indian are ya"

Ignoring him, Raven's pale gaze lifted until it settled on Little White Dick's narrow-eyed face.

"How about jerking on your boy's leash here. I don't need any trouble."

White smirked and didn't answer.

Aaron had stopped and come back. He rattled off some rapid-fire Lakota at Dick White that was too fast for Chris to follow. One of the other goons stood up and shoved Aaron back.

Chris absently noticed that once again the bar had become abnormally quiet.

The vice tightened on his wrist as the drunk jerked and pulled Raven closer as though he wanted to whisper something. Chris, trying desperately to hold back the fury, complied. He leaned close and held his breath. The man reeked of cheap booze and sweat.

"Hey. I wanna show ya somethin'."

Raven's eyed were locked into the man's glaring stare, so he didn't see where it came from. Later he would remember how the Indian had moved and would realize that the gun had been strapped to his leg.

Moving fast for as drunk as he was, the goon stuck the muzzle of a snub-nosed .38 up under Raven's chin and cocked it. Raven didn't move. He barely dared to breath.

"How ya like my gun? I just wanna show it to ya ... see what ya think," he slurrred.

Inside of Raven a war was being fought; fear was trying to push his rage aside. It wanted him to yield to his survival instincts and plead for his life. In the last micro-second before submitting, his pride teamed with his rage and pushed his fear out of the picture.

The man was so drunk he was swaying in his chair. Inane laughter bubbled from his slack lips as he poked the barrel harder under Chris' chin. Calmly, Raven spoke in Lakota. He said, "I would like to see that gun. I never saw a pistol with its barrel sawed off. Did you do it?"

Confusion caused the Indian's black eyes to roll around like marbles in a bowl. Drool came from his lips as he stammered, "I never cut ... it come's ..."

The instant Raven felt a slackening of the pressure under his chin, he moved. With blurring speed his right hand grabbed the revolver around the cylinder with a vice-grip of his own and slid a finger between the hammer and the firing pin. The cylinder, clamped in Chris' fist, had to move to enable the gun to fire; Raven had bet his life that the drunk wouldn't have the strength to pull the trigger. He won the bet.

With a twist and jerk the gun came free. The drunk tried to stand up, Chris planted his hand on the man's face and shoved, slamming him back onto his chair. One of the other bodyguards stood up. Raven reversed the pistol, extended his arm, and aimed it between the Indian's eyes.

"You don't really want a piece of this action, do you?"

The goon saw the red flames of rage flickering in Raven's gray eyes and sat down.

The tavern had become as quiet as when Chris had earlier showed his white face in the doorway.

Raven didn't notice; his rage had all but consumed him. It was all he could do to keep from emptying the revolver into the drunk's head. Instead, without once taking his eyes off Dick White and his burly henchmen, Raven pulled his vest aside, exposing the long Colt nestled in its holster and swung the snub-nosed revolver's cylinder out and spilled four of the five rounds onto the sawdust and beer covered floor. He left the fifth bullet inside one of the .38's chambers. Eyes still matching White's narrow eyed stare, Chris slammed the cylinder shut and spun it. Trembling with suppressed fury, he grabbed the drunken Indian by his hair and rammed the muzzle of the gun's short barrel against the man's forehead. The Lakota's eyes widened with fear. His mouth gaped. Raven pulled the trigger. The dry, crisp snap as the hammer struck the empty chamber sounded loud in the deathly quiet room. The Indian sagged. Chris released him as vomit shot from the goon's mouth and splattered over Dick White's shoes. Enraged, he stood up. Raven stepped forward, pistol poised. Pure venom radiated from the pale eyes.

"Christopher! We must go."

Aaron's voice sliced through Raven's rage and instilled some much needed reason. Without breaking eye contact with White, Chris followed Aaron Spotted Horse out the door and into the cool night air. He threw the .38 as far as he could into the dark. The simple act seemed to cleanse his soul of his mindless fury and drain him of energy. It was all he could do to pull himself into Aaron's old Chevy and slam the door. When they pulled out of the parking lot, had he looked back, he wouldn't have seen one red soul brave enough to stick his nose out the tavern's door.

CHAPTER 37

▲▲▲▲▲

Raven stared up past the leaves of the tree at the changing blue sky and absently wondered if it was still July or was it now August. Whatever it is, he thought, it's the here and now, and I can't do a damn thing about it. One thing I can do, he mused, is get the hell out of here and go back to where I belong. What happened at Carlos' he reasoned, tells me I don't belong here anymore. Back there it doesn't matter what your politics are or what month, day, or year it is, the important things being whether you have food in your belly, clothes on your back, shelter from the weather, and weapons to fight off your enemies.

He sat up and looked around him at the dismal terrain. His was the only tree within view from horizon to horizon. In the west the sky was rapidly changing to gold and orange and the day's light was dimming quickly.

Earlier that afternoon when Raven had left, Aaron had not returned from town. He had left a thank you note and a pair of 1874 double-eagle coins. In the note he said that the coins could be worth several thousand dollars if he and Suella could find the right collector. With his parting comment he had told Aaron that he had risked enough for him and he would find his own way back to Sturgis.

Chris got to his feet and began walking west along the county road. After a couple of miles he knew that he had left the res, the land was slowly beginning to look fertile and more prosperous. On the horizon was the blue mass of the

Hills. Enjoying his solitude and the nature of the land, he watched as a hawk swooped down and cruised the adjoining field at grass level. Ahead of the gliding predator a ground squirrel disappeared down a burrow, while a mother meadowlark hobbled away from her nest in an attempt to lure winged death away from her offspring.

A breeze ruffled Raven's hair and brought with it a remembered scent of wildflowers and tilled earth. It was also a reminder of how it had all begun back in April, walking along a similar county road.

The sound of a fast approaching vehicle interrupted his recollections. A new, gray Toyota Land Cruiser pulled up alongside and stopped. A shadowy figure behind the wheel smiled and asked, "Need a lift?"

Raven had covertly checked the license plate to be sure it wasn't a law enforcement truck, so his ready reply was, "Sure thing." He stepped up into the passenger seat, shut the door and looked into a pair of friendly blue eyes that were somehow familiar. The man was a stranger but there was something about him. He appeared to be in his early forties. Shaggy, dark hair went well with his weathered, lean features. He stuck out his hand. Raven shook the surprisingly soft hand.

"Name's Dan ... what's yours?"

"Chris."

Dan released the clutch and they accelerated down the road. While shifting, he glanced at Raven who was sitting relaxed and staring straight ahead. Raven felt his eyes on him and met his blue-eyed gaze.

"Where you headed?"

"Up Sturgis way."

"You're kidding ... that's where I live. Or, rather, near there. I'm about five miles east of Sturgis. I have a little place up on a ridge that overlooks Bear Butte, and the plains north of the Hills."

Raven glanced in the back seat at the easel, camera, tripod and assorted bags of equipment and tablets.

"You a photographer?"

Dan grinned and shifted into fifth gear.

"Artist. I spend a lot of time on the Lakota reservations. I photograph the people and sometimes use them in my paintings. At first I thought you were a Lakota, they're usually the ones you see walking alongside a road."

Being drawn to the man by his good-natured manner, Chris responded in kind. He grinned as he said, "I have a lot of Lakota friends. Of course, only their best qualities would have rubbed off on me."

The artist laughed and replied, "You know, you could be right. That sounded an awful lot like something a Sioux might say. Their sense of humor is one of the things that keeps me coming back."

In spite of the man's good humor, Raven suddenly began to get paranoid. He worried that the man might ask too many questions he couldn't answer. Without being rude, he told the guy he was exhausted and asked him to wake him at his turnoff. Seeing the slightly confused look on Dan's face, Raven turned away. He secretly watched Wi put the finishing touches to his nightly canvas of golden splendor, as he feigned sleep and waited for the night.

Darkness settled in and brought nearby Rapid City to life with a sprawling display of neon and residential lights. Beyond the glittering, serpentine length of the small city rose the dark mass of the Black Hills. Both men were lost in their own thoughts as they moved onto westbound I-90 and soon left the town lights behind. As they moved west and followed the northern edge of the Hills, the only lights to be seen were their own and the other vehicles moving east and west on the busy Interstate.

Raven woke with a start. They had stopped moving. Everywhere he looked he saw motorcycles and bikers; their various chrome and leather accouterments gleamed beneath the bright street lights. He knew at once he was in Sturgis.

"I decided I might as well bring you into town. It'd be tough trying to catch a ride on the Interstate."

"I really appreciate that, Dan."

Making sure there were no cop cars nearby, Chris stepped out of the Land Cruiser and offered his hand. Dan gripped it and handed him a business card, and added, "If you stay in the area or pass through here again, give me a call. Maybe we have some mutual friends on the res."

"Thanks again. I really appreciate the ride."

"No problem. Take it easy."

Raven pocketed the card and watched the Cruiser turn the corner and disappear behind a brightly lit gas station. The steady clamor coming from main street pulled his gaze in that direction. He looked again at the hundreds of motorcycles and mingling bikers lining the street. Chris shook his head, and thought, what great timing I have. I return to the area just in time for the peace and quiet of Sturgis' Annual Motorcycle Rally.

Before passing through the biker area, Raven put his red bandana on his head pirate style. Having seen bikers wearing bandanas in that manner, and with his elkskin vest and jeans adding to the costume, he felt he couldn't miss. They'll think I'm one of them, he thought. Just the same, when he moved in among them he kept a sharp eye out for Big Lou and his dynamic duo.

Social chaos was everywhere. Everything from tattooed cleavage to a fully bearded minister riding a Harley and wearing bib overhauls was on display. He saw one guy wearing nothing but a big smile, colored jockey shorts and engineer boots. His braless 'mama' sat behind him on his Harley in a wet tee shirt, filing her nails. Raven began to think that maybe he wasn't so inconspicuous, after all.

He turned the corner onto a side street and gladly left the din of shouted conversations, revving bikes, and ribald laughter. He walked north. Straight ahead, on the next corner was a sign for a combined bowling alley and lounge. It conveniently bordered the street that would take him out of town to the V.A. hospital at Fort Meade. He made a final adjustment, making sure his revolver was completely out of sight, and pushed open the glass door.

Fifty feet straight ahead a door to the lounge was closing. Loud rock and roll poured from the obviously overcrowded bar as though relieved to find some space of its own. To his right was the normal clatter and bang associated with bowling alleys. Raven glanced at the short order counter on his left before turning right and right again into the men's room.

He wasn't prepared for the sight that was waiting just beyond the door. He pushed the door open and stared in disbelief. The three stooges: Larry, Curly and Big Lou were all crowded into the small rest room. All three displayed shock and instant recognition. Whiner, his right arm in a cast, was at the urinal. The wide-bodied Einstein was on the toilet and of course, Big Lou, gentleman that he was, was taking a piss into the sink.

After his close encounter at Carlos' the other night, the sight of the three bullies brought on an adrenalin rush and immediate rage. Knowing that if he didn't do something fast, he faced the possibility of a three against one beating.

Wasichu's Return

With uncharacteristic viciousness, Raven attacked. A short, hard left to Big Lou's kidney brought a howl of pain from his tangled beard. He made the mistake of trying to put his penis back in his pants before retaliating. Big as he was, he never had a chance. Once, twice, Chris' fists hit him in the face and throat. He gagged and clutched his bruised windpipe. Whiner's fate was equally as swift. A short side kick slammed him face first into the wall and urinal. He screamed when his broken arm made solid contact with the wall. Wide-body's pants weren't all the way up when a kick to his solar plexus followed by a neck strike put him on his knees. Big Lou, his face beet red, was still struggling to get enough air when Chris buried his fist in his enormous stomach. Big Lou's expelled bad breath, mixed with all the other stenches in the rest room, was nearly enough to put Raven down and out.

As he swiftly exited and hit the fresh night air of the street, the last image retained on Chris' retina was that of Big Lou as he slowly slid down the partition that divided the stool and sink. Sticking to the shadows, Raven moved past the park and the high school football stadium. Just as he was approaching the last street light before leaving town, he searched his pockets for something to blot the blood from his scraped knuckles. All he came up with was the card the artist had handed him earlier. Curious, he glanced at the blue lettering. As he drew into the street's halo of light, the printed legend seemed to leap off the card and bury itself in Chris' brain.

DANIEL CALEB STARR
Painter of the Historical Old West
Painter/Illustrator/Muralist
Blucksburg Mt., Sturgis, SD
Phone 347-0099

HOMECOMING

PART
6

EXCERPT FROM THE JOURNAL OF
CETAN CHIKALA (LITTLE HAWK)
ᐱ ᐱ ᐱ ᐱ ᐱ ᐱ ᐱ ᐱ ᐱ

When I returned from 'walking in darkness' the demon was gone. The wasichu medicine man had to open my belly to release him. Since I came to this unusual land, there have been so many strange sights I cannot, and do not, want to remember them all. Okute should have warned me of some of them.

Never in a hundred winters would I have thought that there was a land with giant silver eagles. The day following the night the demon was removed, I saw one fly by my window. It was very big and roared like a grizzly! I was terrified because I could not run. The opening the medicine man had made to remove the demon was very sore, and I was unable to leave my pallet. Another thing that frightened me was what the wasichu apparently did to punish other wasichus. It seemed that the medicine man would shrink them until they were able to fit inside a shiny, wooden box. The small prison had a big glass window so that they could be watched. I don't think they were allowed to sleep. Strangest of all was how the old wasichu I shared my room with, and his visitors, would sit and watch the people in the boxes; sometimes they would even laugh at things they would see inside.

Then there was the time the medicine man put something metal on my chest that had thongs leading to shiny metal sticks that were stuck in his ears. The Hunkpapa woman, Wendy, told me he could hear my heart and other things inside my body. When I asked if he could tell if the demon was gone she became frightened and dropped one of the medicine man's bowls and he became angry. When Wendy spoke to him in their strange tongue, his eyes became big, and when he looked at me I could see the fear swimming in them. In all of my thirteen winters it was the first and last time I ever saw a medicine man afraid. Afterwards, I never saw the shaman again. He must have been called away to another village to remove other demons or shrink bad wasichus to put in the boxes.

Everywhere I looked I would see new and unusual things. Whenever I would ask Wendy about them, it seemed to confuse or bewilder her, so I tried not to ask anymore. I did ask often about Okute and when he was coming to get me. I was anxious to begin our journey home. After spending two nights and a sun in their giant lodge I was able to walk by myself as long as it was done slowly.

During the second sun, I found where they had hidden my clothes. I sensed that Okute would come for me soon, so I hid them again so that I was certain to have them when we left. I was worried that the strange wasichus would make me return home wearing the garment I had been wearing. In my mind I could almost hear the Oglala girl Fawn's teasing voice asking me why my clothing has no back to it. The foolish girl would probably wonder if I had grown a tail while in the land of wasichus.

On the third night, I awoke knowing that someone was in my room. Being in this lodge belonging to the usually treacherous wasichus, I cautiously turned my head. My heart soared like the eagle. Okute was standing beside my pallet!

"Okute!"

He brought his finger to his lips, shushing me. Behind him I saw the smiling face of Wendy. I was glad to see that she was no longer confused and was happy.

Keeping his finger on his lips, Okute nodded toward the other pallet where the aged wasichu was sleeping, and softly said, "Looks to me, Hawk, that you are ready to go home."

"Yes, Okute. I wish to leave soon before I do something to anger the wasichu medicine man."

"Why would he be angry with you," Okute asked, in a whisper.

"I do not know," I told him, "I just do not want to be shrunk and put in a box with all the other little people."

Okute looked at me as though my mind was gone and I had become witke (crazy). He looked at Wendy, who frowned as though she knew that my mind was gone. Okute must not have seen one of the prison boxes, and the Oglala woman must have been around the white man so much she had become used to his peculiar ways.

While Okute talked with Wendy, I pulled my clothes out of hiding and put them on. I still could not move quickly without pain, but it did not matter. I was going home.

With Wendy leading, we followed some tunnels with windows and did not see one wasichu. In no time at all I smelled the sweet night air. Wendy came to me to say goodbye. She pulled me gently to her and held me close. She smelled like wild flowers and made me think of my mother and how I would be seeing her soon.

The moon was up and I waited in the shadow of the big lodge while Okute spoke with Wendy. She gave him something and he put it out of sight before I saw what it was. I saw moonlight reflect off an object that he in turn handed to her. This time I was able to see; it was one of the wasichu coins that had our sacred eagles carved on them. As he was leaving, Okute spoke to her some more and Wendy's face began to show confusion and fear again. Before we moved out of sight behind the building, Wendy and I waved goodbye.

Moving at a slow pace so that I didn't stumble and injure myself, Okute led me through the shadows to the edge of the building, then beyond and in among some trees and brush. Beyond the trees there was the prairie. I watched as Okute pulled the pumpgun out of a hollow tree. He then moved a deadfall aside and brushed away some dirt and grass that had hidden his blanket and his travois pack, with the holes cut for my legs. Okute glanced at the pack then looked at me and grinned.

"Let's put you in this for the walk and climb. We must hurry. I am anxious to see your mother," he said.

I was also anxious to see my mother. But, being almost a warrior, I did not wish to tell Okute.

In no time at all, I was comfortably seated inside the travois pack. Before Okute lifted me onto his back like a cradle-board, he smiled as he placed my two-shot gun in my hand, and said, "Take this in case the buffalo has objections to our crossing his grass."

It was then that I noticed the looming profile of Bear Butte. I was totally perplexed. I had been to the sacred mountain many times with my people. Never before had I ever seen this strange tribe of wasichus around here. Why must we climb Bear Butte again and anger Sky Father? It was all too confusing for me. Perhaps, I thought, if I had more winters I would understand. I decided that when we returned home, I would ask Okute.

A sharp pain pierced my lower belly as I was lifted onto Okute's back. Shortly after he settled me onto his back the pain went away. While Okute was preparing, I was still facing the butte and the open prairie. It looked like we were standing next to a narrow gray river, but I knew that it could not be; not only could I not smell it, I could not hear it either. I could hear something, though. It was a frightening noise that was getting louder. And the noise was accompanied by a bright light. Both came toward us with an amazing speed unlike anything I had ever seen or heard before. I became terrified! The light had become so bright I tried to shield my eyes with my hand.

"Okute!"

Hearing the fear in my voice, Okute spun around. In doing so, he spun me around also and I did not see what caused the bright light and the horrible roaring noise. As it passed us, I did catch a glimpse of what looked like a man crouched on top of some beast that was going so fast I could not see its legs. There was a bright, red glow coming from its behind. Could its tail have been on fire? What kind of animal could it have been!? My heart was pounding and I felt short of breath.

"Hawk, did you see?"

"Han (Yes). What was it, Okute?"

"I am not sure. I hoped that you could tell me. Well, at least it is gone now. Let us go home."

Okute crossed the gray ground that looked like a river but was as solid as stone. We soon entered a ravine that led down to the prairie where it gradually undulated and spread out toward Bear Butte. Suddenly, I felt exhausted. I decided that I was glad to be leaving this land of strange wasichus and unbelievable sights. It was not a place that I would have been happy to live in, and I did not think other

Lakota would like it, either. I closed my eyes and thought of Bear's Foot, my mother, Fawn, and all my other friends as I prayed to Sky Father for thunder and lightning.

CHAPTER 38

▲▲▲▲▲

Raven opened his eyes to darkness. The stench of sulphur was in his nostrils. Am I back, he thought, or is the smell of brimstone coming straight from hell? Rolling onto his side, Chris peered to the east and saw color forming on the distant horizon. Thank God, he muttered. Stumbling to his feet, he checked Little Hawk and found him to still be asleep but breathing easily. He quickly dressed and moved to the western edge of the summit. After the remembered view from Bear Butte in the daylight, his view at the moment was very disappointing. He could see absolutely nothing except a black void. He couldn't even see the lake where Bear's Foot was camped. When he looked to the south and southwest, he was overjoyed by the sight of absolute darkness. Had he still been in the twentieth century there would have been lights.

"I'm back," he murmured. "Thank God we're back."

By the time Raven reached the bottom of the butte, the fresh morning air had invigorated him, and the rising sun's rays had spread across the land and bathed the rolling prairie in golden sunlight. So close to home, his thoughts turned to Blue Feather. The last time he had seen her had been in the early morning's light. Perhaps now, he thought, they would be together for a prolonged period of time.

Climbing a slight rise, he saw the sun reflect off the distant lake near their former campsite. He wondered if he was going to catch Bear's Foot still asleep in his blankets.

311

Chris smiled as he thought of the relentless teasing he would inflict on his friend. Little Hawk, still asleep, stirred and muttered unintelligible words. As he walked, Raven adjusted the pack's shoulder straps and stared ahead to where their camp should have been. He began to feel uneasy. I should be able to see the horses by now, he thought. The lake was to the left of where their camp had been. There. Bear's Foot stepped from the bushes and waved. Relieved, Chris enthusiastically waved back..

"Freeze, motherfucker!"

Raven's heart plummeted as he stopped in mid-step.

"You so much as twitch, I gonna blow the Injun brat right off your back!"

He felt Little Hawk start and awaken because of the man's harsh voice.

"Okute. What has happened? A black wasichu is pointing a rifle at me."

"Don't do anything to anger the man, Hawk. Everything will be fine." Raven's mind whirled with confusion as he sought to understand this new attack. While he listened to the man closing in, Chris carefully watched the Indian he mistook for Bear's Foot. How could I be so foolish, he silently berated himself.

"Ears said he had a feelin' we should be careful with you ... shit, you don't look like you're anything worth worryin' about."

With his words came the identity of his assailants; they had to be the other time-travel friends of the dead man, Big John.

The pumpgun was snatched out of Raven's hand and a rifle muzzle poked him in the back of the neck. The same black voice exclaimed, "Git your ass movin'; we ain't got all day. Where you been? We're anxious ta climb the butte and get the fuck outta here."

As they approached the camp, Chris' stomach tightened with dread. Where's Bear's Foot? Is he alive?

After a closer look at the Indian, he couldn't understand how he mistook him for his friend. The Indian in question was a little over average height, well built and had a small, sculpted nose; just the opposite of Bear's Foot. Judging by his hair style he appeared to be Crow. He watched as the Indian removed a pair of feathers from his hair. He placed the feathers in his shirt and put a large black hat squarely on his head. He grinned at Raven and turned away. I guess, Chris reasoned, my mind played a trick on me because I was expecting to see Bear's Foot.

"Hey, Larry! Look what we got here."

A tall skinny man with scraggly hair and a full beard had stepped out of the cluster of trees and walked toward the camp, carrying an armful of dry wood.

Raven stopped on command and quickly checked out the campsite. He only had time to notice some blankets spread out in the grass close to the water. Where, he wondered, is that blood-thirsty little monster, Ears? He glanced at Larry who walked past him, apparently on his way to the lake. Larry returned Chris' look with huge eyes. That one look into his eyes was all it took to scare the hell out of Raven. Behind the beard and the hair, the man called Larry was badly frightened. His fear was so close to the edge, it made him a very dangerous man.

A sharp pain exploded alongside of Raven's face. A huge black man, obviously their captor, had stepped in front and slapped him. Somewhere deep inside Christopher Raven, another fuse had just been lit.

"What you starin' at, boy?"

313

The man had ex-military written all over him. He was wearing a faded fatigue jacket and scuffed jump boots. His size was so immense he reminded Raven of Bear's Foot. As though reading Chris' mind, he asked, "Where's your Injun friend?" His question was followed by another hard slap on the side of his head.

Calming himself, Chris shrugged and fought to ignore the ringing in his ear and the fury that was sizzling in his soul. He was very conscious of Little Hawk trapped on his back. He knew that if he was knocked down, he could possibly land on Little Hawk and hurt his new incision. Raven stayed loose and glanced toward the Indian tracker who was standing nearby, impassively watching.

The tracker was dressed in a skin shirt and some wool trousers. The rifle cradled in his arms looked cleaner than he did. Beneath the straight hat brim, he had a big white smile on his dark face as though he enjoyed witnessing Raven and Little Hawk's dilemma.

The black ex-soldier gestured toward the Indian before he proclaimed, "John Crow here ... he saw your buddy's tracks right along with yours. He was here when you left and damned if he wasn't here alone, just before we got here. Looks like he saw us and took a fuckin' hike. Would he do that, or is he still out there?"

Raven was saved from having to answer by an unexpected ally. There was a sudden rustle in the bushes over near the small group of trees. Ears Riley stumbled out of the trees. He pulled suspenders up over his narrow shoulders and buttoned his baggy trousers. Trying to look important, he slapped a cartridge belt on that was weighted down with pistol and knife and swaggered toward them. He angrily addressed the black man, "Goddamn it, Cruiser. I told you to wait. I wanted in on this!"

"Fuck you, you little piss-ant. Who put you in charge?"

Raven's mind was desperately seeking a way out. He couldn't think. He knew he had to get Little Hawk off his back and out of the line of fire.

"Okute, who are these *wasichus*? Where is Bear'?"

"Tell that goddamned kid to quit his jabberin' or I'll cut his lips off," Cruiser said.

Chris was momentarily concerned that Little Hawk didn't understand English. He had no way of knowing if the man's baleful stare and vicious manner frightened Little Hawk; he did know that it scared the hell out of him.

"Let me take Little Hawk off my back so he can rest, and I'll answer your questions. The boy just had surgery a few days ago."

Both Ears and Cruiser stared aghast at Raven.

With Chris' tracks having lead to Bear Butte, and with no returning sign, they hung around knowing he must have been on that butte or back in the future. When Raven spoke of Little Hawk's surgery, now for the first time, it dawned on them that he really had just returned from the future. Talking about going back was one thing, but knowing that the man standing before them had actually done so, momentarily blew their minds.

Quick to take advantage of their surprise, Chris slipped the pack's straps off his shoulders and lowered Little Hawk to the ground. He straightened in time to catch a glancing blow from Cruiser's big fist. The punch caught Raven high on the cheekbone and stunned him enough so that he dropped to one knee.

"Nobody said you could put the fuckin' kid down," the big man snarled.

When Cruiser stepped forward to hit him again, Chris straightened and buried his fist in the much bigger man's crotch. Cruiser bellowed like a gelded bull! Raven followed with a short, power punch that landed just below the man's left ear, dropping him to his hands and knees.

"One more punch, and I'll gut the boy like a fish!"

Raven's eyes, dark with rage, swivelled like twin cannons and zeroed in on the hated, shrill voice of Ears Riley. The demented little man was crouched beside the sprawled form of a terrified Little Hawk. He had one fist buried in Little Hawk's hair and the other was wrapped around his rusty Bowie knife. The point of the huge blade was pressed against the boy's taut, brown belly. At the junction, a crimson tear of blood made a single tacky trail across Little Hawk's skin until it disappeared down his lean side.

A chill climbed Raven's spine and drove an icicle of dread into the base of his skull. Fear for his son's life pulled the strings that moved him away from the battered soldier, Cruiser.

Ears' crazy eyes were jumping here and there like drunken water bugs.

"It wouldn't bother me a bit ta give this kid another incision; one that no doc can ever fix." Ears' utterance was all the more sinister because of its quiet delivery.

There was nothing quiet about Cruiser's scream of fury. He lunged to his feet and viciously grabbed the front of Raven's shirt and vest and raised him up onto his tip-toes as easily as if he were Little Hawk's weight. Raven couldn't breath very well, but he rejoiced that he wasn't searched. The Colt's weight hanging beneath his left arm gave him hope.

"Larry! You got that fire goin!?"

"Yes, Sergeant," Larry replied meekly.

"Goddamn it, quit callin' me that!"

316

Larry, busy feeding small sticks into the fire, rolled his eyes in fear and nodded emphatically.

Unnoticed by all, the sun had risen and created a golden morning by bathing the prairie in its light.

Putting his face inches from Chris', Cruiser grinned maliciously as he softly said, "We gonna burn your honky ass, motherfucker. We gonna do it first, and then ask you how we can get back to the real world."

He grinned and dragged Raven toward the small fire.

Little Hawk tore loose from Ears' grip and got to his knees and shouted, "Who are these men, Okute? Give them what they want before they hurt you!"

John Crow looked on with a bemused expression on his dark, handsome face as Ears yanked hard and pulled Little Hawk back to a sitting position. The boy gasped and grabbed at his abdomen, his small face twisted with pain.

Little Hawk's cry of pain was all the motivation Chris needed to break Cruiser's iron grip on his shirt front. He grabbed the big man's thumb and yanked it back. There was a sharp snap and scream as Cruiser's thumb broke as easily as one of the twigs Larry was busily feeding to the fire. He abruptly released Raven, who tripped over a rock and fell. He scrambled quickly to his feet and stepped out of reach. Too late, he saw his revolver lying in the sand near the big man's feet. It must have fallen from his shoulder rig when he fell.

Cruiser stared incredulously at his broken thumb as it dangled from his huge hand. Cradling his injury, his eyes focussed on Raven and quickly filled with evil and pending malice.

Inexplicably frightened, Larry jumped to his feet and stepped back. His feet splashed into the shallow waters of the lake; not noticing that the morning sun had painted the water a burnished gold.

Releasing his damaged hand, fury contorted Cruiser's broad features into a mask from hell as he reached inside his army jacket and pulled out Bear's Foot's Randall Fighting Knife.

Chris' heart seemed to stop beating. God, no ... tell me he's not dead. Please God, he thought, not Bear's Foot.

Cruiser pushed the knife out in front of him, edge up, and growled, "I'm gonna have ta cut you for that, mother-fucker. I gonna feed ya your own balls."

Raven tensed and assumed his fighting stance. Rage and grief battled for control as he awaited the man's attack.

Cruiser stepped forward and reality vanished in an explosion of water, reeds and mud. Behind him, a few feet from shore, a small island of brush, grass, and reeds rose suddenly into the air with a towering eruption of flying water and mud.

Mouth agape, Raven stared.

Shedding weeds, mud, and water like an attacking sea monster, Bear's Foot charged from the lake. The sun's golden light glanced off the dripping, great knife clenched in his massive hand.

Cruiser barely had time to turn before Bear's glistening, naked body slammed into him like a land-locked killer whale. The sound the two huge men made as they came together made Raven cringe. As if agreed upon, the combatants each stepped back.

Cruiser stared and exclaimed, "Who the fu ..."

With unbelievable speed for such a big man, Bear's Foot lunged forward, caught Cruiser's rising knife hand, and buried his own blade to the hilt beneath the man's left nipple.

Wasichu's Return

A strangled grunt and groan emitted from Cruiser's gaping mouth as he remained upright and stared into Bear's Foot's enraged glare. The Minneconjou stared into the dying man's eyes and said, "There is a time for talk and a time to fight. You did not choose your time wisely."

The spark of life left Cruiser's eyes. Bear's Foot, looking ludicrous with mud, grass, and reeds piled onto his head and shoulders, pulled on his knife; it came loose with a liquid sucking sound as Cruiser's body collapsed onto the sand.

"I'm gonna skin this little sonuvabich alive, if you don't show me how I can leave this place!"

Ears' shouted threat turned every head in his direction. Raven, seeing the Bowie knife at Little Hawk's throat, didn't move.

CHAPTER 39

∆∆∆∆∆

No one moved ... except for Larry. Chris didn't dare look away from Ears, but he could hear splashing noises. When Raven had last seen him, the man was belly deep in the lake and still walking toward the middle.

The Indian, John Crow, was still a bystander. Cautiously keeping his rifle cradled, he watched Ears' antics and waited.

"Brave up, Hawk."

Bear's quiet rumble took the fear out of Little Hawk's eyes.

Ear's jittery gaze bore into Raven's pale eyes with all the intensity of a rabid wolf as he demanded, "What's that Injun jabberin' about!?"

Chris glanced at Bear's Foot's stoic expression and the flint hard look in his eyes and said, "He told Little Hawk to be brave."

"Bein' brave ain't goin' to help him when I slit his throat. And I will, soon."

A crafty look passed over his ferret-like features as he flourished his knife overhead, and shouted, "I told you I want to leave this place!"

"Ca-raack!"

Ears' head changed shape and blood shot out of his left ear. Smoke billowed from the trees, near the small hill to his left. The knife spun through the air as Ears' diminutive form crumpled onto the sandy ground and lay still.

320

The metallic clatter of another bullet being levered into a rifle chamber kept everyone from moving. A slim figure, wearing a battered, gray hat, stepped through the gunsmoke and moved to another tree. His rifle was still pressed to his shoulder and aimed at John Crow.

The Indian stared in disbelief. He spoke in what must have been Crow. His voice was angry; the Crow's near perfect smile was nowhere to be seen. The man with the rifle answered him in the same dialect. Obviously disgusted, John Crow said something that sounded threatening. He threw a menacing glance at Raven and Bear's Foot, then turned and stalked off into the trees. A moment later they heard the sound of hooves as the Indian rode away. They watched him skirt the west side of the lake as he galloped toward the hills. Without saying a word to the survivors, the rifleman stepped back among the trees and disappeared from sight.

Raven was bewildered but jubilant. He hurried to Little Hawk's side and helped him to his feet. He was unharmed, merely sore. Grinning happily, Little Hawk put aside his boyish pride and slipped his arms around Chris and squeezed. Raven peered again at the trees and wondered who their savior could have been.

Bear's Foot, his body covered with wet streaks of mud and dirt, ambled to Raven's side and placed his huge paw on Little Hawk's shoulder. While doing so, his eyes never left the small patch of woods where the shooter had vanished.

"Once again, you have saved my life," Raven said.

Bear's Foot smiled and exclaimed, "As I have said before, Okute, we have suckled from the same breast; we have shared the same belly. We are brothers."

321

The smile turned into a grin, then faded as he looked again toward the trees and quietly said, "The man in the trees was a Crow."

Raven's eyes scanned the area where the man had been. Nothing.

"How do you know?"

Bear shrugged. In lieu of a reply, he began scraping mud from his torso.

Perplexed, Chris turned away. He turned a speculative eye toward the small lake. There wasn't so much as a ripple to act as a grave marker. Larry was gone, apparently drowned. At least he's not afraid anymore, Raven mused. He looked beyond the lake to a distant copse of trees near the edge of the Black Hills and wondered if that was where Bear had hidden The Black and their other horses. When he turned to ask, he was too late. Bear's Foot and Little Hawk had silently moved away from Raven and had walked to the lake shore.

After wading in until waist deep, Bear submerged. He rose from the depths like a bronze whale and spewed water in all directions as he began to cleanse the mud and dirt from his body.

Walking tentatively, Little Hawk waded into the water to be close to his friend. After warning him not to get his bandage wet, Chris watched for a moment as they chatted and teased. Noticing the knife lying beside the dead Cruiser's hand, he moved over and picked it up. Right away Raven saw that it wasn't quite identical to the one he had given Bear's Foot. It also was a Randall, the only difference between the two knives was a long strip of brass along the top six inches; the dull edge of the ten inch blade that was designed to catch an opponent's knife edge on the softer metal. He absently hefted it and examined the nicks in the brass as he walked to retrieve the pumpgun. He looked up and stopped in his tracks.

A horseman was sitting his horse about thirty feet away and was quietly watching him. Recognizing the hat, Chris saw that it was the rifleman who had saved Little Hawk. He slowly moved closer, then stopped.

Surprise struck a hard blow to Raven's stomach! Momentarily stunned, he remained mute and simply stared. It was the blue-eyed Indian youth whom he had spared at the Little Big Horn. He don't look so Indian now, he thought, dressed in white man's clothes. Chris noticed that he had also done something with his hair, but there was no mistaking those pale blue eyes and the penetrating stare. It was the same look he'd given Raven during the tornado when he, in turn, had saved him from his Crow comrade.

"Many thanks, friend," Raven said in Lakota. "You saved the life of my son."

No response, so he repeated it in English. The blue eyes blinked and a small smile twisted the youthful lips. He glanced at Bear's Foot and Little Hawk.

Raven followed his line of sight.

Bear's Foot and Little Hawk were both still in the water. They were standing still, both silently returning the young man's stare. Bear's expression appeared chiseled from granite, while Little Hawk's countenance was full of awe and gratitude. He raised his hand in greeting.

The boy/man returned Little Hawk's wave and again looked at Raven. In English he said, "It is dangerous to be a friend of the Lakota these days."

He was surprised again ... this time, by the boy's grasp of English.

"I'm not just a friend. I am a Lakota now. They are my family," Chris replied.

"I have heard that you are different from most whites. You have no hate in your heart for the Indian."

Raven smiled, proclaiming, "This is true." He looked in the direction John Crow had gone before continuing, "It looks like you have made an enemy."

He shrugged, and said, "He is one of those people that will do anything for profit. I do not need friends like that."

The youth looked toward the hills and gathered his reins. When his gaze again met Raven's, he smiled and said, "My father sent me to find you and give you a warning. He saw the little one ...," he gestured toward Ears' body, "spying on you as you left town. I also have a message from my father ... 'Come and sit a spell, Christopher. The coffee pot's always hot'."

He turned his horse and moved away without a backward glance. Dazed, Raven stared at the brand on the horse's rump. It was a five pointed star within a large C.

Chris' voice cracked with surprise as he queried, "Nathanial?"

The youth looked back over his shoulder. He grinned and waved before urging his mount into a canter. A thick, single braid, just like his father's, bounced between the boy's shoulder blades.

Elated, Raven jumped on a nearby rock, cupped his hands around his mouth and shouted, "You tell Caleb, I'll be there!"

Nathanial Starr continued to ride away but raised his hand in acknowledgment of hearing Raven's words.

Chris was so happy; his grin wouldn't leave his face. He thought of his beautiful wife, Blue Feather, awaiting his return and his wonderful son, Little Hawk. How lucky can a man get? His silent question remained unanswered.

Wasichu's Return

His roving eye ignored the sprawled bodies of his would be murderers. Raven refused to let their presence mar the joy and elation he felt.

He looked toward the shining lake where Bear and Little Hawk were happily splashing water on each other just like a pair of infants. His thoughts turned to his closest friends, Bear's Foot, Ptecila, Caleb Starr, and now ... Nathanial. Christopher Raven knew, in his heart, that everything important to his life was within his grasp.

Raven drank in the clean fresh air and savored the soothing breeze that stirred his long dark hair. He absorbed the grand panorama of the enchanted Black Hills, felt the mysticism, and knew why his people thought them to be sacred.

For some obscure reason he thought of the famous book, Brave New World by Aldous Huxley. He recalled how the author had predicted that 'Utopia' wasn't due to arrive for over six hundred years. A grin flashed white on Raven's weathered face as he thought, everyone has a different Utopia. Mine is not in the future, but in the past. This is *my* brave new world.

The End

ABOUT THE AUTHOR

Born in Menomonie, Wisconsin, Barry grew up in Wisconsin and Minnesota. After a stint with the Marines, he obtained his first art job in Owatonna, Minnesota. After nine years there, he moved to the Black Hills, South Dakota, to pursue his career as a wildlife/western painter. But lack of money forced him to take employment in the gold mines where he met and became close friends with a person who was destined to open the door to a writing career. Joe Four Bears, a Minneconjou Sioux Indian, now deceased, shared stories of his people that had amazed Brierley and cultivated his interest in writing about the Sioux. Another art job brought him back to Minnesota (Winona) for a few years, but his call was in the West, and it was in 1987, when he and his wife, Barb, moved their family to Arizona that his writing began.

Wasichu was his first book, then Timeless Interlude at Wounded Knee was published in 1995. White Horse, Red Rider has just recently been released, and now, Wasichu's Return. Planned books for 1997 are the third in the Wasichu series and the sequel to Timeless Interlude at Wounded Knee. Barry is currently working on a movie project of his novel and script Spirit Riders. The feature film will start production in the fall of '96 and will be filmed in Arizona. The book will be available in 1997.

The Brierley's combined families of five children are now grown. Barry and Barb currently live in Mesa, AZ, with their two dogs, Ninja and Sammy.